SHORT STORIES OF THE 'NINETIES

To

MARGARET

DEREK STANFORD

Short Stories
of
the 'Nineties

A BIOGRAPHICAL ANTHLOOGY [sic]

Anthology

ROY PUBLISHERS INC.
NEW YORK 10021

Printed in Great Britain by
Clarke, Doble & Brendon, Ltd., Cattedown, Plymouth

Contents

CONTENTS

Plates

Plates

Preface

A newly awakened interest in the 'nineties, Aubrey Beardsley, and the Age of Art Nouveau is one of the cultural fashions of our time. In 1965 there were three exhibitions of Art Nouveau at London galleries. These were followed in 1966 by the magnificently mounted massive exhibition of Aubrey Beardsley at the Victoria and Albert Museum. The degree in which these artistic interests have permeated popular culture can be seen in the Art Nouveau patterns in dress design and advertising lay-out which have recently become a feature of London's boutiques and tube stations. Or ride down Oxford Street and there, outside Forte's Restaurant, one will find Beardsley's *Three Waiters*, drawn in Dieppe, serving as an inn-board in the swinging 'sixties.

Because of this generally revived interest in the eighteen-nineties and because the short-storyists gathered here have largely been neglected or forgotten, I have chosen to collect fifteen of them between these two covers.

'Largely neglected,' I have written, and this applies to all these authors with two honourable exceptions: Henry James, the doyen of the 'nineties for all the 'aesthetical' younger men (*'mon maître . . .* the supreme prince of the short-story writers,' was how one of them, Henry Harland, phrased his tribute); and George Gissing who is better known for his novels than for his short stories. Both these authors have a place in any 'nineties anthology of fiction: the first as constituting a *beau ideal* of style, the second as representing the cult and practice of realism.

My principle of choice has been a clear one: to gather together stories written or published within the decade of the 'nineties. Only in one instance have I included an author the date of whose selected contribution did not come within the 1890-1900 limits. This was Arthur Symons, whose story 'Esther Khan' appeared in the volume *Spiritual Adventures* published in 1905. Both the author and his work—and this was his only collection of fiction—are so essentially 'ninety-ish,' that to have omitted them, on chronological grounds, would have been a silly severity.

The term 'ninety-ish' suggests the second consideration upon which I have made my choice. It explains my preference for *The Yellow Book–Savoy* nexus, the Art-for-Art's-Sake storyists, the manners-maketh-man style of writing as opposed to the no-damn-nonsense approach. Yet here, too, I have left a loophole in my rigorism, so that two such interesting writers as H. D. Lowry and Arthur Morrison might be included within my net. These were both contributors to W. E. Henley's journal *The Scots Observer* —later the *National Observer*—a fiery forum of Imperialism and a deadly enemy to the cult of Wilde.

Henley's 'young men'—or 'the Henley Regatta' as Max Beerbohm ironically called them—numbered such names as Kipling, Barrie, Kenneth Grahame, and Thomas Hardy, all of whose work is well enough known and readily accessible elsewhere.

Names I *might* fitly have represented here were those of Wilde, whose volume *Lord Arthur Savile's Crime and Other Stories* was published in 1891; Max Beerbohm, whose fantasy *The Happy Hypocrite* appeared in *The Yellow Book* in 1896; and George Moore, whose volume of tales entitled *Celibates* came out in 1895. The minds of these three authors are central to a 'ninety-ish' notion of letters, and the styles of each of their works are 'ninety-ish' styles. But Wilde's short stories, of course, are easily available in several editions; Max's tale has been reprinted since the war and, like the stories in *Celibates*, is too long for convenient inclusion here. Length, in fact, has been a great deterrent here. Many of the best short stories of the period are between fifty and one-fifty pages long. A supplementary volume 'Novellas of the 'Nineties' might usefully gainsay this statute of limitation.

A word as to the purpose of this collection. I would like to believe that it springs from an assessment of dual factors: my private pleasure and a public need. At least, I know that there exists no such anthology of stories of the 'nineties in or out of print at the moment.

Apart from the entertainment-value of these tales, apart too from their 'period' interest and the way they contribute to our sociological knowledge, these fictions of the 'nineties are significant as being examples of a new thing in English writing: the short story conceived as a *genre* on its own—a fresh art-form conscious of itself—not something that 'just growed' or a cut-down novel.

I have endeavoured to explore some of the aspects of this new form of fiction—social, moral, and artistic—in my Introduction.

Since the names of two-thirds of these authors will be, at most, names only to half my readers, I have introduced each story with a short biographical note. In such brief space there is room, of course, for no more than a minimum of information and opinion.

The short-storyists of the 'nineties have received even less attention than the verse-writers of that decade. In seeking a little to make good this lack, I should like to think of this book as a companion volume to my *Poets of the 'Nineties*.

Here, as elsewhere, I should like to express my thanks to Margaret Holdsworth for her acute and pertinent comments in reading and revising this manuscript.

Bedford Park
September 1967

Introduction

I

Two things mark the short story of the 'nineties as distinguished from the fiction of earlier decades: a greater artistic stringency, and a broader moral permissiveness.

Aesthetically, the period was characterized by a devotion to style and form which derived from sources as different as Flaubert, Stevenson, and Pater. Ethically, the climate of the time was increasingly anti-conventional; though a lively debate still waged between non-conforming and conforming elements. These were the days of Shaw's iconoclasm; of Havelock Ellis' sexological studies, and the freer handling of the passions in the fashionable yellow-backed French novel. The birth of new periodicals—*The Hobby Horse, The Yellow Book, The Savoy, The Dome*, not mere magazines but books with covers (to adapt Max Beerbohm's words upon the second)—substantially fostered the 'serious' short story.

Together, these factors and influences gave rise to what was the English short story proper: an art-form clearly to be distinguished from the magazine pot-boiler or the novelist's by-product. For the first time, the minds of English men of letters were humming with a conscious new concept of what this *genre* was, of what it might be: its privileged possibility, its exacting limitations.

Looking back on those years, in 1912, H. G. Wells summarized some of the excitement and achievement of the time:

> The Nineties was a good and stimulating period for a short-story writer. Mr. Kipling had made his astonishing advent with a series of little blue-grey books, whose covers opened like window shutters to reveal the dusty sun-glare and blazing

colours of the East; Mr. Barrie had demonstrated what could be done in a little space through the panes of his *Window in Thrums*. *The National Observer* was at the climax of its career of heroic insistence upon lyrical brevity and a vivid finish, and Mr. Frank Harris was not only printing good short stories by other people, but writing still better ones himself in the dignified pages of *The Fortnightly Review*. *Longmans' Magazine*, too, represented a *clientèle* of appreciative short-story readers that is now scattered. Then came the generous opportunities of *The Yellow Book*, and *The National Observer* died only to give birth to *The New Review*. No short story of the slightest distinction went for long unrecognised. . . . Short stories broke out everywhere. Kipling was writing short stories; Barrie, Stevenson, Frank Harris; Max Beerbohm wrote at least one perfect one, *The Happy Hypocrite*; Henry James pursued his wonderful and inimitable bent; and among other names that occur to me, like a mixed handful of jewels drawn from a bag, are George Street, Morley Roberts, George Gissing, Ella D'Arcy, Murray Gilchrist, E. Nesbit, Stephen Crane, Joseph Conrad, Edwin Pugh, Jerome K. Jerome, Kenneth Grahame, Arthur Morrison, Marriott Watson, George Moore, Grant Allen, George Egerton, Henry Harland, Pett Ridge, W. W. Jacobs. . . . I do not think the present decade can produce any parallel to this list, or what is more remarkable, that the later achievements in this field of any of the survivors from that time, with the sole exception of Joseph Conrad, can compare with the work they did before 1900. It seems to me this outburst of short stories came not only as a phase in literary development, but also as a phase in the development of the individual writers concerned.[1]

Wells here was talking, of course, with that optimism, exuberence, and generosity which marked most of his early writings; and it would be wrong to believe that all his listed geese were swans. Even so, his inventory is certainly impressive; and one would be hard put to find—with some singular exceptions—work half as good as this in previous decades.

The profits of Victorian commercialism were yielding new social and aesthetic dividends. From the industry of hard-working forefathers a vastly extended leisure-class was being born; and

[1] *The Country of the Blind and Other Stories* (1913) by H. G. Wells.

to the rigid moralists of virtuous labour—Carlyle, Tupper, and Samuel Smiles—succeeded the aesthetes, Pater and Wilde. A refinement, freshly conscious of itself, looked askance at the naïver relaxations of the reading public. The tone of this high dismissal is heard in the *Postscript* to Pater's book of essays, *Appreciations* (1889), when he spoke of 'the stupidity which is dead to the substance, and the vulgarity which is dead to form.' The men of the 'nineties tended to equate this stupidity with convention, this vulgarity with the inartistic—with literature as a penny-a-line affair, subject to the market's laws of demand. Frederick Wedmore—critic, collector, connoisseur, as well as a short-storyist himself—in one of the first essays on the *genre*, speaks of the new interest in 'the artistic treatment of the short story . . . a medium for the exercise of the finest art, as a medium, moreover, adapted peculiarly to that alert intelligence, on the part of the reader, which rebels sometimes at the *longueurs* of the conventional novel: the old three volumes or the new fat book.'[1] The beauty of economy, the brevity of the intense—the 'nineties had a passion for the short and neat.

This revolt against the vulgarity and stupidity of the Victorian ethos, of which Pater spoke, had been slowly gaining ground from the turn of the century. By the 'seventies, the Pre-Raphaelite Movement was established as a fashionable success. Hardy's novel *Tess of the d'Urbervilles* (1891) provocatively entitled by him 'the story of a pure woman' and *Jude the Obscure* (1895), with its marital antinomianism, might scandalize the middle classes and offend the bench of bishops in much the same way as George Moore's *Esther Waters* with its tale of an unmarried servant-girl mother. But Gladstone declared himself grateful for the latter which showed him how the other half lived; and more and more the forward intelligence of the nation proved itself prepared to hear Hardy speak out plainly.

Even by the 'seventies, doubts were being felt as to the measure of truth permitted in fiction. In a Preface to his first volume of short stories, *Pastorals of France* (1877), the conservative-minded Frederick Wedmore observed that 'At a time when the

[1] 'The Short Story' (1896) included in *On Books and Arts* (1899).

under-currents of English thought have passed into places un-
suspected by the stationary eye that has watched the surface, one
cannot but conjecture that to many novelists perfect sincerity
in their work has become hard of attainment, for while the
novelist may think one thing, the society he depicts may think
another, or while both may be thinking alike, it may still be
expected of him that he shall shape his work in polite and gentle
accordance both have inherited and both cast aside.'

The way out of this dilemma which he proposed and employed
in his first book was 'to deal, in remote places, with the tender-
ness of the old and the fancies of the simple'—in other words,
fictionally to accept a terrain, on which the disturbing currents
of Darwinism, Ibsenism, in short, 'the New Spirit,'[1] had not
made themselves felt. But this arbitrary exclusion of true con-
temporaneity could not, necessarily, suffice. 'Our curious, complex, aspiring age,' wrote Pater, 'still abounds in subjects for
aesthetic manipulation of the literary,'[2] and in his academic
romance *Marius the Epicurean* (1884) had spoken of 'life in
modern London' as 'stuff sufficient for the fresh imagination of
youth to build his "palace of art" of.' There was, in truth, as
Le Gallienne noted, retrospectively, in *The Romantic 'Nineties*
(1926) 'quite a cult of London and its varied life, from costers
to courtesans.' With sophisticated urban experience more and
more becoming the theme of fiction, the disturbing 'under-
currents' which Wedmore noted rose to the surface in the novel
and the short story.

II

It was, however, essentially the French who taught the short-
storyists of the 'nineties their most important lessons both as to
treatment of style and subject.

Stevenson, in his short romances, it is true had set standards
of new artistry in prose, finely contemptuous of 'the British pig,'
the common reader with his 'love of the style-less . . . the shape-

---

[1] Title of a book by Havelock Ellis (1890).
[2] *Appreciations* (1889).

less . . . the slapdash and the disorderly.'[1] But, for the most part, this select expression was expended upon the writing of traditional adventure stories such as *The Pavilion on the Links* or *The Sire du Malétroit's Door*. Stevenson, in fact, penned a sort of grown-boy's fiction with all the dedication of the aesthete—a curious alliance some may think, between incongruous means and end. Even when, as in *The New Arabian Nights* (1882), he gives us a peep at Bohemia, there is still, as Henry James remarked, 'the placidly ingenuous tone of Scheherazade.'[2] We remember, along with James, that 'Oyster Bar in the immediate neighbourhood of Leicester Square' into which Prince Florizel and Colonel Geraldine were driven one evening in March by a sharp fall of sleet. But what follows after is Chestertonian—a Soho-Ruritanian extravaganza.

A greater influence, no doubt, than Stevenson was Pater, both as to precept and example. *Marius the Epicurean*, ostensibly a novel, helped to set the fashion for 'a sequence of scenes, woven around a sequence of moods.'[3] This fashion was strengthened by the nearness with which Pater himself came to the short story in *Imaginary Portraits* (1897)—his own favourite book because it seemed to him more 'natural' than any other of his own work. But what might appear natural to Pater was very far from being natural narrative, natural fiction. Pater's imagination moved in the contemplative world of the essayist, and with infinite effort he imparts to it the semblance of motion. But if Pater saw things in still-life terms, without a doubt he did at least *see* them. His eye and senses as a whole were deft enough to catch, retain, and reproduce 'a breath, a flame in the doorway, a feather in the wind.' With all their passive treatment of life's activity, Pater's shorter fictions do come home to us as pictures—'the picturesque form of the narrative to which indeed the term portrait is very happily applied.'[4]

Again and again, in a story of the 'nineties, not otherwise

---

[1] Letter to the author quoted by Richard Le Gallienne: *The Romantic 'Nineties* (1926).
[2] *Partial Portraits* (1888).
[3] *Studies in Prose and Verse* by Arthur Symons (1904).
[4] 'Walter Pater' *(Studies in Prose & Verse)* by Arthur Symons.

memorable perhaps for action, the description of some scene stays in the mind as if one looked into a *camera obscura*.

Pater in his unfurnished autobiographical fragment *The Child in the House*[1] describes how:

> The old-fashioned low wainscoting went round the rooms, and up the staircase with carved balusters and shadowy angles, landing half way up at a broad window, with a swallow's nest below the sill, and the blossom of an old pear-tree showing across it in late April, against the blue, below which the perfumed juice of the find of fallen fruit in autumn was so fresh. At the next turning came the closet which held on its deep shelves the best china. Little angel faces and reedy flutings stood out round the fireplace of the children's room. And on the top of the house, above a large attic, where the white mice ran in the twilight— an infinite, unexplored wonderland of childish treasures, glass beads, empty scent-bottles still sweet, thrum of coloured silk among its lumber—a flat space of roof, railed round, gave a view of the neighbouring steeples; for the house, as I said, stood near a great city, which sent up heavenwards, over the twisting weather-vanes, not seldom, its beds of rolling cloud and smoke, touched with storm or sunshine.

Here is the sharply vivid perception, the same precisely focusing eye as one encounters in much descriptive writing of the 'nineties short-storyists. Sometimes this invisaging, 'realizing' power manifests itself in the paragraph form, as in the account of Piccadilly in a thunderstorm by Hubert Crackanthorpe:

> The hansoms whirled their yellow, gleaming eyes down west : hot flapping gusts went and returned aimlessly : and the mirthless twitterings of the women fell abruptly on the sluggish crowd. All the sin of the city seemed crushed to idleness; vacant wistful, the figures waited by the street corners.
>
> Then the storm burst. Slow, ponderous drops; a clap of the thunder's wrath; a crinkled rim of light, unveiling a slab of sky, throbbing, sullen, and violet; small giggling streams of alarm, and a stampede of bunchy silhouettes. The thunder clapped again, impatient and imperious; and the rain responded, jealously hissing. Bright stains of liquid gold struggled across the roadway; a sound of splashing accompanied the thud of

[1] *Miscellaneous Studies* by Walter Pater (1895).

hoofs, the rumble of wheels, the clanking of chairs, and the ceaseless rattle of the drops on the hurried procession of umbrellas.[1]

At others, it may concentrate itself in a phrase or two or a sentence, as when, in a tale by Frederick Wedmore, the Vicar of Pimlico, dining in a house 'on the North side of the Park' sees for the first time the girl he is to love 'across the table, over the yellow-shaded candles, the pine, the bananas, the *marron-glacés*, the tulip-bed on the table-cloth.'[2]

Again, the same author can summarize the whole temperament and way of life of a character when in another story[3] he describes the entourage of Pelse the chemist in the suburbs, a man with a taste above his position :

> Winter succeeded to autumn. A thick fog had lain for days over Orchard Street. Then there came a little snow. But in the parlour over the shop—with three windows closely curtained— one could have forgetfulness of weather. There was the neat fire- place; the little low tea-table; a bookcase in which Pelse—before that critical event at Aix-les-Bains—had been putting, gradually, first editions of the English Poets; a cabinet of china, in which— but always before Aix-les-Bains—he had taken to accumulate some pretty English things of whitest paste or finest painting : a Worcester cup, with its exotic birds, its lasting gold, its scale- blue ground, like lapis lazuli or sapphire; a Chelsea figure; some- thing from Swansea; white plates of Nantgarw, bestrewn with Billingsley's greyish pink roses, of which he knew the beauty, the free artistic touch. How the things had lost interest for him ! 'From the moment,' says some French art critic, 'that a woman occupies me, my collection does not exist.' And many a woman may lay claim to occupy a French art critic; only *one* had occu- pied Richard Pelse.

This adaptation of *belles-lettres* standards to the practice of fiction was very largely Pater's contribution. Both he and Henry James insisted on the fact 'that fiction is one of the *fine* arts.'[4] for confirmation of which belief they turned to performance

---

[1] 'A Commonplace Chapter' (*Sentimental Studies*, 1895).
[2] 'The Vicar of Pimlico' (*English Episodes*, 1894).
[3] 'The Chemist in the Suburbs' (*Renunciations*, 1893).
[4] 'The Art of Fiction' (*Partial Portraits*) by Henry James.

across the Channel. 'To write our English language as the Latins wrote theirs, as the French write, and scholars should write'[1] became, after Pater, the 'nineties ideal.

To achieve a choicer grain of prose, to work with a greater sense of finessing was something that attracted the practising poet to the hitherto less elevated medium of fiction. Bauderlaire had already had this dream of 'the miracle of poetical, musical prose, without rhythm, without rhyme, supple enough and apt enough to adapt itself to the movements of the soul, to the swaying of a dream, to the sudden throbs of conscience,'[2] and had himself shown how it could be done. Huysman had followed with *Croquis Parisiens* (1880), and Mallarmé with his rarer volatilizations—work which contained, in different proportions, notes of the prose poem, the narrative, the sketch. 'Impressionistic writing' became the fashion; and in an essay by that title Arthur Symons quotes a typical mosaic-piece which the *avant-garde* were elaborately contriving—a sort of shop-front imagism in prose: 'the old gold and scarlet of hanging meat; the metallic green of mature cabbages; the wavering russet of piled potatoes; the sharp white bits of fly-bills, pasted all awry,'[3] all of which pales beside 'Le Gousset' from *Croquis Parisiens* 'in which the capacities of language are strained to define and differentiate the odours of feminine arm-pits.'[4]

Excited by these fresh discoveries which gave to prose a creative new look, the poets joined the ranks of the short-storyists of the 'nineties, including such names as Oscar Wilde, W. B. Yeats, Ernest Dowson, Lionel Johnson, John Gray, Victor Plarr, and Arthur Symons. Praising Pater as 'the English Flaubert,' the 'nineties reviewer Richard Le Gallienne declared that 'it was the art of prose rather than that of verse that occupied most of our minds. . . . Prose was a more plastic medium, lending itself more sensitively to the impress of individual temperaments. . . . At all events, it seemed to have more future than verse; less had been done with it; and many young pundits declared it the greater

[1] 'Postscript' (*Appreciations*) by Walter Pater.
[2] Preface to *Petits Poèmes en prose* (1869).
[3] *Dramatis Personae* (1925).
[4] *The New Spirit* by Havelock Ellis (1890).

art of the two. What solemn talks I have heard on the subject in the elaborate periods of Oscar Wilde and in the vivacious whimsical harangues of Henry Harland.'[1]

One minor poet of distinction, Ernest Dowson, certainly lent support to this fashion by stating that he preferred his prose to his verse.

But the treatment of prose, a care for style, was only a part of what the short-storyists of the 'nineties learnt from the French.

III

Writing a literary causerie on 'Edmund de Goncourt' and his brother in his own magazine *The Savoy*,[2] Arthur Symons remarked that he had 'frequently heard Pater refer to certain of their books, to *Madame Gervaisais*, to *L'Art d'un XVIII Siècle*, to *Chérie*, with a passing objection to what he called the "immodesty" of the last book, and a strong emphasis in the assertion that "that was how it seemed to him a book should be written." ' An Anglo-Saxon, *malgré lui*, a don as cautious as he was cultivated, Pater in the word 'immodesty' here uncovers the very pith of the problem.

To begin with, he had good personal reasons for his reservation concerning *Chérie*. Between the higher sensuousness and an *homme-moyen-sensuel* hedonism, it is not always easy to discriminate. In genteelly proselytising for the former, he risked being thought to defend the latter. The whole tenor of Pater's thinking—his sedulous gospel of sensuous awareness—contained within itself the unanswered questions: what are the senses for, and which are their legitimate uses? It took all of Pater's discursive subtlety, not to mention his masking style (worn rather as a yashmak or motoring-veil), to leave these final issues unclarified —to give them, in fact, a recessive background charm. Nor, for him, did these issues need to be thought through, made explicit in any ethic of action; since in Pater, as Havelock Ellis pointed

---

[1] *The Romantic 'Nineties.*
[2] No. 5, September (1896).

out, 'we see a refined development of the passive sensory sides of the human organism with corresponding atrophy of the motor sides.'[1]

But the question of a literature of the senses, a fiction explicitly and frankly sensual, was sure to come up sooner or later; and it was Maupassant, not the Goncourts, who emphatically highlighted its existence. For this there were a number of reasons. The Goncourts, like Pater, were aesthetes: critics of art, collectors, connoisseurs; and their excursions into the fiction of the sordid might be interpreted as 'the pose of one . . . who . . . in a chic ballet/ [Performs] an apache role in rags of cleverly-cut silk.'[2] No such understanding of the erotic and sordid in terms of fictional choreography could be placed on the novels and short stories of Maupassant. As Henry James remarked of him in 1888, 'His point of view is almost solely that of the senses'[3]—that of an author who 'would doubtless affirm that where the empire of the sexual sense is concerned, no exaggeration is possible.'[4] For James, an older man than the 'nineties generation, a man with his roots in a puritan tradition, this made Maupassant 'a very interesting case . . . but also an embarrassing one, embarrassing and mystifying for the moralist.'[5] James's praise for Maupassant's formal talents—for his pure story-telling gifts—is almost unstinted. But, again, there is moral reservation, with just a suggestion of two standards—one for the English and one for the French. 'The impression of the human spectacle,' comments James, 'for him who takes it as it comes has less analogy with that of the monkey's cage than this admirable writer's account of it.' 'I speak,' he adds, 'of the human spectacle as we Anglo-Saxons see it—as we Anglo-Saxons pretend we see it, M. de Maupassant would possibly say.' Younger by some two decades, and more infused with the spirit of revolt against a respectable

---

[1] *The New Spirit.*
[2] 'A Vagrant', *Collected Poems* by David Gascoyne (1965).
[3] *Partial Portraits.*
[4] Ibid.
[5] Ibid.
[6] *Partial Portraits*

ethic of restraint, the men of the 'nineties were prepared to profit by the Frenchman's freer presentation, even when they did not quite share his vision of life as 'the monkey's cage.'

Then, too, there was a further cause for the pull which he exerted upon them. On Maupassant had fallen the mantle of Flaubert—'the martyr of literary style'[1] as Pater called him, and founder of the novel as a conscious art-form. Flaubert, a vastly venerated figure, dedicated master of the *mot juste*, had chosen Maupassant as his disciple. Not to harken to his claims—claims well substantiated by talent—would therefore be lese-majesty. Come as he might 'in such questionable form,' his credentials had been vouched for in the highest quarters. Finally, Maupassant was no glorious myth, no shining memory—dead like Flaubert since 1880—but the near-contemporary of these men of the 'nineties, their literary neighbour, their older brother. His first volumes had been published in 1880, and continued to appear year by year till his death, in his forties, in 1893.

'As a novelist,' wrote Arthur Symons, voicing the tribute of the English 'nineties to him, 'Maupassant has done remarkable and admirable work; but it is as a *conteur* that he is supreme, and it is in his *contes* that he will live. As a writer of the nouvelle, or short story, Maupassant has no rival.'[2]

IV

It was Symons too who summarized the other literary attraction which Maupassant had for the men of the 'nineties. 'His sense of desire, of greed,' he wrote, 'of all the baser passions was profound; he had the terrible logic of animalism.'[3] This 'terrible logic,' this animalism' were to become elements in fiction deeply occupying the short-storyists of the 'nineties. A running debate upon this subject continued almost throughout the decade.

Havelock Ellis's article on Zola, which appeared in the first number of *The Savoy* (1896), the magazine of his friend Arthur

---

[1] *Appreciations.*
[2] *Studies in Two Literatures* (1897).
[3] *Studies in Prose and Verse.*

Symons, shows the fascination and repugnance which the reading public felt for this new fiction of exposure.

'Zola's name—a barbarous explosive name, like an anarchist's bomb,' wrote Ellis, "has been tossed about amid hoots and yells for a quarter of a century. In every civilized country we have heard of the man who has dragged literature into the gutter, who has gone down to pick up the filth of the streets, and has put it into books for the filthy to read. And in every civilized country his books have been read by the hundred thousand. . . . But popularity failed to silence the hooting; in England, the classic land of self-righteousness, the decree went forth that this thing must be put an end to, and amid general acclamation the English publisher of such garbage was clapped into gaol. There was only a slight pause in the outcry, more a pause of stupefaction than of reconcilation, when it was known that many respected novelists in Europe and America looked up humbly to this scavenger as to a master; or, again, when a metaphysician stood up in the Concord School of Philosophy and boldly classed him with Jesus and the great masters of moral irony; or, once more, when the garbage-monger himself was welcomed as an honoured guest in the city which had imprisoned his publisher and published his books, and when it was known that he was standing, with some hope, at the sacred portals of the French Academy.' Here it may be noted that along with poorer versions, Zola's 'filthy books' found faithful translations at the hands of three poets of the 'nineties—Ernest Dowson, Arthur Symons, and Victor Plarr, the first two being also short-storyists of genuine distinction.

Other articles in *The Savoy* and *The Yellow Book* also dealt with aspects of this debate, the two more important being attempts to define the nature of 'Reticence in Literature' which appeared in the latter magazine for April and July 1894.

Arthur Waugh, father of Evelyn the novelist, started the attack in the first number of *The Yellow Book*—a cunning gesture on the part of John Lane the proprietor, since his magazine was largely intended to provide these new fashions in freedom with a forum. By voicing, in advance, the claims of morality, he could prove himself on the side of the angels while enjoying from his readers the profits of those who peruse the devil's work.

'We get," he wrote Waugh, 'a realistic fiction abroad, and we begin to copy it at home. . . . A new school has arisen which combines the characteristics of effeminacy and brutality. In its effeminate aspect it plays with the subtler emotion of sensual pleasure, on its brutal side it has developed into that class of fiction which for want of a better word I must call chirurgical . . . but instead of leaving these refinements of lust to the haunts to which they are fitted, it has introduced them into the domestic chamber and permeated marriage with the ardours of promiscuous intercourse.'

The last sentence is particularly revealing, suggesting as it does that passion has no place in the conjugal state. In the year when this article appeared, Havelock Ellis published his first sexological work: *Man and Woman: A study of their Human Secondary Sexual Characteristics*, to be followed in 1897 by the first of his six volumes of *Studies in the Psychology of Sex*, a compendium of 'normal' and 'abnormal' practice. But it was not until 1918 that he declared himself more fully a partial supporter of the feminist cause in his book on *The Erotic Rights of Women*. Meanwhile, feminine emancipation—literary, sexual, and social —came under the batteries of the Establishment, as Arthur Waugh's censures go to show.

'We are told,' he continued, 'that it is part of the revolt of women, and certainly our women writers are chiefly to blame.' 'In fiction,' wrote Waugh of the wave of realism, 'it infects the heroines with acquired diseases of names unmentionable and has debased the beauty of maternity by analysis of the process of gestation.'

To readers sharing Arthur Waugh's point of view, much of the fiction of the 'nineties must have seemed—to adapt a sentence from Harland—'all the breath-taking *unpleasantness* of *reality* made visible, audible, actual.'[1]

As another Harland character puts it, expressing the fashionable *nostalgie de la boue*: 'the truth is in the mire; the real flavour is in the lees . . . I don't pretend that the face of truth is

[1] See his story 'Mercedes' (*Grey Roses*, 1895).

beautiful. It is hideous beyond imagination . . . But it is the face of truth; the sight of it gives . . . a supreme satisfaction.'[1]

That oracle of the Establishment the Grundian Mrs. Humphrey Ward—put in a plea for 'the neutrality of the pen—the sexlessness of intelligence.'[2] Arthur Waugh's recipe for dealing with these feminine stormy petrels would seem to have been largely the same: women would conduct themselves properly in fiction provided they learnt to think like men. 'The man,' stated Waugh, in a facile antithesis, 'lives by ideas; the woman by sensations; and while the man remains an artist so long as he holds true to his own view of life, the woman becomes one as soon as she throws off the habit of her sex, and learns to rely upon her judgment'—namely standards formed by her lord and master.

Waugh, of course, hopelessly misrepresents the essentially androgynous nature of the creative process: its fusion of intelligence, intuition, and feeling; and the subtler fresh influx of these last two qualities into the short story of the 'nineties is due, in no small part, to the women writers.

Nor was Waugh able to hit on a formula which properly expressed the fit operation of reticence in writing. 'The standard of taste in literature,' he remarked,' should be regulated by the normal taste of the hale and cultured man of its age [no reference again to the woman] . . . it should steer a middle course between the prudery of the manse, which is for hiding everything vital; and the effrontery of the pot-house, which makes for ribaldry and bawdry.'

No doubt, this was easier in theory than in practice. Waugh's generalities did not, artistically, define the limits—the elasticity of which the younger writers were in any case chafing to stretch. Where was the snapping point? Henry James touches ironically on the subject in his short story *Greville Fane* (1893), where the rather pretentious son of a popular woman novelist comes to the narrator to ask 'how far . . . in the English novel, one might really venture to go.' 'He wasn't resigned to the usual pruderies, the worship of childish twaddle . . . He struck out the brilliant idea

---

[1] 'The Rewards of Virtue *(Grey Roses)*.
[2] *Bookbuyer*, August 1894.

that nobody knew how far we might go since nobody had ever tried.'

Writing on the same side of the issue, in the next number of *The Yellow Book* (July, 1894) Philip Gilbert Hamerton, LL.D. just had to admit that Waugh's answer would not do: 'He defends the principle of reticence, but the only sanction that he finds for it is a temporary authority imposed by the changing taste of the time.' 'A good proof of the complete laxity of the present taste,' he added, 'is that Mr. Waugh himself has been able to print at length three of the grossly sensual stanzas in Mr. Swinburne's "Dolores." '[1]

In the same number of *The Yellow Book*, the short-storyist Hubert Crackanthorpe gave Waugh a balanced if ironical answer. 'Throughout the history of literature,' he argued, 'the jealous worship of beauty—which we term idealism—and the jealous worship of truth—which we term realism—have alternately prevailed.' Neither of these two principles, working exclusively, seemed to Crackanthorpe to produce mature art. The present climate, he admitted, was one of realism; and he thought that the existence of a literary and public opposition would serve to prune its more eccentric extravagances.

For the most part, however, his answer was mocking, as his portrait of 'the gentleman who objects to realistic fiction on moral grounds' nicely demonstrates. 'He has been labelled Philistine,' wrote Crackanthorpe, 'he has been twitted with his middle-age; he has been reported to have compromised himself with that indecent old person Mrs. Grundy. It is confidently asserted that he comes from Putney, or from Sheffield, and that, when he is not busy abolishing the art of English literature, he is employed in safeguarding the interests of the grocery or tallow-chandler's trade.'

This cavalier treatment of orthodoxy was a fashionable move with men of the 'nineties. Wilde had prefaced his novel *The Picture of Dorian Gray* (1891) with a series of moral-artistic squibs, and employed the same approach, with disastrous results, when conducting his case in Court in 1895. To question the autonomy of art, these aesthetes maintained, was to show oneself ill-bred.

---

[1] *The Yellow Book*. A criticism of Volume 1.

Morality was part of the shop-keeping mind; and Wilde, it was known, would not speak to shopkeepers.

Two years later, in *The Savoy*,[1] Vincent O'Sullivan threw a Chinese cracker among the still squeamish public who patronized that emporium for the middle-brow, Mudie's Library. 'Nowadays,' he noted, 'we seem to nourish our morals with the thinnest milk and water, with a good dose of sugar added, and not a suspicion of lemon at all.' Fiction in England crawled painfully along through the fog of Anglo-Saxon conventions. Beyond the Channel things were different: There, a clear, dryer light prevailed. 'In France,' wrote O'Sullivan, 'people appear eager to watch how art triumphs over any matter. "Charles Baudelaire," says Hamerton, "had the poetical imagination with all its worst inconveniences;" but one inconvenience he had not—the inconvenience of a timid public not interested in forms, and with a profound hatred of the unusual.'[2]

O'Sullivan's essay is representative of the short-storyists' polemic: an aristocrat assumption of disdain towards middle-class standards, a snobbism derived from a passion for perfection; and lastly, the inevitable tribute to France.

V

'Science and morals,' Havelock Ellis might write, 'are subservient to the reproductive activity;'[3] but it would be wrong to think that the English short-storyists of the 'nineties were exclusively obsessed by sex. Maupassant's great example had helped to free them from their cultural apron-strings; and the claims they made for sex, in literature and life, were—though admittedly paramount—part of the general broader climate of moral permissiveness which was dawning in their day.

Sex was certainly a strong fermenting factor. The study of animal magnetism—those operations of affinity, attraction, and repulsion—was clearly going to react upon the social sense and the sense of class.

[1] No. 2, April, 1896.
[2] 'On the Kind of Fiction called Morbid.'
[3] *The New Spirit.*

There is, for example, in Walt Whitman's work—a poet prized by many forward spirits of the 'nineties—what may perhaps be called a democracy of the emotions. Havelock Ellis, who devotes an essay to him in his book *The New Spirit,* expresses it thus: 'This "love" of Whitman is a very personal matter; of an abstract Man, a *solidaire* Humanity, he never speaks; it does not appear ever to have occurred to him that so extraordinary a conception can be formulated; his relations to men generally spring out of his relations to individual men. He has touched and embraced his fellow's flesh;[1] he has felt throughout his being the mysterious reverberations of the contact.'

Class in British society in the 'nineties was not without its assumption of a rigid caste system. For the upper-middle class and the aristocracy, the workers, 'the people,' the unemployed were too often quite literally 'the untouchables.' Even within middle-class echelons, the distinction of lower, middle-middle, and upper could be of a segregationist nature. Nothing perhaps is quite so potent at breaking down barriers and dissolving prejudice as the operation of love between those who sit either side of the seat. What was once alien, *verboten,* becomes now desirable, along with its attendant associations. 'For the lover,' writes Ellis, in his essay on Whitman, 'there is nothing in the loved one's body impure or unclean; a breath of passion has passed over it, and all things are sweet.'

This new democracy of the touch, this egalitarianism of the erotic senses is clearly to be felt as a presence informing the fiction of the period. In one sense, the short story here was a more suitable medium that the novel. It could offer the reader the bare essentials of the encounter, the dilemma, the choice: a victory for love or a victory for class. In the same way the short story could highlight, with no inartistic argumentation, the debate on the claims of erotic attraction and the demands of a sexual morality geared to marriage and solely marital intercourse.

The men of the 'nineties were acutely aware of the potentiality of free sexual attraction and of the hard reality of the class system and social morality. They had, then, to choose one of two

---

[1] Presumably a reference to Whitman's hospital nursing in the American Civil War and not to his homosexual experience.

solutions: to let sexual attraction triumph by an act of iconoclasm; or to present their lovers as defeated—'because the world
is neither yours nor mine'[1]—sacrificed to the *mores* of the day.
This genuine dilemma, with loyalties often felt by the author to
both sides, accounts for the high proportion of short stories
published during the 'nineties which have renunciation as their
theme. Indeed, Frank Wedmore, a somewhat older man than
most of the short-storyists of the 'nineties, entitled one volume
by that very name, *Renunciation* (1892). In his short prefatory
remarks he noted that of these 'three short imaginative pieces
. . . two, at least, deal with the renunciation, voluntary or
necessitated, of a great love—or, I would say, rather, of love's
most obvious privileges.' The last story in the book 'The North
Sea and Eleanor' solves the dilemma by opting for something even
more unorthodox than illegitimate intercourse or miscegenation,
namely, a lovers' suicide-pact. Wedmore, with his conservative
mind, avoids the moral interdiction here by making the lovers'
virtual suicide both largely unconscious and accidental. But the
story shows the social pressure to which these short-storyists
were subjected. Death with honour could easily become the
accepted way out for either a lady or a gentleman; and the fiction
of the period is, in fact, full of the death-wish, in explicit or
implicit form, stemming from the repressed impulses of sex.

The greater awareness and exploration of the workings of
animal magnetism, with all its social and moral repercussions,
was supplemented in the fiction of the 'nineties by fresh
sympathetic and empathic insights—by a general increase, in
fact, of the intuitive powers in writing. Our responses to the
presence of another—temperamental as well as sexual—are something these short-storyists delighted to explore. A *Responsibility*[2]
by Henry Harland, for example, traces a delicate seismograph of
the unspoken appeal for help, unanswered as it happens, from
one man to another:

> It is certain that he made signals of distress—faint, shy
> tentative but unmistakable—and that I pretended not to under-
> stand: just barely dipped my colours, and kept my course. Oh

[1] 'Parting' (*Stone and Flower*) by Kathleen Raine, 1943.
[2] *Grey Roses* (1895).

if I had dreamed that his distress was extreme—that he was on the point of foundering and going down! However, that does not exonerate me: I ought to have turned aside to find out.

In reading the short-storyists of the 'nineties with their subtle awareness of currents of feeling often running counter to social convention, one remembers how D. H. Lawrence declared that fiction 'can inform and lead into new places the flow of our sympathetic consciousness, and [how] it can lead our sympathy away in recoil from things gone dead.'[1] Like Lawrence somewhat later, the 'nineties short-storyists were seeking to reveal 'the most secret places of life . . . the *passional* secret places . . . where the tide of sensitive awareness needs to ebb and flow.'[2]

The art-work of inter-relatedness was another formulation of Lawrence's idea of fiction: the inter-relatedness between person and thing. There is a classic passage in his essay on 'Morality and the Novel' in which he speaks about the sense of imaginative union between a Cezanne apple and himself. This identification or empathy, the short-storyists of the 'nineties sought to locate. Again one may pick on Henry Harland to illustrate this fictional concern. His short story *Rooms*[3] is, in fact, no more than a voyage into the past—a *recueillement*, or 're-plucking in memory of the flowers that time has plucked already.'[4] But what is unusual, fictionally, is that this *recueillement* concerns only the inanimate past: the atmosphere or spirit of a number of rooms belonging to the hero's boyhood home:

> I don't know, I can't think why this room should always have awakened in me a feeling of strangeness and mystery, why it should always have set me off day-dreaming and wondering; but it always did. The mahogany bureau, the tapestried four-post bed, the portrait of my grandfather, the recurrent landscape on the wall-paper, the deep black closet where the dresses hung, the faint smell of orange-flower water—each of these was a surface, a curtain behind which, vaguely, wonderingly, I divined

[1] *Lady Chatterley's Lover*, 1928.
[2] Ibid.
[3] *Comedies and Errors*, 1898.
[4] *The Modern Writer & His World* by G. S. Fraser, 1964.

strange vistas, a whole strange world . . . They were hieroglyphs full of meaning, if only I could understand.

This is a long way, of course, from Proust's re-savouring of the madelaine, in his celebrated novel, or from James Joyce's 'epiphany' (or 'sudden spiritual manifestation . . . when the soul of the commonest object . . . leaps to us from the vestment of its appearance') in *Stephen Hero* (1944). It is more like the intimate interior scenes which one meets in Katherine Mansfield's stories; but, in terms of nervous-psychic awareness, there is little of Harland's *sense of things and place* between the time of Charles Dickens and the 'nineties.

'The moods of men! There I find my subject, there the region over which art rules,'[1] writes Arthur Symons in 1896, and the short stories of the period, as much almost as its verse, present us with a literature of moods. The 'nineties can claim to have given birth to the atmospheric short story and novel as far as our English culture is concerned. From it, there develops the subjective fiction of Dorothy Richardson, Virginia Woolf, D. H. Lawrence, and, of course, James Joyce. As Richard Le Gallienne remarked: 'Those last ten years of the nineteenth century properly belong to the twentieth century,' whose achievements he thought to be no more than 'extension of what the men and women of the 'nineties began.'[2]

This boast has something more to it than that of a minor figure inflating his own past.

VI

The atmospheric art which the 'nineties practised is suggested by the titles to their volumes of short stories: George Egerton's *Discords* (1894) and *Keynotes* (1893); Ella D'Arcy's *Mono-chromes* (1895); Hubert Crackanthorpe's *Vignettes* (1896) and *Sentimental Studies* (1895); Eric Count Stenbock's *Studies of Death* (1894); and Ernest Dowson's *Dilemmas: Stories and Studies in Sentiment* (1895). Given their common concern for

[1] Preface to the Second Edition of 'London Nights' (*Studies in Prose and Verse*, 1904).
[2] *The Romantic 'Nineties*.

style, their broader social and moral approach, their intuitive feeling and impressionist vision, what fresh forms or adaptations of the old were these authors to employ in their fiction? What, in fact, distinguished the short story from the novel proper; or, was there no distinction?

These were questions difficult to answer; and outside of French literature there existed no body of theory or precedent to inform these short-storyists as to their art.

Fiction, in this country, seemed to Henry James, 'a paradise of loose ends.'[1] 'Only a short time ago,' he wrote in 1884, 'it might have been supposed that the English novel was not what the French call *discutable*.' Until recently 'there was a comfortable good-humoured feeling that a novel is a novel as a pudding is a pudding, and that our only business with it could be to swallow it.' Now, he agreed, things were changing—'the era of discussion would appear to have been to a certain extent opened.'[2]

But James in his essay was dealing with *The Art of Fiction* in terms of the novel; and the prefaces which he was to write to the volumes of his short stories included in 'the sumptuous plum-coloured expensive New York Editions of his work'[3] had yet to be composed. Meanwhile, there was hardly a single disquisition which sought to treat of the short story as a structure with potentials and limits all its own. Frederick Wedmore's essay on the subject[4] which appeared in 1898 is thus all the more important both for the scarcity of critical comment and because it represents the opinions of a widely cultivated man and a delicate practitioner of this craft.

Wedmore begins his inquiry 'what is, and is *not* a short story?' His answer proves multiple:

> It may be an episode . . . a fancy-tale . . . the presentation of
> a single character with the stage to himself (like Mr. George

---

[1] *The Art of the Novel: Critical Prefaces by Henry James* (New York 1935).

[2] 'The Art of Fiction' (*Partial Portraits*, 1888).

[3] Richard P. Blackmur: Introduction to *The Art of the Novel: Critical Prefaces by Henry James*.

[4] 'On the Short Story' reprinted in his collection *On Books and Arts*, 1899.

Gissing); a tale of the uncanny . . . a dialogue of comedy; a panorama of selected landscape, a vision of the sordid street, a record of heroism, a remote tradition or an old belief vitalised by its bearing on our life today, an analysis of an obscure calling, a glimpse of a forgotten quarter.'

It would not be difficult to allocate those phrases to various short stories of Wedmore's day.

One thing he noted is the lack of stress placed on the narrative element: 'Plot, or story proper, is no essential part of it.' The end-impression is more important than the means of artificial suspension and progression.

Next, he asserts its self-identity, its independence from the longer and more popular form of fiction: 'One thing it can never be . . . "a novel in a nut-shell" . . . It is a separate thing—as separate, almost, as the Sonnet is from the Epic—it involves the exercise almost of a different art."

Wedmore then considers the methods of approach which the short story may share with the novel, and then those approaches which belong to it alone. He notices how both novel and short story may employ the form of the personal narrative as well as that of the epistle (employed by him in his story To Nancy);[1] and how they redound to the advantage of the short story, since in this *genre* there are fewer characters, thus avoiding inconsistency, weariness, confusion.

Of the forms of approach for the short story only, he names 'the simple dialogue' and 'the diary form,' the second of which he used in The New 'Marienbad-Elegy'[2] and The Poet on the Wolds.[3] But the nub of the affair, whatever form is used, is that if the short story is well done, 'it has become quintessence; it has eliminated the superfluous, and it has taken *time* to be brief.'[4]

As an illustration of the 'pregnant brevity,' he instances Daudet's Les Deux Auberges 'a little piece that has no story at all; but a "situation" depicted, and when depicted, "left." '

[1] *Orgeas and Miradou with other pieces*, 1896.

[2] *Renunciations*, 1894.

[3] *Orgeas and Miradou with other pieces.*

[4] 'On the Short Story' reprinted in his collection On Books and Arts.

Wedmore summarizes this masterpiece in a dozen or so appreciative lines:

> There is an open country; leagues of Provence; a long stretching road; and, on the roadside, opposite each other, two inns. The older one is silent, melancholy; the other, noisy and prosperous. And the landlord of the older spends all his time in the newer; taking his pleasure there with the guests who were once his own, and with a handsome landlady, who makes amends for his departed business. And in his own inn, opposite, a deserted woman sits solitary. That is all—but the art of the master![1]

It was this art—this laconic obliqueness—which the 'nineties short-storyists prized. 'The indispensableness of compression . . . an unbroken continuity of excellent style'—here in two phrases one has the formal criteria of the age; the criteria of men 'who may not claim to be geniuses, but who . . . must claim to be artists.'[2]

Naturally, these counsels of perfection would not recommend themselves to the penny-a-liners, the mercenary wooers of a lazy-minded public. The reading public of the new short story was, in numbers, choice though few, a receptive élite. 'What,' concluded Wedmore, quoting an old German proverb, 'has a cow to do with nutmegs?'

VII

The themes most frequently met with in the 'nineties short story are three: the life of sex, the life of art, bohemian and *declassé* existence.

The most significant element in the treatment of the first—that which gives it, in Henry James's phrase, the sense of a 'larger latitude'—is the new image of woman just then emerging. No longer part of her lord and master's chattels, no longer a slave to the masculine mind and will, she is seen as a creature with resources of her own, equal if not superior to man in strength, tenacity, and cunning.

[1] Ibid.
[2] Ibid.

And what is remarkable about this new image is the faith placed in it by the women short-storyists whatever their relations to the feminist movement. In the work of Ella D'Arcy and George Egerton (a convenient pseudonym for a thrice-married female author) one is given, so to speak, the heads and tails, the black and white side of the feminine psyche. For George Egerton woman is the new hero of fiction, the daring champion of liberty and passion. Egerton writes as a literary suffragette, very much romantically in love with her bold and beautiful espousers of freedom. If it were not for affection 'that crowning disability of my sex,' a pregnant wife tells her passing lover, 'we women would master the world. I tell you men would be no match for us. At heart, we care nothing for laws, nothing for systems. All your elaborately reasoned codes for controlling morals or man do not weigh a jot with us against an impulse, an instinct. We learn these things from you, you tamed, amenable animals; they are not natural to us. It is a wise disposition of providence that this untameableness of ours is corrected by our affections. We forge our own chains in a moment of softness, and then (bitterly) we may as well wear them with a good grace. Perhaps many of our seeming contradictions are only the outward evidences of inward chafing ... the qualities that go to make a Napoleon —superstition, want of honour, disregard of opinion and the eternal I—are oftener to be found in a woman than a man. Lucky for the world perhaps that all these attributes weigh as nothing in the balance with the need to love if she be a good woman, to be loved if she is of coarser fibre.'[1]

No such glamorous rhetoric of emancipation passes the lips of Ella D'Arcy's women who are mostly shown as cold, trite, and empty, but with a persistent strength of cunning. In nine-tenths of her fiction it is woman who is the villain of the piece. Her favourite theme was unhappy marriage, and she sent her lovers to the altar 'as if their blood was to be shed.'[2] As a female commentator has herself remarked, 'Unlike many men authors of the period, who portrayed gentle femininity trampled by the male's unprincipled brutality, Miss D'Arcy showed the superior

[1] 'A Cross Line' (Keynotes, 1894).
[2] The Beardsley Period by Osbert Burdett.

and well-intentioned man caught in the snares of a designing or stupid woman. For all that was wrong in these marriages the blame rested on the heroine's drooping shoulders.'[1]

The theme of woman's sexual freedom is burdened in Egerton's short stories by a narcissistic sentimentality. She delights in drawing her heroines as free, untramelled spirits of the air; then promptly proceeds to cripple them by telling the reader, admiringly, how kind and warm-heartedly thoughtful they are; ministering angels of charity, in fact, though unbound by their religious sisters' vows of obedience and chastity. No such nice consideration fetters the trivial though terrible harpies one encounters in Ella D'Arcy's tales. Detached, analytical, and merciless, she presents without comment her empty-headed women who ruthlessly exploit and destroy their men. The conclusion of her short story A Marriage[2] has all of Maupassant's famous 'cruel point.' A wife and a woman friend are busy choosing material for a dress:

> 'I do think the green quite heavenly, Mini, in colour,' she repeated, holding a scrap up at arm's length, so that the lamp light might slant over it; 'and yet the black is a softer, richer silk, and would make up awfully well with jet trimmings, as you say. I don't know which I had better have.'

Then comes the sound of her sick and unloved husband's cough as he descends the stairs from his study:

> 'After all,' she said in her curious drawling voice, 'it would be more prudent, I suppose, to decide on the black.'

Writing side by side in the same magazines, these two short-storyists must have left many a contemporary reader (particularly of the weaker male sex) puzzling more fatuously upon the time-honoured 'enigma of woman.'

But both these women short-storyists, in their treatment of the theme of sex, pale before the work of Hubert Crackanthorpe. Beside the brilliant incisive writing of this young author, who committed suicide at the age of twenty-six, the realism of George

[1] A Study in Yellow: The Yellow Book & its Contributors by Katherine Lyon Mix (1960).
[2] Modern Instances, 1898.

Egerton and Ella D'Arcy appears sadly stereotyped. In the first, there is a kind of feminist romanticism distorting both judgment and observation—an audacity disturbed by feverish propaganda. In the second, the limiting factor is a sort of pragmatic realism—a doctrinaire vision of human behaviour applied too literally to every situation.

Crackanthorpe, for all the 'juvenility of his candour,'[1] recognized the danger of the latter approach. 'There is,' he wrote in *The Yellow Book*, 'but scanty merit in the mere selection of any particular subject, however ingenious or daring it may appear at first sight . . . a man is not an artist, simply because he writes about heredity or the *demi-monde* . . . to call a spade a spade requires no extraordinary literary gift . . . the essential is contained in the frank, fearless acceptance by every man of his entire artistic temperament, with its qualities and its flaws.'[2] It was this reservation which gave Crackanthorpe's stories their fuller sensibility, their wider vision.

Maupassant provided him with the ground-plan; but this he modified according to the more flexible insights of his own nature. A besetting obsession of the French mind has often been its trust in *la logique:* the extension of a train of reasoning, a rational theory, to its extreme conclusions. Given la Rochefoucauld's master-key of cynicism, it was inevitable that, sooner or later, someone should apply its workings to the theme of sex in fiction. This is exactly what Maupassant does; and in so doing he makes of many of his characters, not men and women but mere sex-machines.

It is not that Crackanthorpe, by contrast, indulges in any optimistic flights of humanity's final free-will. As much as Maupassant he would seem to believe in 'the irresistible force of circumstance.' As the reviewer Le Gallienne expressed it, commenting on Crackanthorpe's first volume *Wreckage* (1893):

> The poor woman who has just left her drunken husband hugging a prostitute at the public house, will, for a little while, resist the temptation that offers her starving baby a little food,

[1] *Last Studies* by Hubert Crackanthorpe, with an Introduction by Henry James, 1897.
[2] 'Reticence in Literature' (*The Yellow Book*, Vol. II).

but in the end she gives in to the little man who tempts her as she stands looking over the bridge into the river; the drunken wife has her moments of remorseful love, but she will go on drinking; the successful sharper's wife may despise him in her heart but when he comes home with six hundred odd pounds she must go on 'loving' him.[1]

Here, instead of the French 'traite principal' of sex is necessity presented in different guises. We mostly do what we have to do —we accept what fate imposes on us; but the fate to which we resign ourselves is different for each one of us; and within each respective fate there are still contending factors and limited choices.

During his brief life-time Crackanthorpe appeared to many as 'the young hope of English realism;'[2] and of all the short-story-ists of the 'nineties his tales would best bear complete reprinting.

Seduction, prostitution, animal magnetism, the sudden change of a personality under the impact or revelation of sex, the state of concubinage, the social status of the divorcee, and even alcoholism in marriage—the 'nineties short-storyists treat of all these : the first generation of English writers completely to ignore the taboo of silence.

It is, pre-eminently, the old master—the old pretender, as H. G. Wells called him—the venerable, subtle, convoluted Henry James who set down the problems of the author in society with a fine complex lucidity in his tales.

In the preface to the New York edition of the volume entitled The Lesson of the Master, he tells how its four stories (three of which appeared in The Yellow Book[3]) have in common 'some noted adventure, some felt embarrassment, some extreme predic-tion of the artist enamoured of perfection, ridden by his idea or paying for his sincerity.'[4] They deal, as the critic Matthiessen said 'with the split between life and art;'[5] and if to more activist-

[1] Retrospective Review: A Literary Log 1891-95 (1896).
[2] Ibid.
[3] The Death of the Lion (1894), The Coxon Fund (1894), The Next Time (1895).
[4] The Art of the Novel: Critical Prefaces by Henry James, 1935.
[5] Henry James: Stories of Writers and Artists edited with an Introduc-tion by F. O. Matthiessen.

minded readers 'the choice that [James] insists upon between the world and the supremely exacting mistress of art may sound curiously dated,'[1] it is not necessarily in error on that charge.

The invitation by Henry Harland, editor of *The Yellow Book*, to contribute to his 'small square lemon-coloured quarterly'[2] appeared as a stimulating welcoming gesture to the scrupulous author in his fifties who was finding a number of doors no longer open. James' own rhetorical gratitude—a kind of inimitable aesthetic gush, if gush can be sincere, as his clearly was—is worth reproducing for its own sake, and for its expression of the possibilities which he felt inherent in the situation:

> I was invited, and all urgently, to contribute to the first number, and was regaled with the golden truth that my composition might absolutely assume, might shamelessly parade in, its own organic form. It was disclosed to me, wonderfully, that —so golden the air pervading the enterprise—any projected contribution might conform, not only unchallenged but by the circumstances itself the more esteemed, to its own true intelligible nature. For any idea I might wish to express I might have space, in other words, elegantly to express it—an offered licence that, on the spot, opened up the millennium to the short story.[3]

In his time an indefatigable diner-out, a country-house weekender, a spender of leisure, James came to see, as the years unrolled, that even the gracious allurements of society, as well as its cruder temptation, publicity, represented a danger to the artist and his art. It is not poverty and neglect that literally kills the newly celebrated Neil Paraday in *The Death of the Lion* but fame with its asphyxiating embrace. The group of stories in *The Lesson of the Master* combine a kind of divine anecdotage, a blend of infinitely bland gossip, with enacted manifestos of single-mindedness—credos of the utmost commitment.

If the short-storyists of the 'nineties regarded the life of art as

[1] Ibid.
[2] Preface to 'The Lesson of the Master (*The Art of the Novel* by Henry James).
[3] Ibid.

a *beau ideal*, they recognized only too well its often dehumanizing demands. No writers have described better the see-saw between felicity and frustration which this mode of existence tends to produce. George Gissing in *Comrades in Arms*[1] and Hubert Crackanthorpe in *A Conflict of Egoisms*[2] both described the emotional debate between the call of domesticity and the claims of a literary calling. Particularly in the latter story does one find a dramatic analysis of the terrible selfishness or self-obsession which the inward-turning imagination produces almost as a by-product, an occupational disease of the creative mind. In much the same way in George Egerton, the pride of authorship felt by her New Women is seen as being subtly at war with the old-fashioned feminine sensibility which her independent mental Amazons in part, at least, consciously scorn. In her tale *The Spell of the White Elf*[3] the woman author goes out and earns the household income by a career in journalism while her husband stays at home, runs the house and looks after the garden. It is, perhaps, significant that the woman is barren, desires a child, eventually adopts one, and finds herself jealous of an old servant more ready than her with an instinctive gift of baby talk. The servant, Belinda, in turn is jealous of the husband who somehow possesses a temperamental stock of baby lore: 'Master worritted in and out, an' interfered with everything, she never seen a man as knew so much about babies, not for one as never 'ad one of 'is own.' In keeping with advanced opinion of the time, George Egerton's authoress prides herself on being free of the shackles of religion; but for all her certitude on this point is reluctant to have her adopted infant brought up purely to negative beliefs. The child is therefore taught its simple prayers at her husband's knee, since he is not 'emancipated' like her.

The dialectic of the woman's divided nature is clearly felt in the following words:

'You see (half hesitatingly) I have more brains, or at least more intellectuality than my husband, and in that case one is

[1] *Human Odds and Ends*, 1898.
[2] *Wreckage*, 1893.
[3] *Keynotes*, 1894.

apt to undervalue simpler, perhaps greater, qualities. That came home to me, and I began to cry; I don't know why, and he lifted me up, and I think I said something of the kind to him . . . we got nearer to one another someway. He said it was unlucky to cry over a child.'

But no collection of short stories by a 'nineties author deals more authentically with the life of art than Arthur Symons' volume *Spiritual Adventures*, published in 1905—a late-ripening fruit from the *fin-de-siècle* tree.

The arch-modernist Ezra Pound held it in the highest esteem, describing the contents as 'a series of studies in special sensibility.' 'As culture,' he asserted, 'this book is worth all the freudian tosh in existence.'[1]

Like Pater's *Imaginary Portraits*, *Spiritual Adventures* constitute a set of 'studies in strange souls.'[2] They are highly evocative accounts of persons unadjusted to reality who, to make life endurable, must interpose their own vision of the world between themselves and existence. In three stories out of the eight, this vision is the vision of art—of painting in *The Death of Peter Wayderlin*, of acting in *Esther Kahn*, of music in *Christian Travalga*. But the vision is never an entirely happy one, and the chinks through which reality enters, or the self-incarceration which it produces when it more successfully seals off the person, make the book an imposing record of the restless nature of the artistic mind.

The pianist Christian Travalga turns back from a perspective of love which he views as a prison ('Woman, as he saw her, is the beast of prey: rapacious of affection, time, money, all the flesh and all the soul, one's nerves, one's attention, pleasure, duty, art itself') to his music, which presents itself as just another captivity. ('After all, he considered, what was he? Caged already, for another kind of slavery, the prisoner of his own fingers, as they worked, independently of himself, mechanically, doing their so many miles of promenade over the piano.') The escape from reality is all too complete. The last strands connecting the out-

<hr />

[1] *Guide to Kulchur* (1938).
[2] A limited edition title by Symons, 1929.

side world are severed. The notes of music begin to assume a visual existence . . . and Travalga goes mad.

Just the reverse of such a fate is that of the painter in *The Death of Peter Waydelin*, a curious amalgam-image of Aubrey Beardsley and Toulouse Lautrec. Far from shrinking from reality, Waydelin immerses himself in 'the destructive element' in order to come nearer the themes of his art. Consumptive (as was Beardsley) he marries a music-hall model and lives a kind of submerged existence, shut off from his kind, beyond the point of return. 'I have been living,' he tells his narrator who comes to see him when he is dying, 'systematically, not as a stranger in a foreign country which he stares at over his *Baedeker*, but as like a native as I could, and with no return ticket in my pocket.'

Nor is this degradation of his life to be understood for art's sake alone. The elective affinities of the temperament which underlie the creative imagination are powerfully revealed by Waydelin:

> 'And the odd thing is, as you will say, I didn't live in that way because I wanted to do it for my art, but something deeper than my art, a profound low instinct, drew me to these people, to this life, without my own will having anything to do with it . . . I never really chose the music-halls or the public-houses; they chose me.'

Symons' story of the painter Waydelin, as a study of the painterly imagination, takes us well beyond the theories and techniques of Impressionism with what may be called its psychology of the eye. In this tale one understands something of the Fauvist of Expressionist with their identifying 'committed' response to the theme. However much Beardsley may have been the unconscious part-model of Waydelin, it is of neurotic Edward Munch or the psychotic Van Gogh that one thinks as one reads this story. As Professor Frank Kermode has observed, *Spiritual Adventures* remains 'an unjustly neglected book.'[1]

The life of art is naturally related to bohemian and *déclassé* existence; and the short-storyists of the 'nineties gave much attention to these latter themes. It would, no doubt, be true to say that their studies of bohemianism were too often romanti-

[1] *Romantic Image*, 1957.

cized, Henry Harland being a notable offender. Nina, in his story
The Bohemian Girl,[1] does manage at length to have an illegitimate baby, but only after the most improbable balancing acts
of virginity have been tediously and ambiguously paraded.

Harland was a great one for having his cake and eating it:
the virtuous American in wicked Paris. For example, in his tale
of the dancing-girl P'tit-Bleu,[2] the reader is constantly being fed
with hints to the effect 'that a Latin Quarter girl should be soulless was as much a part of the natural order of creation, as that
they should be heartless.' 'They were all of them soulless,' the
narrator reminds us, with 'a stolid implicit cynicism' which, we
are told, 'was the mode of the Quarter.' Yet, after all this talk,
however, of the girl as 'a mere little animal,' the reader is fobbed
off with a taradiddle of P'tit Bleu's dedication of herself to an
elderly opium-taking English painter, with whom, in a state of
chastity, she lives a life of sacrifice in the deep country, existing
only to protect him from his vice. She is, in fact, the 'damned
decent little girl' sacred to the heart of the Puritan playing at
being an artist and a cynic.

It is a pity that this element of dishonesty mars Harland's
accounts of bohemian life since there is a gaiety and grace about
these writings in which he girds at the gods of the Philistines.
Then, too, he is conversant with the jargon of the studio, the
vernacular of the Latin Quarter. But while he proudly brandishes
his key to an *atelier*, we know that he carries deep in his pocket
its twin and opposite, the key to a villa.

This, however, is not quite the whole story. Behind the idealist
in Harland, with his trans-atlantic puritan belief in industrious-
ness and virtue, there lurked the fatalist who seldom spoke out,
and whose wisdom was perhaps derived from a certain streak
of Jewish blood. The Bohemian in *When I am King* is a bohemian
malgré lui. He is no dilettante, no Peter Pan *poseur*. As he says,
looking back upon his career, 'I wanted to earn a decent living;
I wanted to justify my existence by doing something worthy of
the world's acceptance. But the stars in their courses fought
against me.'

[1] *Grey Roses* (1895).
[2] 'P'tit Blue' (*Comedies and Errors*, 1898).

44

There is no flourish in this story—not even the flourishing failure. 'We made the mistake,' the bohemian tells his friend, 'when we were young, of believing, against wise authority, that it was in mortals to command success, that he could command it who deserved it. We believed that the race would be to the swift, the battle to the strong; that a man was responsible for his own destiny, that he'd get what he merited. We believed that honest labour couldn't go unrewarded. An immense mistake. Success is an affair of temperament, like faith, like love, like the colour of your hair.'

There is the same bleak disillusioned wisdom in another of Harland's lates *A Broken Looking-Glass*,[1] set this time in middle-class society; but it was a note he struck all too seldom; and less and less with the passing of time. In the field of bread-and-butter art-for-art's-sake fiction, sedulously cultivated by him, it was not a popular one.

One reason, probably, why the 'nineties short-storyists sentimentalized the bohemian arena was that it represented for them a funk-hole or fortress, a place of retreat. Writers, for the most part, with a limited public, they were in the process of con-tracting out from conventional established society. Bohemia promised a new living-plan, a *modus vivendi* sacred to the figure of the Muses and the forces of freedom.

It was, of course, these writers, unprotected by a middle-class income, who reflected bohemia most truly, the chief of these being George Gissing. For him it was no Chelsea film-set, no site for a chic apache ballet, but rather the seedy residential district of literary promise or failure. Gissing's bohemia was not the temporary middle-class playground of young men down from Oxford, nor the Latin Quarter of the French student. Unlike Dickens' Mr. Gowan, the characters of Gissing have not 'sauntered into the Arts at a leisurely Pall Mall pace,'[2] nor shared with Henri Murger's Musette 'le pain beni de la gaieté.'[3] Bohemia for them consists of cheap lodging, lack of fuel and food and medi-cal attention. It confers no status, it deprives them of class, seek-

---

[1] *Grey Roses* (1895).
[2] *Little Dorrit* (1857).
[3] *Scènes de la Vie de Bohême* (1851).

ing even, as in the tale *Comrades in Arms,* to rob men and women of their sexual distinction. 'But was Miss Childerstone to be judged as a woman? For seven or eight years she had battered in the world of journalism, and with a kind of success which seemed to argue manlike qualities. Since he had known her these last three years, she seemed to have been growing less feminine. At first he had thought of her with the special interest which arises from difference of sex. Now, he rarely, if ever, did so. He liked her, admired her, and could imagine her, in more natural circumstances, a charming woman.'[1] 'More natural circumstances'—the implication being that bohemia denaturalizes.

Gissing's bohemia is a no-man's land; a sordid literary sweatshop, not a nursery of the Muses. In it, no romantic uniform of broad-brimmed hat or floppy tie is worn. Its dwellers dress themselves from the second-hand clothes shop; and measure art quantitatively in terms of labour and rewards: not qualitatively, in terms of style and form: 'By-the-bye, I've been hearing from Tomlinson. He's a better sort of fellow than I supposed. He sent me a cheque for five-and-twenty pounds—on account, he says.'[2]

Gissing's cash-register realism puts him apart from the other short-storyists of the 'nineties, whose leanings to the realistic were psychological, not economic. Gissing exhorted the writer of fiction to 'take himself as seriously as the man of science.'[3] In his own approach there was a 'rigid faithfulness'[4] in which observation stood in place of sympathy. Henry James, who admitted to possessing a 'persistent taste' for Gissing, called him 'an authority . . . *the* authority, in fact, on a region vast and unexplored.'[5] This was the region of the lower-middle class within whose murky precincts Gissing located bohemia, a careful map of which he provided in his novels *The New Grub Street* (1891) and *The Private Papers of Henry Ryecroft* (1903). London has no

[1] 'Comrades in Arms, (*Human Odds and Ends,* 1898).
[2] Ibid.
[3] *Selections Autobiographical & Imaginative from the Works of George Gissing* (New York) 1929.
[4] Ibid.
[5] *Notes on Novelists* (New York) 1914.

Latin Quarter, and Gissing is the master-chronicler of those, who living within the class-system, have none the less become de-classed.

VIII

The Scots poet John Davidson once described the 'nineties as an age of Bovril. Irony aside, the phrase is just. The period was indeed one of compressed literary essence; of saying much in a little space. It is this 'pregnant brevity'[1] which makes it an era of the lyric and short story rather than the narrative in verse or the novel. And if, as has also been alleged, 'the age was short-winded'[2] in its art and 'could only stay over short distances,'[3] at least it had the speed and grace of the sprinter—a streamlined toxophilic attraction. What appealed to the writers of this era was, as Henry James said of Crackanthorpe, 'the situation that asked for a certain fineness of art that could best be presented in a kind of foreshortened picture.'[4]

Like the draughtsmanship of Degas, the painting of Lautrec, the short story of the 'nineties sought its own short-cuts to a climacteric effect.—These new immediacies of art, expressing the intimacies of life more directly, are something fresh in English fiction. We register their workmanship even today.

[1] Frederick Wedmore: 'The Short Story' (*On Books and Arts*, 1899).
[2] Bernard Muddiman: *The Men of the 'Nineties* (1920).
[3] Ibid.
[4] *Studies* by Hubert Crackanthorpe, with an Appreciation by Henry James (1897).

D.S.

Frederick Wedmore
1844-1921

FREDERICK WEDMORE was born at Richmond Hill, Clifton, Bristol, in 1844. Coming of an old Quaker family, he was educated at a Quaker private school before proceeding to study in Lausanne and Paris.

Having early resolved upon a career in journalism and literature he entered a Bristol newspaper office, then came to London in 1869.

His two earliest fictions—A Snapt Gold Ring (1871) and Two Girls (1874)—were, like Henry Harland's first novels, works which he did not wish to re-publish. It was in 1877 that the two types of work best characteristic of him commenced to appear: Pastorals of France, the first of four slim collections of short stories, and Studies in English Art, the initial volume of the author's finely poised and choicely worded critical comments on painting and etching.

'The publication of the Pastorals,' wrote a reviewer in the Bookman, 'may be said to have revealed, not only a new talent, but a new literary genre.' Speaking of this third collection English Episodes (1894), a writer in the Westminster Gazette makes clearer what this new literary genre implied. 'Mr. Wedmore', declares the critic, 'is a singularly fine and sane and carefully deliberate artist. His short stories are not long stories in essence or abbreviation. They abandon the complete narrative for the simpler episode; and in the quality of their difference lies the secret of their literary vitality.'

Wedmore's fine sense of economy and form was matched by a moral fastidiousness which made him no partisan of the purely

49

objective, seemingly amoral, fashionable realism of his day. He refers, for instance, to Gissing as 'a mere student of sordid existence', and, not unnaturally, prefers Anatole France to Maupassant. Again, in his prefatory words to *Orgeas and Miradou, with other pieces* (1896), he speaks of the London vogue 'of a literary "realism" so far from reality that it is ignorantly proud to be bereft of tenderness'. 'Studies in polite realism', was the epithet devised by one reviewer to convey the distinction which Wedmore intended.

The best impression made by these stories is that which Le Gallienne records in noticing the author's *English Episodes*: 'Mr. Wedmore loves to contemplate the grey romances, silver-grey, not dull blanched grey, of men and women who have renounced the dream of their lives, either from an impulse of duty, or from a sort of artistic sense, which forbids them to risk their dream by concrete embodiment—which, so to say, impels them to leave the passion-flower growing, after the manner of the heroine of Madamoiselle de Maupin.' Not without significance did he call his second volume *Renunciations* (1893).

Wedmore's position in the culture of his time is an unusual one. With his shaping sense of formal control, he is with the artistic *avant-garde*: morally and socially, on the other hand, he is an extreme back-number. He is so impossibly high-minded, so reactionary in all his sentiments (against suffragettes, the Board Schools, the Pre-Raphaelites, the aesthetes and the Salvation Army) that his attitude appears to parody itself.

Nor was this 'die-hard' approach, as with Lionel Johnson, aristocratic and romantic. Wedmore's point-of-view is morally middle-class and Victorian. He does not sufficiently distinguish between 'honour', 'conscience', and 'respectability.' This is not to decry the fine enduring element in all of his work—its chaste and purposed lucidity of expression.

Critical books by him include *Masters of Genre Painting* (1880), *On Books and Art* (1899), *Painters and Painting* (1912).

He left a volume of reminiscences—little fertile in personal disclosure—entitled *Memories* (1912). *Certain Comments*, a collection of articles by him published posthumously in 1925, contains two recollections of him by his friends Sir George Douglas and George C. Williamson.

Along with Max Beerbohm, Wedmore was the only noted writer of the 'nineties to receive the accolade of knighthood.

A CHEMIST IN THE SUBURBS*

I

Richard Pelse was the chemist. The suburb was near the 'Angel'; at the top of the City Road; on the confines of Islington. There he led his prosaic life—getting old, and a bachelor. But into the prosaic years—years before Islington—there had burst once the moment of Romance. Then his shop was near Oxford Street. Into the sitting-room over it there had come, one evening, for an hour, the lady of his dream. Unexpectedly; suddenly. She had drawn her chair, by his own, to the fire. They had sat together so; and he had been happy. She had given him his tea; had opened his piano; had played, a while, Xaver Scharwenka's wild music; had kissed him once; and had gone away.

Perhaps his years before and after had seemed at times two deserts, divided by that living stream which was her momentary presence. Or perhaps there was an outstretched darkness on one side of the heavens; then a star; then again outstretched darkness—the life of the shop and the suburb.

Richard Pelse was one of those poor men who are born cultivated: one of the cultivated who are born poor. You had only to look at him now, across the counter and the ranged tooth-powder pots—to see the clear-cut head, against its background of dry drug jars and Latin-labelled drawers—'Alumens;' 'Flor: Sul;' 'Pot: Bitar;' 'Cap: Papav'—to know that he was individual. A sympathetic spectator might call him original; an unsympathetic, eccentric. What fires burnt in the brownness of his quick, keen, restless eyes? What had left his face—not yet really old— topped with a mass of silvery-white hair? There were the delicate

* A *Chemist in the Suburbs* appeared originally in *The Fortnightly Review.*

features, decisive and refined; the nose aquiline, the kindly mouth
with nervous movement at its corners. And, again, the hands,—
thin and white and long: with fingers and thumbs turning back
prodigiously: flexible, subtle, sensitive. And the spare figure,
still quite straight, dressed in the black frock-coat of his business
hours. Original or eccentric: a man whom men and women
looked at: either liked or feared.

At home for years within a stone's throw of the 'Angel,' he
had all his life been a Londoner. Energy and diligence he had
from his boyhood, but country colour had never come into his
cheeks; no robustness of the sea's giving, into his frame. All his
pursuits were of the town—and nearly all his recollections. His
mother was a widowed little newsagent—a withered woman,
once pretty and vivacious—who kept, when he was a child and
a lad, her news-shop in a byway, two doors from North Audley
Street. His father? He never knew him.

When he was twelve years old his mother died, and a customer
of theirs, a druggist of the quarter, took him as 'useful boy.'
Had he ever changed and risen so far afterwards as to be a
famous physician, it would have been told of him, in pride, or
as astonishing, that he had been an errand boy only. As it was,
he had in fact been that, but something besides. He was so
intelligent that gradually he had got into all the work of the
shop. He was civil, and comely too. From selling things behind
the counter, he was put into the dispensary. He educated himself; he passed his examinations; he became an assistant who was
entirely necessary; then he became a partner. At thirty-five he
was a prosperous man and alone; the shop's earlier master having
retired. For Richard Pelse, before that happened, there had been
twenty years of progress, and of self-denial; no doubt of satisfactory, but unremitting work. Then he allowed himself a holiday,
and with a valise by his side and a *Baedeker* in his pocket, started
for Switzerland and Savoy.

II

Mr. Pelse had made more than half his tour and had got over his
surprises, the sense of all that was strange, when he found him-

self, on Sunday, arrived at Aix-les-Bains for two days' rest, and for the charm of its beauty. He had intended to go, rather modestly, to the Hôtel de la Poste. But when the omnibus pulled up, opposite it, in the Place, the landlady, rushing out breathless and busy, announced that the house was full. 'Allez à l'Hôtel Vénat,' she immediately recommended. Then, having seen at a glance that the traveller was an Englishman, 'Hôtel Vénat et Bristol,' she added, by way of encouragement, 'Vénat et Bristol,' and everything was right.

It was there that Mr. Pelse stayed. Though a tradesman, he had tact as well as education; various interests and real kindliness. He could mix quite easily with 'his betters'—found his 'betters' much more his equals than his neighbours had been. At the Vénat, an argument with an English chaplain brought him into contact with a family of three—Colonel Image, a military politician, very well connected, and busy in the House; and his wife, who was above all things fashionable; and his daughter, who was blonde and nineteen.

Richard Pelse must certainly then, with all his earlier deficiencies and disadvantages, have been picturesque, and almost elegant, as well as interesting. The impulsive Miss Image found him so. In the garden, from his ground-floor bedroom, there had been a vision of a tall white figure, of floating muslin, of pale-coloured hair. Nearer, there were seen dancing eyes, large and grey, and a mouth that was Cupid's bow. At table d'hôte there was heard the voice that he liked best, and liked at once. A voice? Hardly. An instrument of music. You listened to it as to a well-used violin.

In the drawing-room he got into talk with her. Was she not, unexpectedly, the ideal realised?—the lady of the dream of all his youth.

But that night he reflected on the distance between them. He was no ambitious snob, scheming for marriage in a sphere not his. The distance—the distance! No, there could never be marriage, or his career must change first. Should he leave to-morrow, and forget the encounter? Should he enjoy her for three days, and forget her then instead, or hug the memory? At all events, he did not go.

And on both sides, in the short three days—prolonged to four and five—there was interest and fascination. Perhaps he should have told her father who he was. Instead of it, he told her. There was a recoil then—and it might have saved them. Her knowledge of the world and of the *convenances*—nineteen, but bred in Society—was suddenly uppermost. Nothing more could be said to him, and she would mention to her mother as a piece of gossip to be heard and forgotten—as the funny adventure of travelling and of chance acquaintance—that the man was a shopkeeper, a chemist; might have sold her sponges, nail brushes, Eau de Cologne. Then the simplicity, the naturalness, warmth, impulsiveness which were in her too—came uppermost in their turn. She would tell none of that. She would keep him to herself, for the time at least—him and his secret. There was mutual attraction, strong and unquestionable. Elective affinities. And such things had their rights.

Wilful and independent—it seemed so then—she laid herself out to be with him. Mrs. Image was indolent, physically. In the morning the military politician was wont to wait in the ante-chamber of a man of science who was great on the healing waters; later in the day he was borne from the Bath House, closely muffled, in a curtained chair, and put to bed till dinner-time at the hotel. He was not seriously ill, however, and the treatment, which had begun a fortnight before Richard Pelse's arrival, would now soon be over. Anyhow their opportunities were numbered. There was an end to meetings—chance meetings, after all, though wished for on both sides—at noon, under the shade of the grouped trees in a sun-smitten park encircled by the mountains; at night, amid the soft illuminations of the Villa des Fleurs, whither Miss Image was chaperoned; again, at breakfast time, when, almost from the open windows of the hotel, could be discerned, here and there, between luxuriant foliage, gold and green—beyond the richness of walnut and chestnut branch, beyond the vines, beyond the poplar marshes and the sunny fields—a level flash of turquoise, which was the Lac de Bourget.

'We go tonight,' said Beatrice, meeting Mr. Pelse by the Roman Arch, when she had deposited her father for his last consultation.

'Should I speak to Colonel Image?' he urged, almost hopelessly.

'I was mad for you to do it; but you never must. Nothing could possibly come of it but harm. You must be loyal and obey me. There is not the very ghost of a chance for us. . . . Oh! you won't think of me very long. You have your own life, you know; and I must have mine. Silly, silly lovers! I might wait; but then it could never, *never* be. Dick!—forget me!'

She had been presented that Season. For a moment there had fallen upon her the smile of the Princess. She had been admired at the Drawing-room; and she and what she wore had been admired afterwards, at a Drawing-room tea. She had danced at great houses, and was there as a native of them. There was reason as well as earnestness in the tone of 'Dick!—forget me!'

'And in England we live almost in the next street,' he said to her. 'There is nothing but class that divides us. I have done something already, if you recollect how I began. I could do more, and go a good deal further. You are the first lady I ever talked to, intimately. You would change me—you would bring me up to you.'

'There is nothing in me to bring you up to, Dick. Think how young I am! I am a little fool, who happened to take a fancy to you. Pretty, am I? But a little fool, after all. You treated me so gravely and so well. I had been flattered often enough. And I was mad to be respected. . . . There is no chivalry left. . . . Your respect was flattery, too. . . . Here is my photograph, because I trust you. But forget me, forget me! My last word. Take my hand. And good-bye!'

He took her hands—both of them—and saw the last of her. And, by another train, he too went back to London, to the chemist's shop.

It was curious, at first, to think, as he was making up prescriptions, or giving them to his assistants, that she was within a stone's throw of that pestle and mortar; almost within sight of the green and red and straw-coloured jars that stood in his shop window and were the sign of his calling. His shop was in Orchard Street; their house in Manchester Square. Once, did she pass the shop? Once, when he was on the Oxford Street pavement, was that she, borne along in a Victoria?

But gradually he was training himself to forget all that. He was loyal, obedient—was accepting the inevitable. Was it not a chance fancy? Was it not in sheer impulsiveness—in recognition of he wondered what in him, besides his deepest admiration —that she had flung him her confidence; honoured him by liking. Could that last with her? Could it anyhow have lasted? Probably he would never see her again. Might he not one day console himself?—he once half whispered. No—it could never be that. He was so dainty about women; he was so particular—he either wanted nothing, or exacted so much—the experience of a rapid fascination would never be repeated. He was an idealist—of those who want, in women, a picture and a vision: not a house-keeper.

III

The autumn dragged along. Pelse had acquired from America the rights to an exclusive sale of a particular preparation of the Hypo-phosphites, and the Society doctors—the men who had charge of Royalty and of over-tasked celebrities, of smart people, and of the very rich—had taken to recommend it. The extra work which that involved made him very busy, and his own more accustomed work, in all its thousand details, was done at his shop with such a singular nicety—of which he, of course, was the inspirer—that the shop was more and more frequented.

Winter succeeded to autumn. A thick fog had lain for days over Orchard Street. Then there came a little snow. But in the parlour over the shop—with three windows closely curtained— one could have forgetfulness of weather. There was the neat fire-place; the little low tea-table; a bookcase in which Pelse—before that critical event at Aix-les-Bains—had been putting, gradually, first editions of the English Poets; a cabinet of china, in which— but always before Aix-les-Bains—he had taken to accumulate some pretty English things of whitest paste or finest painting: a Worcester cup, with its exotic birds, its lasting gold, its scale-blue ground, like lapis lazuli or sapphire; a Chelsea figure; something from Swansea; white plates of Nantgarw, bestrewn with Billingsley's greyish pink roses, of which he knew the beauty, the free artistic touch. How the things had lost interest for him! 'From the moment,' says some French art critic, 'that a woman occupies me, my collection does not exist.' And many a woman may lay claim to occupy a French art critic; only *one* had occupied Richard Pelse.

It was on an evening in December, and Pelse was in the sitting-room, tired with the day's labours, and not particularly happy with the evening newspapers—for, apart from any causes of private discontent, the *Pall Mall* had told him that our upper classes were unworthy of confidence, and from the *St. James's* he had gathered that even the lower could scarcely boast complete enlightenment—it was on an evening in December, when the chemist was so circumstanced, that his neat servant, opening the door of the parlour, held it back for the entrance of a veiled, tall lady. 'Miss Image,' said the servant, for the name had been frankly given her.

The servant vanished. Richard Pelse rose from his seat, with his heart beating. The tall lady was standing there with lifted arms, detaching veil and the broad velvet hat; a minute afterwards, laying aside her furs and her warm wraps, the glowing face of a swift walker in the winter weather was made visible: the blonde head, the slim and straight rounded figure had got up to the fireplace. She put her hand out towards Richard Pelse. He took it; exclaimed to her, by her name: nothing more— "Beatrice!"—wheeled a chair to the fire. And down she sat.

'Yes. I could stand it no longer. I have passed the place so often. I was mad to see you. They are gone into the country on a visit. I could manage it tonight.' She looked quite good and sweet and serious—passionate it might be, as well as young, but at all events, no intriguing Miss. Strange!—the intuitive trust she had in him, to come there, so. 'Perhaps you can give me some tea?'

He flew downstairs to order it—a bell's summons would have been inadequate to the occasion, and would have given no vent to his delight. Ten minutes after, it was in front of the fire. The lamp was just behind her. Might he be calm now? Might he be excited? Might he be paralysed with astonishment? She was so quiet and so bright, he was made quiet too. She sat there as in an old and daily place—the blonde head, the eyes, the figure's lines. He was so happy. Suddenly his house was made a home.

'How have you been? How are you?' But before he answered he had given her a stool, respectfully: had put a cushion at her head. 'How good of you!' she said, with her grey eyes very beautiful: thanking him for his mental attitude: not for his cushion and his stool.

'Well, you know, I have been trying to forget you. Have you changed your mind?' he asked. She gazed into the fire. 'Has the time come for me to speak?' he continued. His chair was beside hers. 'Why did you come here?'

'I supposed I felt you cared about me. And I was sick of *not* coming. I suppose I felt you were a friend. No, I don't think I have changed my mind at all. But I am one of the girls who can do mad things. And girls who can do mad things, once or twice in their lives at all events, are commoner—much commoner—than proper people think. So here I am! 'Tisn't wonderful. Father and mother are at Lord Sevenoaks'.'

His brow clouded. Again, and, as it seemed, with emphasis, the difficulty of class. Difficult? Impossible, was it not? Yet this was what he said:

'You will come again? And one day I will speak. Beatrice, Beatrice,—I am *yours*! Have it as you will—it shall all be as you will—but *you* know that you can never go away for good.'

'If you are nice to me, very likely I shall come ever so *many* times. I can't stay very long to-night. There—my cup. Ah! you have got a piano? Whose is it?'—opening it—'A Bechstein. Sit still there. I will play.'

She tried the instrument a moment, first. Certain chords. Then, with turned head, she waited silently: was making her choice. For, whatever it was, it would have to be from memory. There was not a single music book.

In a minute, she had chosen. It was a plunge into a weird, wild dance. 'You know whose that is?'

'No.'

'Polish. Xaver Scharwenka's. Now the same again, and then

another.' And they were played, and then she rose from the piano. 'My cloak, please. Thank you.'

He went to the window curtain: listened for the rumble of the street, for all the city was about them—they two. But the noises of the town had ceased.

'Snowing fast!' he said, coming back from the red curtain. 'Can you go?'

'It is only two minutes' walk,' she answered. 'And I don't quite think I see them cheeking me. Besides, I will find some excuse or other for wet things. O! you think me mean. You don't approve of prevarications. But prevarications give me to you.' Her smile would have melted mountains. 'Thank you'—near the door. 'I suppose I shall come back many times. Dick! I feel like it.' He looked enraptured. She put her hand out, and he took it. Always respectful, reverential, he had had an angel's visit. From the Heavens, down into Orchard Street, what divine, undreamt of, guest! 'O! but you worship me *too much*,' she said. She brushed his cheek with her lips, and her hand stayed in his.

'You must come back many times,' he almost gasped. For all his manhood yearned for her. And she was gone—and gone as much as the last note of Scharwenka's wild music.

For she never came back. The voice, the figure's lines, the blonde head, and the eyes, and the mouth that was Cupid's bow —no more in Richard Pelse's sitting-room. A flirt, was she? Heartless?—changeable?—a child? Who shall say? For weeks, he waited. Then, a short letter:

O! Dick: it is of no use, you know. You'll have to forgive me, because I was wrong and rash. Only, Dick, understand that it is all over. I could never do that again. If I say I owe Father and Mother something, you know I'm not a fraud—you know I mean it. After all, we should never have done together. Yet, I love you. Think of me kindly. Good-bye!

And she kept her word. And it was over. No lamplight welcomed her; nor fire gleamed for her; nor chairs were placed again on the cosy hearth for two. And, in the closed piano, there slept, for ever, Scharwenka's wild music.

IV

But Pelse had to move from Orchard Street. Change of scene; change of people. And good-bye—with all his heart—to the fashionable custom—to the inroads of the elegant who reminded him of Her, though with a difference. He must seek a new life, in some work-a-day quarter. To be with the busy and the common—not with any chosen or privileged humanity, but just humanity: nothing else. To be with people who really suffered; not with peole who wanted hair-dyes. So it was that when a long-established druggist of Islington passed away, old and decrepit, with a business neglected and lessened, Richard Pelse came near the 'Angel'—to the dingy shop you mounted into by two steep steps from the pavement—to the dingy shop with the small-paned, old-fashioned windows; with the little mahogany desk at which who stood at it commanded the prospect of the City-Road. He sold the Orchard Street business; and, taking with him only the youngest and least qualified of his young men—and the china and the First Editions, to coax his thoughts to return again to these first loves—he established himself afresh, and did his own work. Gradually he was recognised as rather an exceptional person in the quarter. And his energy was great enough to allow him, little by little, year by year, to build up a trade.

Things were slack in the forenoons, and a face sometimes depressed, sometimes preoccupied, looked out in the street; and Pelse would stand at his desk with bright eyes and clenched mouth, rapping a tune nervously with long lean fingers. After Islington's early dinner, important people were abroad—the people who lived in the squares on the west side of Upper Street—and the wife of a City house agent, pompous and portly, patronised (with the breadth of the counter, and all that conveyed, between them) a man whom Beatrice Image had once kissed. Acquaintance with these folk was strictly limited. The shopkeeper, refined and super-sensitive, was not good enough company for the genteel.

But when evening came, he was wont to be too busy to think for an instant of his social place. The prescriptions brought to

him were few, but the shop—and on Saturday night especially
—was crowded with the smaller *bourgeoisie*, with their little
wants; the maid-of-all-work from the Liverpool Road arrived
hurriedly in her cap, and was comforted; Mr. Pelse was the
recipient of sorry confidences from the German clerks of Barns-
bury. He was helpful and generous—kind to the individual and
a cynic to the race. Late in the evening the gas flared in the little
shop. Its shutters were just closed when the cheap playhouse,
almost within sight, vomited forth its crowd, and loafers were
many about the bars of the 'Angel' and at the great street
corner, and omnibus and tramcar followed each other still upon
the long main roads. The night of the second-rate suburb.

And that went on for years; and he was a bachelor with no
relations; getting visibly older and thinner; and a shock of white
hair crowned now the pale forehead, over the dark brilliance
of the keen, quick eyes. Long ago he had read in the newspaper
of the marriage of Miss Image—a day when he had been wondering where of all places in the wide world, the one face might
be?

> 'Where is she now? What lands or skies
> Paint pictures in her friendly eyes?'

Then he had read of her marriage. Hers, at least, was a wound
that had healed. His?—but what sign was there of wound at all?
For in intervals of business he had come again to hug his First
Editions. They knew him at book sales, at Sotheby's. He dusted
his own Worcester carefully. Was it not of the best period?—
with the 'square mark.' As a contract to his quarter's common-
ness, he had begun to cultivate the exquisite with the simple in
his daily ways. His food was sometimes frugal, but it was cooked
to perfection. When he allowed himself a luxury, for himself and
one rare crony—an unknown artist of the neighbourhood,
discovered tardily; a professor of languages who understood
literature; or a brother druggist whom business dealings caused
him to know—it was nothing short of the best that he allowed
himself: he admitted not the second rate: he was an idealist
still. The fruit with which, just once or twice in summer or in
autumn, he regaled a pretty child, was not an apple or an orange,

but grey-bloomed grapes, or a peach, quite flawless. The glass of wine which he brought out from the parlour cupboard to the weak old woman, accommodated with a chair, was a soft Madeira, or a sherry nearly as old as she was. It had known long voyages. It was East India, or it was Bristol Milk. Yes; he was fairly prosperous; and he showed no sign of wound.

Even 'the collector' within him reasserted itself in novel enterprise. To the Worcester, the Swansea, the Nantgarw, the Chelsea, the First Editions, there came to be added bits, that were faultless, of Battersea Enamel—casket and candlesticks, saltcellars, needle-case, and rose-pink patch-box: best of all, the dainty *étui*, with the rare puce ground, or the white thing with the tulip and the pansy—pansies for thoughts—and winding in between its gilded scrolls, the foreign motto, '*Fidèle en amitié*'— a Frenchman's utmost vow. Yes; he was prosperous.

Nor was it Battersea only. Hidden away in the recesses of a cupboard—Pelse questioning a little, within himself, the rightness of its barbaric splendour—there may have lain one specimen of Vernis-Martin, a glow of gold and of red. He was a collector, and fortunate.

Still, the nerves had been strained for many a year; and suddenly were shattered. Speechless and one side stiffened—stricken now with paralysis—Mr. Pelse lay in the bedroom over the shop; understanding much, but making small sign to servant or assistant or medical man. His last view—before a second and final seizure—was of the steady February rain; the weary London afternoon; the unbroken sky; the slate roofs, wet and glistening; the attic windows of the City Road. He had lived—it seemed to him—so long. The Past—that moment of the Past, however vivid—might, one thinks, be quite forgotten.

Yet, wrapped in a soiled paper, in the pocket of his frock-coat, after death, they found a girl's likeness. 'My photograph, because I trust you!' she had said to him at Aix-les-Bains. And what was all the rest!

In all his thought, for all those years, she was his great, dear friend. Once or twice he had held her beautiful hands—looked at her eyes—been strong and happy in the magnetism of her presence.

Ella D'Arcy
1851-1939

ELLA D'ARCY was born in London of Irish parents in 1851. She was educated in France and Germany, and the Channel Islands were particularly well known to her and are featured in a number of her tales. Like George Egerton, she had planned a career in painting and had, in fact, attended the Slade until defective eyesight caused her to yield that ambition and turn to the sister art of letters.

Her début in London was made with the appearance of her story 'Irremediable' in volume one of *The Yellow Book* (1894). This story had been turned down by a number of publishers and editors—*Blackwood's* declaring that the sacrament of marriage could not be so summarily dealt with—and Henry Harland, who accepted the manuscript for John Lane, congratulated himself on his perspicacity.

Miss D'Arcy duly became one of Harland's 'regulars.' She appeared more times in *The Yellow Book* than any author save the editor himself, and in 1895 Lane collected her stories together into a volume *Monochromes* which was published in his famous Keynotes Series. This was followed in 1898 by two other volumes: *The Bishop's Dilemma,* a novel; and *Modern Instances,* a second gathering of short stories. With her translation of Maurois' *Ariel* in 1924 her writing life was over.

Ella D'Arcy is certainly the most astringent author of her sex in the 'nineties. She is the perfect antidote to George Egerton's feminist romanticism, and her style differs as much from that lady's as Jane Austen's from Charlotte Brontë's. Place George Egerton's story *Wedlock* beside Ella D'Arcy's *A Marriage* and the greater realism of the latter effects one like an icy day.

Socially, it is *Wedlock* with its drink and working-class brutality which seems to be nearer the bone of existence, while A *Marriage* appears middle-class and suburban. Psychologically, however, it is the latter which, without stress or strain of style, makes its chilling deadly point.

However George Egerton understood men, she could only describe them externally. Ella D'Arcy is better at this and is even prepared to show man—not woman—as the villain of the piece. None the less, it is in those tales when she is exposing her sisters that she writes with the most telling focus.

The story included here—*At Twickenham*—aptly justifies what William C. Frierson writes in *The English Novel in Transition* (1942) of this author and her place in literature: 'Her insistence upon the narrowness and triviality of feminine interests is of sufficient importance . . . to attract our interest. The intimate and unromantic detail which characterized her presentations forecast the unsentimental analyses of the late English realists.'

Nor can there have been before Ella D'Arcy's day, so cool, collected, and cogent a study of the psychology of a nymphomaniac as her tale *The Pleasure Pilgrim*.

Not equally at home with all her subjects, here was an author whom one could have wished to have written not less, but more. Netta Syrett, a friend of Ella, put down her low productivity to 'her incurable idleness;' and Henry Harland is reported to have locked her in a room on one occasion until she had completed her next *Yellow Book* story.

She spent her latter years in Paris, though she died in England in September 1939.

AT TWICKENHAM

When John Corbett married Minnie Wray, her sister Lœtitia, their parents being dead, came to live under his roof also, which seemed to Corbett the most natural arrangement in the world, for he was an Irishman, and the Irish never count the cost of an

1. FREDERICK WEDMORE

II. ELLA D'ARCY
From the *Bookman* (New York), II (1895)

extra mouth. 'Where there's enough for two, there's enough for three,' is a favourite saying of theirs, and even in the most impecunious Irish household no one ever dreams of grudging you your bite of bread or your sup o' th' crathur.

But Corbett was not impecunious. On the contrary, he was fairly well off, being partner in and traveller for an Irish whisky house, and earning thus between eight and nine hundred a year. In the Income Tax returns he put the figure down as five hundred, but in conversation he referred to it casually as over a thousand; for he had some of the vices of his nationality as well as most of its virtues, and to impress Twickenham with a due sense of the worth of John Corbett was perhaps his chief preoccupation out of business hours.

He lived in an imitation high art villa on the road to Strawberry Hill; a villa that rejoiced in the name of 'Braemar,' gilded in gothic letters upon the wooden gate; a villa that flared up into pinnacles, blushed with red-brick, and mourned behind sad-tinted glass. The Elizabethan casements let in piercing draughts, the Brummagem brass door-handles came off in the confiding hand that sought to turn them, the tiled hearths successfully conducted all the heat up the chimneys to disperse is generously over an inclement sky. But Corbett found consolation in the knowledge that the hall was paved with grey and white mosaic, that the 'Salve' bristled at you from the door-mat, that the dining-room boasted of a dado, and that the drawing-room rose to the dignity of a frieze.

Minnie Corbett, whose full name was Margaret, but preferred to be called Rita, although she could not teach her family to remember to call her so, and Lœtitia, who had recently changed the 'Tish' of her childhood to the more poetical 'Letty,' dressed the windows of 'Braemar' with frilled Madras muslin, draped the mantel-pieces with plush, hung the walls with coloured photographs, Chinese crockery, and Japanese fans. They made expeditions into town in search of pampas graas and bulrushes, with which in summer-time they decorated the fireplaces, and in winter the painted drain-pipes which stood in the corners of the drawing-room.

Beyond which labours of love, and Minnie's perfunctory ordering of the dinner every morning, neither she nor Lœtitia found anything to do, for Corbett kept a cook, a house-parlourmaid, and two nurses to look after Minnie's three children, in whom her interest seemed to have ceased when she had bestowed on them the high-sounding names of Lancelot, Hugo, and Guinevere. Lœtitia had never pretended to feel any interest in the children at all.

The sisters suffered terribly from dulness, and one memorable Sunday evening, Corbett being away travelling, they took first-class tickets to Waterloo, returning by the next train, merely to pass the time.

When Corbett was not travelling, his going to and fro between Twickenham and the City lent a spice of variety to the day. He left every morning by the 9.15 train, and came home in the evening in time for a seven o'clock dinner. On Saturdays he got back by two, when he either mowed the lawn in his shirt-sleeves, or played a set of tennis with Lœtitia, or went with both girls for a row on the river. Or, if Minnie made a special point of it, he escorted them back into town, where he treated them to a restaurant *table d'hôte* and a theatre afterwards. On Sundays he rose late, renewed his weekly acquaintance with the baby, read through the *Referee* from first line to last, and, accompanied by his two little boys dressed in correct Jack Tar costume, went for a walk along the towing-path, whence they could watch the boating.

Humanly speaking, he would have liked to have followed the example of those flannel-shirted publicans and sinners who pushed off every moment in gay twos and threes from Shore's landing-stage, but consideration for the susceptibilities of Providence and of Twickenham held him in check.

It is true he did not go to church, although often disquieted by the thought of the bad effect this omission must produce on the mind of his next-door neighbour; but he salved his conscience with the plea that he was a busy man, and that Sunday was his only day of home life. Besides, the family was well represented by Minnie and Lœtitia, who when the weather was fine never missed morning service. When it was wet they stayed away on account of their frocks.

Sunday afternoons were spent by them sitting in the drawing-room awaiting the visitors who did not come. The number of persons in Twickenham with whom they were on calling terms was limited, nor can it be maintained that 'Braemar' was an amusing house at which to call. For though Corbett was one of the most cordial, one of the most hospitable of young men, his women-folk shone rather by their silences than by their conversational gifts.

Minnie Corbett was particularly silent. She had won her husband by lifting to his a pair of blankly beautiful eyes, and it did not seem to her requisite to give greater exertion to the winning of minor successes.

Lœtitia could talk to men providing they were unrelated to her, but she found nothing to say to members of her own sex. Even with her sister she was mostly silent, unless there was a new fashion in hats, the cut of a sleeve, or the set of a skirt to discuss. There was, however, one other topic which invariably aroused her to a transitory animation. This was the passing by the windows, in his well-appointed dog-cart, of a man whom, because of his upright bearing, moustache, and close-cut hair, she and Minnie had agreed to call 'the Captain.'

He was tall, evidently, and had a straight nose. Lœtitia also was straight-nosed and tall. She saw in this physical resemblance a reason for fostering a sentimental interest in him.

'Quick, Minnie, here's the Captain!' she would cry, and Minnie would awake from the somnolency of Sunday with a start, and skip over to the window to watch a flying vision of a brown horse, a black and red painted cart, and a drab-coated figure holding the reins, while a very small groom in white cords and top-boots maintained his seat behind by means of tightly folded arms and a portentous frown.

'He's got such a pretty horse,' observed Minnie on one occasion, before relapsing back into silence, the folding of hands, and a rocking-chair.

'Yes,' Lœtitia agreed pensively, 'it has such a nice tail.'

Although she knew nothing concerning the Captain, although it did not seem probable that she ever would know anything, although it was at least a tenable supposition that he was married already and the father of a family, she saw herself, in fancy, the wife of the wearer of the drab coat, driving by his side along the roads of Twickenham, up the High Street of Richmond. She wore, in fancy, a sealskin as handsome as Minnie's and six inches longer, and she ordered lavishly from Gosling and the other tradesmen, giving the address of Captain Devereux of Deepdene, or Captain Mortimer of the Shrubberies. The names were either purely imaginary, or reminiscent of the novels she constantly carried about with her and fitfully read.

She sat nearly always with an open book upon her knee, but neither Hall Caine nor Miss Marie Corelli even in their most inspired moments could woo her to complete self-forgetfulness. She did not wish to forget herself in a novel. She wished to find in it straw for her own brick-making, bricks for her own castle-building. And if a shadow fell across the window, if a step was heard along the hall, she could break off in the most poignant passage to lift a slim hand to the better arrangement of her curls, to thrust a slim foot in lace stocking and pointed shoe to a position of greater conspicuousness.

On Sunday evenings at 'Braemar' there was cold supper at eight, consisting of the early dinner joint, eaten with a salad scientifically mixed by Corbett, the remains of the apple or gooseberry pie, cheese, and an excellent Burgundy obtained by him at trade price. When the cloth was removed he did not return to the drawing-room. He never felt at ease in that over-furnished, over-ornate room, so darkened by shaded lamps and pink petticoated candles that it was impossible to read. The white, untempered flames of three gas-burners in the dining-room suited him better, and here he would sit on one side of the hearth in an armchair grown comfortable from continual use, and read over again the already well-read paper, while Minnie, on the other side of the hearth, stared silently before her, and Lœtitia fingered her book at the table.

Sometimes Corbett, untaught by past experience, would make a hopeful appeal to one or the other, for an expression of opinion concerning some topic of the day; the last play, the newest book. But Minnie seldom took the trouble to hear him at all, and Lœtitia would answer with such superficial politeness, with so wide an irrelevance to the subject, that, discouraged, he would draw back again into his shell. At the end of every Sunday evening he was glad to remember that the next day was Monday, when he could return to his occupations and his acquaintances in the City. In the City men were ready to talk to him, to listen to what he said, and even to affect some show of interest in his views and pursuits.

The chief breaks in his home life, its principal excitements, were the various ailments the children developed, the multifarious and unexpected means they found of putting their lives in jeopardy and adding items to Dr. Payne's half-yearly accounts. Corbett would come home in the happiest mood, to have his serenity roughly shattered by the news that Lancelot had forced a boot-button down his ear, and was rolling on the floor in agony; that Hugo had bolted seventeen cherry-stones in succession and obstinately refused an emetic; that the baby had been seized with convulsions; that the whole family were in for chicken-pox, whooping-cough, or mumps.

On such occasions Minnie, recovering something of her ante-nuptial vivacity, seemed to take a positive pleasure in unfolding the harrowing details, in dwelling on the still more harrowing consequences which would probably ensue.

When, on turning into Wetherly Gardens on his way from the station, Corbett perceived his wife's blonde head above the garden gate, he knew at once that it betokened a domestic catastrophe. It had only been in the very early days of their married life that Minnie had hurried to greet his return for the mere pleasure it gave her.

The past winter had brought rather more than the usual crop of casualties among the children, so that it had seemed to Corbett that the parental cup of bitterness was already filled to overflowing, that Fate might well grant him a respite, when, returning from town one warm May Saturday, his thoughts veering riverwards, and his intention being to invite the girls to scull up and have tea at Tagg's, his ears were martyrised by the vociferous howls of Hugo, who had just managed to pull down over himself the kettle of water boiling on the nursery fire.

While the women of the household disputed among themselves

as to the remedial values of oil, treacle, or magnesia, Corbett rushed round to Payne's to find him away, and to be referred to Dr. Matheson of Holly Cotage, who was taking Payne's cases. At the moment he never noticed what Matheson was like, he received no conscious impression of the other's personality. But when that evening, comparative peace having again fallen upon the Villa, Lœtitia remarked for the twentieth time, 'How funny that Dr. Matheson should be the Captain, isn't it?' he found in his memory the picture of a tall fair man, with regular features and a quiet manner, he caught the echoes of a pleasantly modulated voice.

The young women did not go to service next morning, but Lœtitia put on her best gown nevertheless. She displayed also a good deal of unexpected solicitude for her little nephew, and when Matheson looked in, at about 11 a.m., she saw fit to accompany him and Corbett upstairs to the night-nursery, where Minnie, in a white wrapper trimmed with ribbons as blue as her eyes and as meaningless, sat gazing into futurity by her son's bedside.

Hugo had given up the attempt to obtain illuminating answers to the intricate social and ethical problems with which he wiled away the pain-filled time. For when by repeated interrogatives of 'Mother?' 'Eh, mother?' 'Well, mother?' he had induced Minnie at least to listen to him, all he extracted from her was some unsatisfying vagueness, which added its quota to the waters of contempt already welling up in his young soul for the intelligence of women.

He rejoiced at the appearance of his father and the doctor, despite some natural heart-sinkings as to what the latter might not purpose doing to him. He knew doctors to be perfectly irresponsible autocrats, who walked into your bedroom, felt your pulse, turned you over and over just as though you were a puppy or a kitten, and then with an impassive countenance ordered you a poultice or a powder, and walked off. He knew that if they condemned you to lose an arm or a leg they would be just as despotic and impassible, and you would have to submit just as quietly. None of the grown-ups about you would ever dream of interfering in your behalf.

So he fixed Matheson with an alert, an inquiring, a profoundly distrusting eye, and with a hand in his father's, awaited developments. Lœtitia he ignored altogether. He supposed that the existence of aunts was necessary to the general scheme of things, but personally he hadn't any use for them. His predominate impression of Auntie Tish was that she spent her day heating curling-irons over the gas-bracket in her bedroom, and curling her hair, and although he saw great possibilities in curling-irons heated red-hot and applied to reasonable uses, he was convinced that no one besides herself ever knew whether her hair was curled or straight. But women were such ninnies.

The examination over, the scalds re-dressed and covered up again, Matheson on his way downstairs stopped at the staircase window to admire the green and charming piece of garden, which ending in an inconspicuous wooden paling, enjoyed an illusory proprietorship in the belt of fine old elm trees belonging to the demesne beyond.

Corbett invited him to come and take a turn round it, and the two young men stepped out upon the lawn.

It was a delicious blue and white morning, with that Sunday feeling in the air which is produced by the cessation of all workaday noises, and heightened just now by the last melodious bell-cadences floating out from the church on the distant green. The garden was full of flowers and bees, scent and sunshine. Roses, clematis, and canariensis tapestried the brick unsightlinesses of the back of the house. Serried ranks of blue-green lavender, wild companies of undisciplined sweet pea, sturdy clumps of red-hot poker shooting up in fiery contrast to the wide-spreading luxuriance of the cool white daisy bushes, justled side by side in the border territories which were separated from the grass by narrow gravel paths.

While Corbett and his guest walked up and down the centre of the lawn, Minnie and Lœtitia watched them from behind the curtains of the night-nursery window.

'He's got such nice hands,' said Lœtitia, 'so white and well kept. Did you notice, Minnie?' Lœtitia always noticed hands, because she gave a great deal of attention to her own.

But Minnie, whose hands were not her strong point, was more

impressed by Matheson's boots. 'I wish Jack would get brown boots, they look so much smarter with light clothes,' she remarked, but without any intensity of desire. Before the short phrase was finished, her voice had dropped into apathy, her gaze had wandered away from Matheson's boots, from the garden, from the hour. She seemed not to hear her sister's dubious : 'Yes, but I wonder he wears a tweed suit on Sundays?'

Lœtitia heard herself calling him Algernon or Edgar, and remonstrating with him on the subject. Then she went into her bedroom, recurled a peccant lock on her temple, and joined the men just as the dinner gong sounded.

Matheson was pressed to stay and share the early dinner. 'Unless,' said Corbett, seeing that he hesitated, 'Mrs. Matheson . . . perhaps . . . is waiting for you?'

'There is no Mrs. Matheson, as yet,' he answered smiling, 'although Payne is always telling me it's my professional duty to get married as soon as possible.'

Lœtitia coloured and smiled.

From that day Matheson was often at 'Braemar.' At first he came ostensibly to attend to Hugo, but before that small pickle was on his feet again and in fresh mischief, he was sufficiently friendly with the family to drop in without any excuse at all.

He would come of an evening and ask for Corbett, and the maid would show him into the little study behind the dining-room, where Corbett enjoyed his after-dinner smoke. He enjoyed it doubly in Matheson's society, and discovered he had been thirsting for some such companionship for years. The girls were awfully nice, of course, but . . . and then, the fellows in the City . . . he compared them with Matheson, much to their dis-advantage. For Matheson struck him as being amazingly clever —a pillar of originality—and his fine indifference to the most cherished opinions of Twickenham made Corbett catch his breath. But the time spent with his friend was only too short. Minnie and Lœtitia always found some pretext to join them, and they would reproach Matheson in so cordial a manner for never coming into the drawing-room, that presently, somewhat to Corbett's chagrin, he began to pay his visits to them instead.

Then as the summer advanced, the fine weather suggested river picnics, and the young women arranged one every week. They even ventured under Matheson's influence to go out on a Sunday, starting in the forenoon, getting up as far as Chertsey, and not returning till late at night. Corbett, half delighted with the abandoned devilry of the proceedings, half terrified lest Wetherly Gardens should come to hear of it, or Providence deal swift retribution, was always wholly surprised and relieved when they found themselves again ashore, as safe and comfortable as though the day had been a mere Monday or Wednesday. And if this immunity from consequence slightly shook Corbett's respect for Providence, it sensibly increased his respect for his friend.

Corbett would have enjoyed this summer extremely, but for the curious jealousy Minnie began to exhibit of his affection for Matheson. It seemed to him it could only be jealousy which made her intrude so needlessly on their tête-à-têtes, interrupt their conversation so pointedly, and so frequently reproach Corbett, in the privacy of the nuptial chamber, for monopolising all the attention of their guest.

'You're always so selfish,' Minnie would complain.

Yet, reviewing the incidents of the evening—Matheson had been dining perhaps at 'Braemar'—it seemed to Corbett that he had hardly had a chance to exchange a word with him at all. It seemed to Corbett that Lœtitia had done all the talking; and her light volubility with Matheson, so different from the tongue-tiedness of her ordinary hours, her incessant and slightly meaningless laugh, echoed in his ears at the back of Minnie's scoldings, until both were lost in sleep.

But when the problem of Minnie's vexation recurred to him next morning, he decided that the key to it could only be jealousy, and he was annoyed with himself that he could find no excuses for a failing at once so ridiculous and so petty. The true nature of the case never once crossed his mind, until Minnie unfolded it for him one day, abruptly and triumphantly.

'Well, it's all right. He's proposed at last.'

'What do you mean? Who?' asked Corbett bewildered.

'Why Jim Matheson, of course! Who else do you suppose? He proposed to Tish last night in the garden. You remember how long they were out there, after we came in? That was why.'

Corbett was immensely surprised, even incredulous, although when he saw that his incredulity made his wife angry, he stifled it in his bosom.

After all, as she said with some asperity, why shouldn't Matheson be in love with Lœtitia? Lœtitia was a pretty girl . . . a good girl . . . yet somehow Corbett felt disappointed and depressed.

'You're such a selfish pig,' Minnie told him : 'You never think of anybody but yourself. You want to keep Tish here always.'

Corbett feared he must be selfish, though scarcely in respect to Lœtitia. In his heart he would have been very glad to see her married. But he didn't want Matheson to marry her.

'Jim's awfully in love,' said Minnie, and it sounded odd to Corbett to hear his wife call Matheson 'Jim.' 'He fell in love with her the very first moment he saw her. That's why he's been here so often. You thought he came here to see you, I suppose?'

Her husband's blank expression made her laugh.

'You *are* a pig!' she repeated. 'You never do think of anyone but yourself. Now hurry up and get dressed, and we'll go into town and dine at the Exhibition, and after dinner we'll go up in the Big Wheel.'

'Is Letty coming too?' Corbett asked.

'Don't be so silly! Of course not. She's expecting Jim. That's why I'm taking you out. You don't imagine they want your society, do you? Or mine?' she added as an afterthought, and with an unusual concession to civility.

Henceforward Corbett saw even less of Matheson than before. He was as fond of him as ever, but the friendship fell into abeyance.

It seemed too that Matheson tried to avoid him, and when he offered his congratulations on the engagement, the lover showed himself singularly reticent and cold. Corbett concluded he was nervous. He remembered being horribly nervous himself in the early days of his betrothal to Minnie Wray, when her mother had persisted in introducing him to a large circle at Highbury as 'My daughter Margaret's *engagé*.'

On the other hand, Corbett could not enough rejoice at the

genial warmth which the event shed over the atmosphere of
'Braemar.' Both young women brightened up surprisingly, nor
was there any lack of conversation between them now. Corbett
thankfully gathered up such crumbs of talk as fell to his share, and
first learned that the wedding was to take place in October, when
Minnie informed him she must have a new frock. She rewarded
him for his immediate consent by treating him to a different description of how she would have it made, three nights in the
week.

Lœtitia thought of nothing but new frocks, and set about making some. A headless and armless idol, covered in scarlet linen,
was produced from a cupboard, and reverentially enshrined in
the dining-room. Both sisters were generally found on their knees
before it, while a constant chattering went on in its praise. Innumerable yards of silk and velvet were snipped up in sacrifice,
and the sofas and chairs were sown with needles and pines, perhaps to extract involuntary homage from those who would not
otherwise bow the head. The tables were littered with books of
ritual having woodcuts in the text and illuminated pictures
slipped between the leaves.

There were constant visits to Richmond and Regent Street,
much correspondence with milliners and dressmakers, a long succession of drapers' carts standing in the road, of porters laden
with brown-paper parcels passing up and down the path. Lœtitia
talked of Brighton for her wedding tour, and of having a conser-
vatory added to the drawing-room of Holly Cottage. Friends and
acquaintances called to felicitate her, and left to ask themselves
what in the world Dr. Matheson could have seen in Letty Wray.
Presents began to arrive, and a transitory gloom fell upon 'Braemar' when Lœtitia received two butter dishes of identical pattern
from two different quarters, neither of which, on examination
by the local clockmaker, proved to be silver.

In this endless discussion of details, it did occasionally cross
Corbett's mind that that which might perhaps be considered an
essential point, namely, Matheson's comfort and happiness, was
somewhat lost sight of. But as he made no complaint, and maintained an equable demeanour, Corbett supposed it was all right.
Every woman considered the acquisition of fallals an indispens-

able preliminary to marriage, and it was extravagant to look for an exception in Lœtitia.

Matters stood thus, when turning into Wetherly Gardens one evening at the end of August, Corbett perceived, with a sudden heart-sinking, Minnie awaiting him at the gate. He recited the litany of all probable calamities, prayed for patience, and prepared his soul to endure the worst.

"What do you think, Jack," Minnie began, with immense blue eyes, and a voice that thrilled with intensity. "The most dreadful thing has happened——"

"Well, let me get in and sit down at least," said Corbett, dispiritedly. He was tired with the day's work, weary at the renewal of domestic worry. But the news which Minnie gave him was stimulating in its unexpectedness.

"Jim Matheson's been here to break off the engagement! He actually came to see Tish this afternoon and told her so himself. Isn't it monstrous? Isn't it disgraceful? And the presents come and everything. She's in a dreadful state. She's been crying on the bed ever since."

But Lœtitia, hearing her brother-in-law's step in the hall, came downstairs, her fringe, ominous sign, out of curl, her eyes red, her face disfigured from weeping.

And when she began, brokenly, 'He's thrown me over, Jack! He's jilted me, he's told me so to my face! Oh, it's too hard. How shall I ever hold up my head again?' then, Corbett's sympathy went out to her completely. But he wanted particulars. How had it come about? There had been some quarrel surely, some misunderstanding?

Lœtitia declared there had been none. Why should she quarrel with Jim when she had been so happy, and everything had seemed so nice? No, he was tired of her, that was all. He had seen someone else perhaps, whom he fancied better, someone with more money. She wept anew, and stamped her foot upon the floor. 'I wish you'd kill him, Jack. I wish you'd kill him!' she cried. 'His conduct is infamous!'

Matheson's conduct as depicted by the young women did seem infamous to Corbett, and after the first chaotic confusion of his mind had fallen into order again, his temper rose. His Irish pride was stung to the quick. No one had a right to treat a woman belonging to him with contumely. He would go up to Matheson, at once, this very evening, and ask him what he meant by it. He would exact ample satisfaction.

He swallowed a hurried and innutrious meal, with Lœtitia's tears salting every dish, and Minnie's reiterations ringing dirges in his ears. She and Lœtitia wanted him to 'do something' to Matheson; to kill him if possible, to horsewhip him certainly. Corbett was in a mood to fall in with their wishes, and the justice of their cause must have seemed unimpeachable to them all, since neither he nor they reflected for a moment that he could not have the smallest chance in a tussle with the transgressor, who overlooked him by a head and shoulders, and was nearly twice his size.

This confidence in righteousness is derived from the story-books, which teach us that in personal combat the evil-doer invariably succumbs; no matter what the disparity of physical conditions may be; although it must be added that in every properly written story-book it is always the hero who boasts the breadth of muscle and length of inches, while the villain's black little soul is clothed in an appropriately small and unlovely body.

Corbett, however, set off without any misgivings.

He found Matheson still at table, reading from a book propped up against the claret-jug. He refused the hand and the chair Matheson offered him, and came to the point at once.

'Is this true what I hear at home? That you came up this afternoon to break off your engagement with Lœtitia?'

Matheson, who had flushed a little at the rejection of his hand-shake, admitted with evident embarrassment that it was true.

'And you've the—the cheek to tell me that, to my face?' said Corbett, turning red.

'I can't deny it, to your face.'

'But what's your meaning, what's your motive, what has Letty done? What has happened since yesterday? You seemed all right yesterday,' Corbett insisted.

'It's not Letty's—it's not Miss Wray's fault at all. It's my mistake. I've made the discovery we're not a bit suited to each

77

other, that's all. And you ought to be thankful, as I am, that I've discovered it in time.'

'Damn it!' exclaimed Corbett, and a V-shaped vein rose in the centre of his forehead, and his blue eyes darkened. 'You come to my house, I make a friend of you, my wife and sister receive you into their intimacy, you ask the girl to be your wife. . . . I suppose you admit doing that?' he interpolated in withering accents; 'and now you throw her away like an old glove, break her heart, and expect me to be thankful? Damn it all, that's a bit steep.'

'I shouldn't think I've broken her heart,' said Matheson, embarrassed again. 'I should hope not.' There was interrogation in his tone.

'She feels it acutely,' said Corbett. 'Any woman would. She's very——' he stopped, but Matheson had caught the unspoken word.

'Angry with me? Yes. But anger's a healthy sign. Anger doesn't break hearts.'

'Upon my soul,' cried Corbett, amazed at such coolness. 'I call your conduct craven! I call it infamous!' he added, remembering Lœtitia's own words.

'Look here, Jack,' appealed the other, 'can't you sit down? I want to talk the matter over with you, but it gets on my nerves to see you walking up and down the room like that.'

Corbett, all unconscious of his restlessness, now stood still, but determined that he would never sit down in Matheson's house again. Then he weakly subsided into the chair which his friend pushed over to him.

'You call my conduct craven? I assure you I never had to make so large a demand upon my courage as when I called upon Lœtitia today. But I said to myself, a little pluck now, a bad quarter of an hour to live through, and in all probability you save two lives from ruin. For we should have made each other miserable.'

'Then why have engaged yourself?' asked Corbett with renewed heat.

'Yes . . . why? Do you know, Jack, that the very morning of our engagement, five minutes even before the fateful moment,

78

I'd no more idea . . . but you know how such things can come about. The garden, the moonlight, a foolish word taken seriously . . . and then the apparent impossibility of drawing back, the reckless plunging deeper into the mire. . . . I don't deny I was attracted by Letty, interested in her. She is a pretty girl, an unusually pretty girl. But like most other girls she's a victim to her upbringing. Until you are all in all to an English girl you are nothing at all. She never reveals herself to you for a moment; speaks from the lips only; says the things she has been taught to say, that other women say. You've got to get engaged to a woman in England, it seems, if you're ever to know anything about her. And I engaged myself, as I told you, in a moment of emotion, and then hopefully set to work to make the best of it. But I didn't succeed. I didn't find in Letty the qualities I consider necessary for domestic happiness.'

'But Letty is a very good——'

Matheson interrupted with 'In a way she's too good, too normal, too well regulated. I could almost prefer a woman who had the capacity, at least, for being bad! It would denote some warmth, some passion, some soul. Now, I never was able to convince myself that Lœtitia was fond of me. Oh, she liked me well enough. She was satisfied with my position, modest as it is, with my prospects. My profession pleased her, principally as she confessed to me, that it necessitates my keeping a carriage. But *fond* . . . do you think she is capable of a very passionate affection, Jack?

'Of course. I know this is going to do me a lot of harm. Twickenham, no doubt, will echo your verdict, and describe my conduct as infamous. I daresay I shall have to pull up stakes and go elsewhere. But for me, it has been the only conduct possible. I discovered I didn't love her. Wouldn't it be a crime to marry a woman you don't love? I saw we could never make each other happy. Wouldn't it be a folly to rush open-eyed into such misery as that?'

Which was, practically, the end of the matter, although the friends sat long over their whisky and cigarettes, discussing all sublunary things. Corbett enjoyed a most delightful evening, and it had struck twelve before he set off homewards, glowing outside and in with the warmth which good spirit and good fellowship impart. He reaffirmed to his soul the old decision that Matheson was undoubtedly the cleverest, the most entertaining, the most lovable of men—and suddenly he remembered the mission on which he had been sent nearly four hours ago; simultaneously he realised its preposterous failure. All his happy self-complacency radiated off into the night. Chilled and sobered and pricked by conscience, he stood for a moment with his hand upon the gate of 'Braemar,' looking up at the lighted windows of Minnie's room.

What was he going to say to her and to Lœtitia? And, more perturbing question still, what, when they should hear the truth, were his womenfolk going to say to him?

H. D. Lowry
1869–1906

HENRY DAWSON LOWRY, the son of a bank official, was born on February 22, 1869, at Truro. He was educated at Queen's College, Taunton, and then as a non-collegiate student at Oxford where he graduated in the honours school of chemistry in 1891.

Almost alone among the men of the 'nineties—with the brilliant exception of Havelock Ellis—Lowry had a scientific training. He did not, however, seek to apply it, since literary ambitions woke early within him. After contributing to the *Cornish Magazine*, he was encouraged by the acceptance, in 1891, of his Cornish stories by W. E. Henley, who published them in the *National Observer*.

Lowry maintained his connection with Henley, coming to London in 1893. Many of the sketches, stories, and studies of his prose writing appeared in Henley's pages: *Wreckers and Methodists* (1893), *Women's Tragedies* (1895), *A Man of Moods* (1896), *Make Believe* (1896), and *The Happy Exile* (1897).

Warm-hearted, impulsive, sociable, and popular with both friends and colleagues, Lowry has left an account of his novice days in London in the last book. 'Once upon a time,' he wrote, 'there was a group of young men who worked hard for little money, living gaily the while. They made a play of their work, and the responsibilities which came with settled means, positions of greater of less dignity, had not yet fallen on them.' Among this band of writing brothers was one (a *persona* for Lowry himself) who would often abruptly disappear from their meetings in order to revisit the land of his birth. 'For, indeed, he was no less truly a dweller beyond the Tamar than in his London chambers near the sky. There, as here, he had his friends. The interminable journey he must take who would reach the real West Country "Where roses grow that have no thorns," daunted him not at all. He was a veritable lover, and would travel twenty dreary hours for the sake of scarce as many in the land of his desire.'

It was, doubtless, this dual existence which most fully nourished the artist in Lowry. His steam pilgrimages to the Principality fed his senses and braced his imagination while lively and urbane talk in London stimulated his intellect.

Reviewing *Women's Tragedies* enthusiastically, Le Gallienne hails its author as 'the latest of Mr. Harding Hardy's several promising disciples,' namely an artist in the fiction regionalism. Le Gallienne is careful to insist that 'These country lives seem to have the more dramatic intensity and contrast from the very smallness of the stage. Indeed, from one point of view, if it be not actually its essence, limitation is one of the essential conditions of tragedy. . . . There is a Venusberg, and the heavenly mount of Beatrice in every village.'

Le Gallienne selects for special attention the story *Beauty's Lover* which has been included in this collection. As he says, 'the tragedy of beauty and beauty-loving works itself out in Cornwall as elsewhere. The love born of beauty, logically, dies with beauty. Strangely enough, beauty begets no gratitude.' For all its outward rustic dress, Lowry's story is a cogent critique of the beauty-cult of extreme aestheticism. The point is made more tellingly here because Rosetta—the woman of the story—is not, by nature, a *femme fatale*. What proves to be her undoing is no siren-psychology—no sultry luring suggestion of D. G. Rossetti's *Astarte Syriaca*—but just a great beauty which is, without her intending it, accurst.

Almost entirely forgotten today, Lowry held various journalistic posts. He worked on the staff of the *Pall Mall Gazette*, edited the *Ludgate Magazine*, joined the *Morning Post*, and wrote as 'independent' in the *Daily Express*.

Besides his work in prose, he was also a facile writer of tasteful verse, publishing in 1904 a book of poems *The Hundred Windows*.

Lowry died at Herne Hill on October 21, 1906.

BEAUTY'S LOVER

It was a surprise to everyone that Rosetta Curnow should consent to become the wife of Jim Penhallow. She had gained the name and fame of the loveliest girl in all the neighbourhood during the four or five years which had elapsed since she began to be noticeable among the maidens of the place. It would have seemed most natural if some new Cophetua of the countryside had raised her to the rank for which she was plainly made. Many who might have played the part had been seduced by her exquisite beauty to forgetfulness of the dictates of common prudence; and each had been vastly surprised when he found himself unmistakably rejected. Already there were wiseacres who declared that Rosetta played the fool in trifling with opportunities which would not always be hers. When it was told that she would marry Penhallow, the village cried out with one voice, proclaiming her mad.

Indeed, it was not easy to understand her choice.

Penhallow was but a common labourer, and so her social inferior. Moreover, he had the misfortune to be not exactly like other men, and was therefore looked upon by the majority as undeserving of their entire approbation. He was sufficiently industrious; he did not drink; and, though he made no great pretentions to religion, he was moderately regular in his attendance at the chapel. Perhaps his strongest characteristics was his love of flowers, to which he devoted the whole of his small garden, thereby scandalising a community essentially practical in all its views.

It is reported that the manner of his introduction to Rosetta was after this fashion.

She was going one day, dressed in her prettiest, towards the

Big House; the roadway took her past Penhallow's cottage, and there she lingered, looking over the low white wall of the garden to where the man himself was working. The dahlias were almost over; but in the centre of the garden, where all could see, he had a treble row of chrysanthemums all in full flower. He was looking over them with something of the artist's affection for work that is plainly good; and now and again he carefully removed imperfect blooms. Rosetta had stopped in the first instance to look at the flowers. Very soon she found herself watching the man and faintly smiling. And when at last he looked up and deigned to take notice of her she laughed outright.

'They're lookin' wonderful!' she exclaimed. 'But so would any flowers that had their treatment. They might have human souls!'

All this time Penhallow had been gazing at her with a curious look of surprise; Rosetta paused and blushed slightly, for it was borne in upon her that until this moment the man had never rendered the proper homage to her beauty. She had a sudden desire to win his admiration.

'Can 'ee spare me one or two?' she asked coquettishly.

A few seconds passed, during which Penhallow continued to stare at her, plainly wondering that he had never recognised her beauty until now. Then he stepped to the gate.

'Come and help yourself,' he said eagerly. 'Take as many as you mind to.'

Rosetta thanked him, and began rather nervously to gather the flowers, while Jim Penhallow watched her. Presently he came forward, and, without speaking, picked cluster after cluster, until Rosetta told him she had enough. He paused, looking contemptuously at the nosegay he had gathered her.

'Well!' he said. 'Come again when you do want more. Good af'noon to 'ee.' And he watched her as she proceeded on her way, dexterously avoiding the pools that stood in the road.

Once, and once only, she glanced back, and saw that he still watched.

An hour or two later she returned, one of the young men of the village walking at her side. Jim was still working in his garden, but he kept his eyes fixed upon his work, refusing to perceive that Rosetta sought to greet him again in passing. He looked up as they retreated into the dusk, and immediately his resolve was taken.

People had hardly realised that Rosetta was being courted by Jim Penhallow, when they heard that the marriage was decided on. It was duly solemnised at the chapel, and Rosetta went to live in the cottage by the roadside.

'There's one good thing about it,' said a matron discussing the matter with her peers. 'Rosetta's a sensible girl. She'll make him till 'taties in that garden and root up all his ol' flowers. 'Tis a rig'lar eyesore to see a good bit o' garden like that bringin' forth nothin' but a pa'cel o' flowers, that's good neither for man nor beast.'

As a matter of fact Rosetta did nothing of the sort. She became Penhallow's eager pupil, and the staid and sober villagers perceived with a sort of pious horror that the newly-married pair were living a life which was simply a prolongation of courting-days. Rosetta was manifestly well content with the husband she had chosen.

Once she confided to a friend the reason of her affection for him. 'Is it any shame to say I'm proud of my pretty face? A woman has failed if she is not beautiful: to one, or to many. And there have been many would have done much for me because of the face God gave me. But to Jim 'tis all the world. He would give his life for it—ay, and his very soul. And I can't but love the man.'

And so things went, until Rosetta was taken with a deathly sickness.

Penhallow seemed endowed with superhuman endurance, and for weeks he hardly slept at all. Rosetta grew weaker day by day, and daily there was a change in her bearing towards her husband. For a space she continued mindful of her beauty: she would ask frequently to be given a mirror, that she might know what injury had been wrought by sickness against her good looks.

But gradually, as the strength left her, she forgot her attitude of superiority: she seemed to long passionately for a simple human love that should be hers merely because she was herself. Penhallow did not understand, and still treated her rather as the incarnation of all loveliness than as a simple human creature. When he was told that she must surely die, he was taken with an insanity of grief; but he spoke as one believing that it lay with her to consent or refuse to accept the change of death.

And while he cried on her as to a creature of Divine attributes, Rosetta, conscious of mortal infirmity, yearned for some expression of a love for that part in her which suffered or was glad, which would be still the same though her beauty had been long ruined by accident or the relentless hand of time. But very soon she was overtaken with a heavy torpor, and lay unconscious with the mark of death upon her.

The last night came. Penhallow's grief had been hardly human. He had watched rebelliously the dreadful change which made her face a livid and inhuman mask; now it appeared he had forgotten his old passion, or, rather, that he could not be persuaded that this creature of so hideous an aspect was indeed the wife whose beauty he had worshipped. The night went on. The husband had with him an old woman of the village accustomed to the work of watching. From time to time she endeavoured to comfort him; but presently she ceased from troubling: she was, indeed, disconcerted, and in some degree affrighted, by the man's demeanour.

He was watching the still figure of his wife as if held fast by some horrible attraction. Her face was all discoloured, distorted to the semblance of an obscene mirth; through the shut eyelids a narrow line of the eyeball glistened. And it seemed to the husband, standing by, that this unsightly body was no longer inhabited by the spirit of his wife: she was gone from it, leaving it to become the ambuscade of a fiend, whose evil nature now reinformed its features.

Presently he began to mutter incoherently, seeming wholly unconscious of everything save that dreadful face which mocked him. The nurse had almost forgotten the patient in growing fear of Penhallow. Presently she could no longer be quiet. She rose and moved to his side; then, finding he gave her not the slightest attention, she took him by the arm and shook him roughly. Doubtless, some sharp remonstrance was in her mind, but she had no time for speech.

Penhallow started at the touch of her hand; then he laid a hand upon her shoulder and spoke, regarding her with vacant eyes. 'It is not Rosetta,' he said. 'Night and day I watched, and she lay there beautiful in sickness as she was before. Look at this thing that lies where she lay. It is not Rosetta; I am afraid of it.'

He paused, and the old woman strove ineffectually to bring him back to reason.

'Your head is light, Jim, after so much watching. No wonder! Lie down a bit, an' I'll see that Rosetta's all right.' Her tones became more urgent and she recognised the uselessness of her entreaties. 'Be quiet, man,' she cried. 'Don't 'ee know Rosetta's near to death?'

And the man laughed aloud.

'Rosetta's gone this long time,' he said. 'She was beautiful. This thing . . . it is a devil. I am afraid of it.'

He walked clumsily to the door.

'I can't stay under the same roof with it,' he said, as he left the room. A moment later the nurse heard him quit the house, and when the sound of footsteps had died away she turned to the bedside again.

Rosetta was regarding her curiously with wide-open eyes; her face had once more changed, so that Penhallow, could he have seen her, would have known that she was in very truth the wife he had loved. And while the nurse still wondered Rosetta spoke, weakly, but very eagerly. 'Where is he gone to?' she asked. 'What was it he said?'

The nurse strove to quiet her curiosity. 'He's gone out to get a mouthful o' fresh air,' she said. 'He've been watchin' with 'ee night an' day, this long time past. He didn' say nothin' particular.'

But Rosetta was not deceived.

'Give me the looking-glass,' she said; and when the nurse had brought it she raised herself laboriously and studied her face in the glass. And presently she fell back upon the pillows with a sob. 'He spoke true,' she said. 'But it was cruel.' Yet from that moment she progressed towards recovery.

Thirty years later, on a most dismal autumn day, I drove up

to The Crown, an hotel whose front commands a full view of the single narrow street which constitutes the town. I could not attract the attention of the hostler, and discovered that everyone was greatly interested in a funeral that came slowly down the street. There were hardly half a dozen mourners; and these, so far as one could judge, were by no means deeply afflicted. A moment later, as the procession came nearer, I perceived that the interest of the people centred rather in a small shop at the roadside than in the funeral itself. The shutters were up, the door closed, the white blinds of the small upstairs windows drawn.

And as the bearers reached this point the door was opened and a tall woman, dressed in deep mourning, stepped into the roadway. She took her place in the procession. She held a black-edged handkerchief to her dry eyes. A small crowd had gathered, and now followed the coffin. In a little while the funeral had passed out of sight in the direction of the cemetery. Inquiring afterwards, I learned the story I have told, with its concluding passages.

From the night when he left her to die alone Rosetta hardly spoke again to her husband. He was found the next morning wandering at a great distance from the village; coming home, he met the doctor quitting the cottage, and from him he learned that his wife would live. And from that hour, his madness over, he tended Rosetta with more than the old devotion. When she was sufficiently recovered he got the loan of a spring-cart, and offered to take her for a drive in the fresh air. 'Take me home,' she said. 'Take me to see mother.' And she was strangely impatient to start.

She was still silent, but for Penhallow there was sufficient joy in the contemplation of her beauty, which rapidly came back to her. They reached the cottage, and drove into the little yard. Penhallow helped his wife to descend, and almost carried her to the open door. Then he went back to lift the cushions out of the cart: but, hearing a sound behind him, he once more turned.

Rosetta had shut the door; even now he heard her fastening the bolt. And immediately, with a strange understanding of the thing which had befallen him, he dashed forward and began to hammer with his fists upon the panels, crying, 'Open the door, Rosetta! Let me in!'

A faint laugh reached him.

'Go back alone,' she said. 'Did you not take me for better or for worse? And because I had been sick a long time, and lost my good looks, you would have let me die alone. You shall live alone. Go back, and do not fool yourself with hoping.'

It would seem that Penhallow realised—perhaps one should rather say he was a fool to believe—that her resolve was inexorable. At any rate, it is said he never once troubled his wife again. When she had quite recovered her strength she opened a small shop in the village; being, further, a skilled needlewoman, she found it very possible to make a living. And, though there were many attempts to shake her resolution, she lived until the day of Jim Penhallow's funeral as if he had ceased to exist when she sent him from her at the door of her mother's cottage.

Frank Harris

1856-1931

ACCORDING to his own accounts—which are often extremely untrustworthy—Frank Harris was born in Galway, Ireland, on February 14, 1856.

He claimed to have been awarded a scholarship at fifteen to Cambridge, but on account of his youth this was commuted and a sum of ten pounds granted to him. With this money he made his way by steerage to the U.S.A. where in turn he worked as bootblack, ditch-digger, hotel clerk in Chicago. From Chicago he ventured to Texas where, he stated, he became a cowboy.

After qualifying at the Kansas Bar as a lawyer in 1875, he drifted back to Europe, reaching England in the 'nineties.

As editor of the *Saturday Review*, he claimed to have 'discovered Shaw and Wells.' Later, as editor of *Vanity Fair*, he served a brief prison sentence for libel. Oscar Wilde—a study of whom Harris was to write in 1916—said that he was 'invited to all the great houses in London—*once.*' Bernard Shaw called him a ruffian and a monster; and Joseph Wood Krutch, the American critic, 'an exhibitionist satyr.'

Harris returned to America during the First World War, and from 1922 made his home on the Riviera. His last days were spent in increasing poverty writing unreliable gossip sheets for English and American tourists.

Harris's heyday was the 'nineties, during which decade he combined the editorial role of talent scout with that of original creator—particularly in the short-story form. Reviewing Harris's first fictional volume *Elder Conklin and Other Stories* (1894), Richard Le Gallienne remarked that it seemed 'a little curious that a man who can write such stories . . . should prefer, for the most part, to devote himself to journalism.' Le Gallienne found the answer to this mystery in Harris's 'passion for action' as represented by 'militant journalism.'

A less kind way of putting this would be to say that the sensationalist too often took precedence over the artist in him. Even so, the tales contained in *Elder Conklin, Montes the Matador* (1900) and *The Bomb* (1908) constitute the fascinating harvest of a raffish yet authentic humanism, for whom nothing human is alien.

Harris left a number of memoirs, the most noteworthy of which is his four-volume *My Life and Loves* (1923-7), printed first in Germany on account of its erotic forthrightness. He has also reported—sometimes wildly—on a number of 'nineties colleagues (including Wilde, Dowson, Symons and Crackanthorpe) in his *Contemporary Portraits* (four series, 1915-30).

FIRST LOVE. (A CONFESSION)

My boyhood and youth were passed in Brighton. I entered the College there as a boy of ten, and went through every class on the Modern side in the usual seven years. I only tell this to show that from the beginning my father intended me to go into business, and that I was not particularly clever at books. I loved football as much as I hated French, and I learned more of 'fives' in half an hour than I knew of German after eight years' teaching. In fact, if it had not been for mathematics I should not have got my 'remove' each year regularly as I managed to do. There were lots of fellows who could beat my head off at learning; but there were very few as strong or as good at games, and I'd have been Captain of the School if Wilson, who was one of the best 'bats' of his day (he played afterwards for the 'Gentlemen'), had not been a contemporary of mine. I was not bad-looking either. I do not mean I was handsome or anything of that sort; but I was tall and dark, and my features were fairly regular, and, as I had more of a moustache than almost any fellow in the school, I rather fancied myself.

After leaving Brighton College, my father got me a clerkship with Lawrence, Loewenthal and Co., stockbrokers, of Copthall Court. My father was rector of a Brighton parish, and knew Mr. Lawrence, who came regularly to his church. The two old boys were great 'pals,' because, as my father said, they were both Protestants and not Catholics in disguise; but I always thought that my father's liking for Mr. Lawrence's port and Mr. Lawrence's respect for my father's birth and learning had more to do with their mutual esteem. However, that may be, old Lawrence gave me a good start and I turned it to account. From the first I took to business. The school work at Latin and Greek had had no meaning for me; but in the City the tangible results of energy and skill were always before me, interesting me in spite of myself, and exciting me to do my best. And rivalry soon came to lend another spur. In Throgmorton Street my chief competitors were young German Jews, keen as mustard in everything relating to business, and preternaturally sharp in scenting personal profit. Their acuteness and boldness fascinated me: I went about with them a good deal, picked up conversational German without much effort, and soon learned from my mentors how fortunes were to be made. A little group of us pooled our savings, and began to speculate and, after a succession of gains and losses which about balanced themselves, turned our tens into hundreds over a 'slump' in American rails. Our success was due to Waldstein— the Julius Waldstein who has since made a great fortune, and whom I should like to write about some day or other, as I look upon him as the first financial genius of the age. But now I must get on with my story. It was a remark I made after this lucky 'deal' that drew Mr. Lawrence's attention to me and gave me my first step up in the house. I had gone into his private room with some transfers to be signed. He was reading a letter; in the middle of it he rang for the managing clerk, and asked him:

'How are Louisvilles going?'

'I'll see,' was the reply; and in a minute or two old Simkins returned with:

'Steady at 48.'

I could not help muttering 'They'll be steadier at 35.'

'What do you know about it?' asked Lawrence, with an air of amused surprise. His tone put me on my mettle, and I laid my reasons, or rather Waldstein's, before him, and he soon saw that I knew what I was talking about. A year afterwards I, too, was a managing clerk and a member of the Stock Exchange; and from that time on have never found it very difficult to lay by something each year. It's curious, too, how the habit of saving grows on one—but I am forgetting my story.

As I became interested in my work and confident of success I wanted someone to talk to, to brag to if the truth must be told, and life, I have noticed, generally furnishes us with the opportunity of gratifying our desires. I still kept up the custom of going home to Brighton from Saturday till Monday. And one Sunday, coming out of church, my sister introduced me to some people whom I took to immediately, Mrs. and Miss Longden. Mabel Longden was tall and good-looking, but too dark for my taste. Still, we chummed at once, and perhaps got along together better than if we had fallen in love at first sight—a thing, by the way, which I have never believed in. Mrs. Longden was the widow of a major in the army, and lived in a small house in Kemp Town. She had only a hundred a year or so beyond her pension, and her one ambition in life was to keep herself and her two daughters like ladies. Her love of gentility was so passionate that when the rumour got about that she was the daughter of a small tradesman, everyone believed it. Mabel had a sister whom I have not mentioned yet, perhaps because I saw little of her for some time, and the little I saw did not interest me. She could not have been more than thirteen or fourteen years of age when I first met her, and she seemed to me an ordinary schoolgirl—all ribs and ankles. Her face was not even pretty; the eyes were all right, greyish and large, but the nose was inclined to be thick and the oval of the face was too narrow; the jaws seemed pinched in, and this pecularity gave her an uncomfortably sharp look. She was a strange child in every way, and I did not like her. I remember the first time I really noticed her. I had been talking to Mabel about business; telling her how I had nabbed a fellow who had tried to cheat me, when suddenly

I looked up and found Blanche gazing at me. As our eyes met she looked away quietly, and then got up and went out of the room, leaving me under the impression that she disapproved of me, or did not like what I had been saying. I put this down to 'cheek' that deserved to be snubbed; but she never gave me the opportunity of snubbing her; she seemed rather to avoid me.

A few weeks later I was waiting one afternoon in the little parlour. Mabel had gone up to dress to go out with me, when suddenly Blanche came into the room with her cheeks aglow, crying. 'Where's mother?' She had been skating, and her spark-ling eyes and rich colour so improved her that I exclaimed, 'Why, Blanche, you're quite pretty!' I suppose the astonishment in my voice was rather marked; for as I looked her eyes grew indignant; the colour in her cheeks flamed from pink to scarlet, and she turned and stalked out of the room with her chin in the air. An absurd child; she annoyed without interesting me, and I resolved to take no further notice of her.

It was easy to keep that resolution; for about this time my companionship with Mabel became close: we began to spoon in fact, and soon tried to believe ourselves very much in love with each other. But there was always something lacking in our intimacy, and now, looking back, I see that there was no real bond between up, and I begin to suspect that kisses often stand youth in lieu of sympathy. For even if I would, I really could not tell much of my flirtation with Mabel Longden. She was good to look at and good to be with, too uniformly sweet-tempered ever to have cared much about me, I imagine; but I knew nothing of her true character and temperament; for love was not in her, love with its terrible need of self-betrayal. There were moments, it is true, when we seemed drawn together, moments when her eyes sought mine with timid abandonment, and when pride in her looks and pity of her weakness grew in me to unselfish tender-ness; but there was no enduring strength in the feeling, no roots of life in it, and a few days' separation chilled us both. I am glad now to think that the play was pure comedy on both sides, though at the time I was often vaguely disappointed with our aloofness from one another, and tried by dwelling on her beauty to bring myself to the passionate ardour I ought to have felt for her. Mabel never really loved me at all; at the height of our intimacy I noticed that she used to lead me on to talk of the fortune I should make, and the great house we should have and the horses and carriages, and it seems to me now, though I am half ashamed to say it, that it was some picture in her mind of dress and jewellery and distinction which made her try to like me. In any case the matter is not worth thinking about any longer, and I only mention it now because it belongs to my story.

I had known Mabel Longden for nearly two years, and for six or eight months had spent three-fourths of the time I passed in Brighton, with her, when I called early one Saturday evening and found that she was out. I was a little hurt—more in vanity than in affection, I think—and disappointed, which I took to be a proof of feeling, whereas it was merely the result of baulked habit. True, I was later than usual, much later in fact; but then my father had kept me talking of my younger brother Tom, and I had bought tickets for the theatre to make up for my late coming. I found it difficult to disguise my bad humour when I was told that Mabel had gone out for the evening and would probably not be home till eleven.

'You see,' said Mrs. Longden apologetically, 'you never sent her word, and I presume she thought you were not coming at all.' While she was speaking, my eyes, wandering about in hesitation and annoyance, suddenly caught sight of an expression of indignant contempt on Blanche's face as she sat looking into the fire.

'But what am I to do with these tickets?' I asked, in helpless irritation. As I spoke Blanche kicked the fender and got up hastily, and an idea came into my head.

'Would you let me take Blanche?' and I turned to Mrs. Longden.

'Yes,' said Mrs. Longden after a moment's hesitation, only to be noticed because of her unvarying suavity; 'yes, certainly; and I think Blanche would enjoy it. She loves music.'

'Well, Blanche?' I asked; but there was no need of an answer, for the girl's eyes were dancing.

'Oh,' she said in a low voice, as if to excuse her joy, 'it is "Le Nozze di Figaro" isn't it? and I love music, and Titiens and

III. Richard Le Galliene

iv. Henry Harland
From the *Bookman* (New York), 1 (1895)

Trebelli are both in it, Oh,' and she drew in her breath with delight and clasped her hands, 'it is kind of you!'"

'What will you wear, dear?' asked her mother, and the girl's face fell so lugubriously that I could not help laughing. 'Anything will do: we must start at once,' I said, and bustled them both upstairs. I like music as much as most people, but I like, too, to talk between the acts, and my companion that night was more than silent; still Titiens was very good in spite of her bulk, and Trebelli the most enchanting page that was ever seen. When she sang 'Voi che sapete' with that angelic voice of hers, I was carried off my feet.

As she finished the song my companion gave a queer, little, hysterical squeak that turned all eyes upon her. I saw that the child was overwrought; her face was pale and pinched, and the eyes blazing, so I whispered, 'Let us go, Blanche, eh?'

'Oh, no!' she said. 'No! It is too beautiful—please, please don't go.'

'If we stay,' I insisted, 'you mustn't cry out; the people are all looking at you.'

'What do the people matter?' she snapped, and then, pleadingly, 'please, let me listen.' Of course there was nothing more to be said, and we stayed to the end.

It was a fine night, and we walked home together, Blanche taking my arm.

'Are you glad I took you?' I asked, feeling that I should like her to thank me; she pressed my arm. But I wanted to talk, so I went on:

'You liked the play, didn't you?' That started her off; she was so excited with enthusiasm and admiration that she talked like one out of breath.

'The music,' she said, 'was divine; so beautiful, it hurt. I ache with it still. I can never, never forget it.'

I laughed at her exaggerations, and brought her down to common sense, and then she began to attack the play.

'It was beastly,' if you please; 'all falsehood and deceit and cheating. I hope life isn't like that,' she burst out, 'if it is, I shall hate it. How could Mozart have given that perfect music to those horrid words and horrid people? How could he?'

There seemed to be some sense in what she said, but as I knew very little about it, I preferred to change the subject. And then the conversation died away.

When we reached her house I left her at the door. Somehow or other I did not feel inclined to go in and make up my little difference with Mabel. It seems to me now as if our estrangement began that evening; but, indeed, I did not trouble much about it, either then or later. And it was not any affection for Blanche that put Mabel out of my head: no, the child excited my curiosity, and that was all; she was evidently clever, and I liked that; but she was so intensely emotional, which seemed odd rather than pleasant to me.

For some weeks I did not call at the Longdens, and when I called I noticed that Mabel was affected in manner and speech. Her coldness I didn't mind; in fact, I felt relieved by it; but her graceful poses and little slang phrases of gentility seemed ridiculous to me. I wondered that I had never been disagreeably impressed by them before. I felt too, that they were characteristic of her; she was affected and vain. I did not want to be alone with her, and though we spent several afternoons together I maintained my attitude of polite carelessness. Mabel scarcely seemed to notice my change of manner; she was often out when I called, and I fell upon the idea of asking Blanche to accompany us whenever Mabel happened to go out with me. At first Blanche used to refuse point blank; but as I returned to the charge she consented now and then, evidently in accord with her sister; indeed, Mabel often pressed her to say 'Yes.'

I remember one Saturday evening taking them both to dine at Mutton's. We had a private room and the best dinner the place could afford; for success and Waldstein's example were teaching me to be extravagant in such matters. The week had been a red-letter one for me; I had cleared a thousand pounds in it and naturally was cock-a-hoop, though I did not conceal from myself, or even from the Longdens, that my success was due to Waldstein. In fact, towards the end of the dinner I set his whole plan before them and gave all his reasons for the course he took. Before I had got half through the story it was impossible not to notice that Blanche was my only listener. Mabel made polite

exclamations of attention at the proper places; but she was manifestly rather bored by the account, whereas Blanche asked about
everything she didn't understand, and appeared to be really
engrossed by the dramatic elements in the struggle for wealth.
Piqued by Mabel's manner, I did my best to interest Blanche and
succeeded, I suppose, for Mabel at length left the table and took
to drumming on the window pane to show her impatience.

'I must go!' she exclaimed at last. 'I expect Captain Burroughs
to call this evening to try over a song with me, and I don't want
to be late.' After that there was nothing left for us but to put on
our wraps and go. I had met Captain Burroughs at the Longdens
more than once, but had not paid much attention to him. He was
an ordinary-looking man, I thought, with nothing particular
about him except that he was well set-up and had large blue
eyes. Now as Mabel spoke his image came before me, and I understood that he was good-looking, that she thought him exceedingly
attractive, and had more than consoled herself with his court-
ship for my inattention. Perhaps even she had begun to go her
own way before I had thought of going mine. Yes, she had; a
hundred little signs unnoticed at the time assured me that she
had. The discovery relieved and pleased me greatly; I grew
excited and felt quite cordial to her. She was a fine girl after all,
and deserved a handsome husband like Burroughs. Was it this
elation or the wine I had drunk that made me act as I did? I
don't know; the bare facts are not flattering to me, but I'll set
them down. Mabel went out of the room first, as if in a hurry
to get to her Captain; she disappeared just as I took up Blanche's
jacket to help her on with it. As the young girl swung round
before me I noticed for the first time that she had a figure, a
figure that promised to be a very pretty one, and after putting
on her jacket I could not help taking her slender waist in my
hands. Of course I said something to cover my action: 'Go along,
let us catch Mabel,' or something of that sort; but the words died
on my lips, for she turned abruptly and faced me with an im-
perative: "Don't!'

'Go along,' I repeated awkwardly, 'you're only a child.'

She moved away haughtily, without a word, and followed her
sister downstairs.

The cab was waiting for us, and as soon as we were seated in it I forced a conversation with Mabel on the subject of her song and Captain Burroughs' voice.

After this incident Blanche avoided me persistently. At first, feeling rather uncomfortable, I was not at all sorry to get out of a complete explanation. But as the feeling of shame wore off I began to contrive opportunities of being alone with her. 'I don't care for her,' I used to say to myself, 'but I don't want her to think me a howling cad.' But though I did not care for her she was in my thoughts a good deal, and knew how to pique my vanity at least by continually avoiding me. She was more successful in this than she could have been a few months before; for now I never went to the house without finding Burroughs in the little parlour on the ground floor, filling the place I had formerly occupied beside Mabel. In fact, about this time Mrs. Longden confided to me that the pair were engaged, and when I congratulated Mabel I noticed that she was prettier and less affected than I had ever imagined she could be. Love is like youth for hiding faults and enhancing merits. After this event my chances of meeting Blanche alone became too slight to be worth the risk of disturbing the lovers, and so I gave up going to the house at all regularly. Mere chance soon helped me where purpose had failed. One afternoon late, as I reached the house I found the servant at the door, who told me that everyone was out except Miss Blanche. I was very glad to hear it. Blanche was in the parlour alone, and as I entered she stood up hastily, and returned my greeting with a cold 'I'll see if mother or Mabel is in.' But I stopped in front of the door, and said:

'Won't you speak to me, Blanche? If I've offended you, I beg your pardon. Forgive me, and let us be friends again.' I caught myself speaking with an intensity far greater than I had thought of using; and, as her face did not relax and she kept her eyes obstinately bent on the ground, I began again with an extraordinary eagerness:

"Why will you bear malice? I had no idea you could be so cross. Just remember what a great talk we had that night, and forgive me." Still the same silence and little downcast face, scarcely to be seen in the gathering shadows. I began again:

'Really, Blanche, you ought to be ashamed of yourself. It is childish to sulk so: yes, childish,' I repeated, for she had looked up at last. 'If you were older you would know that every woman forgives when the man apologises and asks for pardon.' She looked me straight in the face, but said nothing. Had I excited myself by my own pleading, or what was it? I don't know; but I began again in a different tone:

'Upon my word, if you won't speak, I'll treat you like the little girl you are, and kiss you into a good temper.'

'You daren't,' she said, and stood rigidly.

'You mustn't dare me,' I cried, and I threw my left arm round her waist, and held her face to mine with my right hand. At first she struggled desperately, and writhed so that I could hardly hold her. Then gradually I overcame her struggles, and kissed her again and again. I shall never be able to describe the strange, keen pleasure I took in the touch of her lips; nor the intimate, intense delight it gave me to hold her tender, panting form against my breast in the darkness. Whilst I was still embracing and kissing her, the idea came to me that her resistance had become merely formal; that she was not trying to avoid my lips. At once conscience smote me, and I felt that I had been a brute. No sort of excuse for me—none. I pulled myself together, and stopped kissing her. Then I began pleading again.

'Little Blanche, have you forgiven me? Are we friends again? Won't you speak to me now?" And I laid my cheek to hers: the girl's face was wet, and I realised with a pang that she was crying silently. This was worse than I had feared. I was genuinely grieved.

'Oh Blanche,' I exclaimed, 'if you knew how sorry I am! Please don't cry; I didn't mean to hurt you; I'm so sorry—what am I to do? I'll never, never forgive myself.' As I began to speak she slipped from my arms and went to the door.

'Blanche,' I went on—for I couldn't let her go like that—'you must hate me to leave me so; won't you say you'll forgive me, please?' She paused, holding the door ajar; then I heard her say in a little subdued voice.

'There's nothing to forgive,' and then 'It wasn't your fault,' and the door closed behind her quickly, leaving me in the dark, half penitent and half in doubt as to her meaning, though the tone of her voice had partially reassured me.

After she left me I seemed to be possessed by a demon of unrest. Up and down the parade I tramped reproaching myself for what I had done. I had no business to kiss her. It was a shame. I felt very clearly that kisses meant infinitely more to her than they did to her sister. What was I to do? I didn't love her, and yet I had never kissed anyone with such passion. She was an inscrutable mystery to me. Why had she cried? Did she dislike me? Had she grown tired of struggling, or merely affected to struggle, wishing all the time to be kissed? This flattering hypothesis seemed to be true; but, if true, why had she begun to cry? And if she had cried out of vexation, why did she say that there was nothing to forgive, and that it wasn't my fault? I couldn't read the riddle; and it was too fascinating to leave unread. I wanted to return to the house to see her if but for a moment, but that went against my pride. I resolved to write to her. The girl was a mystery, and the mystery had an attraction for me that I could not account for nor explain. That night I went up to my little bedroom and sat down to write to her. I soon found that the task was exceedingly difficult. At one moment I was writing as if I loved her, and the next I was warning her that I did not love her yet. At length I began to quiet myself: "Why write at all?" But I couldn't leave her without a word, and so I decided at last to write just a brief note, saying how grieved I should be to hurt or offend her in any way, and declaring that I would call next Saturday afternoon as soon as I reached Brighton. I began 'Dear little Blanche,' and ended up with 'I shall think of you all through the week; yours, Will Rutherford."

The week passed much as other weeks had passed, with this difference however, that from Monday on I began to look forward more and more eagerly to seeing Blanche again. I did not write this to her in the meantime, partly out of prudence, partly out of the wish to tell it to her when we met. As soon as I reached Brighton on the Saturday I hurried off to the Longdens. The mother met me in the parlour.

'Where's Blanche?' I asked, gaily.

'Blanche! repeated Mrs. Longden, with a slight tone of surprise; 'she had gone into the country to stay with some friends.'

'Into the country,' I muttered, in confusion; 'where to?'

'Near Winchester,' came the calm reply.

'But did she leave no message for me—no letter?'

'Not that I'm aware of,' replied Mrs. Longden smilingly; 'I didn't even know that you took interest enough in each other to write or send messages.'

And that was all. I left the house more bewildered than ever; but my pride was up in arms, and I resolved to put Blanche out of my mind completely. That seemed easy enough at first; but with time it became increasingly difficult. The mystery puzzled me more and more, and the abrupt parting piqued my curiosity. As the weeks passed and I recalled all our meetings and what she had said, I began to see that she was very intelligent and very ingenuous. At length I couldn't stand it any longer; so I wrote to her, telling her how constantly I thought of her, and begging her to let me see her. I took the letter to Mrs. Longden, who promised to forward it, with a request to Blanche to answer it, and next week Mrs. Longden showed me the end of a letter Blanche had written to her: 'I received the letter you sent me; please tell him there's no answer. I have nothing to say.'

I had gone as far as my pride would allow. From that day I never went near the Longdens, but gave myself up to work, and gradually the fascination of business took hold of me once again. Four or five years later I married and bought a little country place near Winchester. A year or so afterwards I took my wife to a ball given by the officers of the —— Hussars, who were quartered in the Cathedral city. I knew a good many people and, as I liked dancing, prepared to enjoy myself; feeling sure that my wife would be well taken care of. After the second or third dance a Captain Wolfe came up to me and said, 'You're in luck, my friend; I'm going to introduce you to the belle of the ball.' With some laughing protestation I followed him and he presented me by simply saying. 'This is Mr. Rutherford.'

The girl certainly deserved his praise; she was one of those astoundingly pretty girls one sees now and then in England and nowhere else in the world. I cannot describe her except by saying that she was above the middle height and of a very perfect round figure, with the most beautiful face I have ever seen.

'Pardon me,' I said, 'but Captain Wolfe forgot to tell me your name.'

'Don't you know it?' she asked, while her blue eyes danced with amusement.

'No,' I replied, 'how should I? I have never seen you before.' I spoke with absolute conviction.

'What a bad compliment—to forget me and deny me! Aren't you ashamed of yourself?' and she pouted adorably.

'The best of compliments,' I retorted warmly; 'the certainty that if I had ever seen you I could never have forgotten you.'

She swept me a low curtsy, and then, with sudden gravity, 'Allow me to introduce myself, Miss Blanche Longden that was, now Miss Longden.'

I was dumbfounded. The grace, the charm, the self-possession, I could understand, even the fine figure : but not the change in face. Blanche's nose had been rather heavy and shapeless, and now it was daintily cut; the pointed chin was rounded, the oval of the face had filled out, the eyes had surely grown darker, the complexion that had been muddy was now dazzling; but even these extraordinary changes did not account for her beauty. I was lost in wonder.

She laughed in a pleased way at my embarrassment :

'You don't recognise me even now?'

'No,' I confessed ruefully. 'You are altogether changed : even your voice has improved beyond recognition.'

'Let us sit down,' she said, 'and talk, if you have this dance free;' and I sat down, careless whether I was free or not. At last I should get the mystery solved. What did we talk about? At first the usual things. Her sister, I learned, was married and had three children. She was in India now with her husband, and Mrs. Longden, in Brittany, was taking care of the little ones. At last I put my question :

'Why did you go away from Brighton, and never answer my letters?'

'I did answer them. Mother told me she showed you my answer.'

'That was no answer. You have no idea how disappointed and hurt I was; how grieved over your silence.' I could not help being much more intense with this girl than I had any right to be 'But tell me why you left me so, and I'll forgive you.'

She seemed to consider, and then:

'I don't know; there *was* nothing to be said;' and then, 'You are married, aren't you?' I nodded; she went on: 'I want to know your wife; you must introduce me.'

'With pleasure,' I replied: 'but my answer; you will explain the mystery now.'

'But you must have understood?'

'No; I did not, I assure you, and even now I can't make out why you acted as you did.'

'How strange!' And she laughed, looking away from me. On reflection afterwards, it seemed to me that this laughter of hers was a trifle forced; but I may be mistaken. At the time I didn't remark the false note. 'How strange!' she repeated; and then, with sudden gravity. 'Shall I dot the "is" and cross the "ts" for you, and confess? I wonder will it be good for my soul. The truth is very simple, and yet very hard to tell. I loved you. Oh! as a child, of course, I mean, but with an ideal passion. You never guessed it? I'm glad. Do you know, I think it began that night at the theatre. You won something of the charm of that fatal music that seemed to me the voice of my soul's desire. It transformed me; the tide of it swept through me, and ebbed and flowed in me, and bore me away out upon it till the sweet tears scalded my eyes and made my heart ache. After that my guard broke down before you; the way was open and you took possession of the empty throne. How I loved you! I invested you with every grace and every power; you were the lay figure and I the artist. Forgive me, I don't mean to hurt you; but that's the truth. You brought the wild fresh air of struggle and triumph into our close narrow life, and I made a hero of you, that was all.

'I think I began by pitying you; even in short frocks some of us are mothers. I saw that Mabel didn't love you and was indignant with her. After seeing her with you my heart has ached for you, and I've gone out of the room hating her make-believe of love and stopped in the hall to talk to your coat. How I used to kiss and stroke it and put my cheek against it and whisper sweet things to it! "Tell him, dear coat," I used to say, "that I love him, and he mustn't be sad or lonely. Tell him—tell him that I love him." I used to believe that unconsciously you must receive some comfort from those assurances.

'Do you remember the dinner when you touched me? I stopped you; I was so glad at heart that I had to pretend to be angry for fear you'd understand. And that afternoon when you kissed me; I provoked it—on purpose? I don't know. I do know that I resisted as long as I could, and when I could resist no longer, *you stopped*. How the passion of shame hurt me then! I thought I should die of it, and then I thought of the sweet unknown affection I had been giving you—all past and at an end— and the tears came. . . . Well, there's my confession. You see now that I could not answer your letters. I had to win back self-respect, and I did.'

There; that's all the story. I know I've told it badly, but I've done my best. What did I say to her? I played the fool. I could find nothing sensible to say; I held my head in my hands and muttered :

'And now?'

'And now,' she repeated, smiling through wet eyes, 'I'm grown up and you're married, and I want to know your wife.'

'And that's all?' I blundered on.

'All?" she said; 'all—and enough too, I should think.' Her voice had changed and grown hard; even as a girl she was quick-tempered : 'Do you know I look at you and can't tell what possessed me, what I could have seen in you? You're not even like the mental picture I had made of you. I don't know how I could have dressed you up in those heroic vestments. When I look at you I wonder at myself. I must really ask your wife what she sees in you. I must——'

At last I came to sense; the beautiful play was over, and I had offended her; but she had gone too far in punishment: the words came to me :

'If you go on hurting me, I shall think you are daring me again.'

The blood surged to the roots of her hair; she rose and took the arm of a man who had just come up, and vanished from my sight; and with her going romance died out of my life, and the grey walls of the ordinary shrank round and hemmed me in for ever.

In the years that have elapsed since, my business instincts have often forced me to try and strike a balance : I was richer by a wonderful memory and poorer by the sense of incalculable loss. Sometimes I try to console myself with the thought that perhaps that is all life holds, even for the luckiest of us.

LONDON,
    September, 1896.

Henry James
1843-1916

HENRY JAMES was born on April 15, 1843, in New York. His father was a theological writer of a somewhat esoteric order, and his brother William, the philosopher, was the founder of the school of Pragmatism.

James's education was unsystematic, but diverse, deriving from many schools and *pensions* as he travelled about Europe with his parents. His book of reminiscences *A Small Boy and Others* (1913), recalls the happenings of these years.

For a while he studied law at Harvard; but it was the Old World of Europe, with its art, manners, and sophistication, which called to him irresistibly. In 1875 he settled in London; and in his novel *The Europeans* (1878) we see him assessing the balance between the Old World and the New. Briefly, the conclusions he then reached were that Europe was morally negative, but positive in terms of taste and *savoir vivre*, while America was morally positive, but negative in terms of *savoir vivre* and taste.

James enlarged upon the loss-side of American experience in his book on Hawthorne (1879). 'It is,' he wrote, 'on manners, customs, usages, habits, forms, upon all those things matured and established, that a novelist lives;' and in the same book he compiled a list of 'the items of high civilization' absent from American life: a court, an aristocracy, an established church; country houses, cathedrals, old universities and schools; the arts, a political society, a sporting class.'

Between 1879 and 1883, James was engaged in 'The Conquest of London' (to borrow the title-phrase of volume II of Leon Edel's biography). 'London,' declared James himself, 'is on the whole the most possible form of life. I take it as an artist and a bachelor; as one who has the passion of observation and whose business is the study of human life. It is the biggest aggregation of human life—the most complete compendium in the world . . . if you learn to know your London you learn to know a great many things.'

And if you learnt your James, the young writers discovered, you had learnt many things besides the processes of art. The glass of fashion, a school of manners, the sacred fount of civilized response—James was all these things to many young authors in the 'nineties. Henry Harland, who had secured James's contribution to *The Yellow Book*, spoke of him as 'the very greatest mind that has ever been devoted to the writing of fiction in any language since the beginning of created literature.'

James's story *The Death of the Lion* appeared in *The Yellow Book*, volume I, *The Coxon Fund* in volume II. *The Next Time* in volume VI, and *He and She*—an essay on the affair between George Sand and Alfred de Musset—in the April number, 1896.

For all James's co-operation, it was clear that he found himself uneasy when confronted by Harland's gathered host assembled beneath the Beardsley-cover banner. 'I haven't sent you *The Yellow Book*,' he confessed to his brother, '—on purpose . . . I say on purpose because although my little tale . . . appears to have had, for a thing of mine, an unusual success, I hate too much the horrid aspects and company of the whole publication. And yet I am again to be intimately, conspicuously associated with the second number. It is for gold and to oblige the worshipful Harland.'

'It is for gold' is very pregnant. Leon Edel informs us that 'With *The Pupil*, published in 1891, James began a productive period of work devoted to the short story and to the stage. He announced to his friends that he was abandoning the writing of novels; these yielded revenue during serialization but had no sale in the bookshops. James would now write for the theatre in the hope of gaining a better livelihood; and by producing many tales, in the margins of his theatricals, he hoped to support himself adequately during this period. This explains the great variety of James's stories during the 1890's, and their appearance in periodicals as diverse as *The Yellow Book* and the *Illustrated London News*, the *New Review*, or *Black and White*.'

Between 1891 and 1899 James published thirty-two tales, a number of them—such as *The Turning of the Screw* (1898) and *In the Cage* (1898)—being what we should today term *novellas*, some hundred or hundred and fifty pages in length.

In 1898 James moved down to Lamb House, Rye, a fine Georgian mansion with wistaria on its walls and a mulberry tree in the grounds. Henry Harland offers the following picture of him, 'with four or five servants keeping bachelor's hall. . . . In the fine weather he does his writing in a pavilion in the garden, but for the rest he has an inside study. Here he spends his time till the London season calls him, when he goes up to town to dine with his duchesses.'

James became a naturalized British subject in 1915, received of Order of Merit in the New Year's Honours of 1916, and died shortly afterwards in Chelsea.

THE MIDDLE YEARS

The April day was soft and bright, and poor Dencombe, happy in the conceit of reasserted strength, stood in the garden of the hotel, comparing, with a deliberation in which, however, there was still something of languor, the attractions of easy strolls. He liked the feeling of the south so far as you could have it in the north, he liked the sandy cliffs and the clustered pines, he liked even the colourless sea. 'Bournemouth as a health-resort' had sounded like a mere advertisement, but he was thankful now for the commonest conveniences. The sociable country postman, passing through the garden, had just given him a small parcel which he took out with him, leaving the hotel to the right and creeping to a bench he had already haunted, a safe recess in the cliff. It looked to the south, to the tinted walls of the Island, and was protected behind by the sloping shoulder of the down. He was tired enough when he reached it, and for a moment was disappointed; he was better of course, but better, after all,

than what? He should never again, as at one or two great
moments of the past, be better that himself. The infinite of life
was gone, and what remained of the dose a small glass scored
like a thermometer by the apothecary. He sat and stared at the
sea, which appeared all surface and twinkle, far shallower than
the spirit of man. It was the abyss of human illusion that was the
real, the tideless deep. He held his packet, which had come by
book-post, unopened on his knee, liking, in the lapse of so many
joys—his illness had made him feel his age—to know it was
there, but taking for granted there could be no complete renewal
of the pleasure, dear to young experience, of seeing one's self 'just
out.' Dencombe, who had a reputation, had come out too often
and knew too well in advance how he should look.

His postponement associated itself vaguely, after a little, with
a group of three persons, two ladies and a young man, whom,
beneath him, straggling and seemingly silent, he could see move
slowly together along the sands. The gentleman had his head
bent over a book and was occasionally brought to a stop by the
charm of this volume, which, as Dencombe could perceive even
at a distance, had a cover alluringly red. Then his companions,
going a little further, waited for him to come up, poking their
parasols into the beach, looking around them at the sea and sky
and clearly sensible of the beauty of the day. To these things
the young man with the book was still more clearly indifferent;
lingering, credulous, absorbed, he was an object of envy to an
observer from whose connexion with literature all such artless-
ness had faded. One of the ladies was large and mature; the other
had the spareness of comparative youth and of a social position
possibly inferior. The large lady carried back Dencombe's imagination to the age of crinoline; she wore a hat of the shape of a
mushroom, decorated with a blue veil, and had the air, in her
aggressive amplitude, of clinging to a vanished fashion or even
a lost cause. Presently her companion produced from under the
folds of a mantle a limp portable chair which she stiffened out
and of which the large lady took possession. This act, and something in the movement of either party, at once characterised the
performers—they performed for Dencombe's recreation—as opulent matron and humble dependant. Where, moreover, was the

virtue of an approved novelist if one couldn't establish a relation between such figures? the clever theory for instance that the young man was the son of the opulent matron and that the humble dependant, the daughter of a clergyman or an officer, nourished a secret passion for him. Was that not visible from the way she stole behind her protectress to look back at him?—back to where he had let himself come to a full stop when his mother sat down to rest. His book was a novel, it had the catchpenny binding; so that while the romance of life stood neglected at his side he lost himself in that of the circulating library. He moved mechanically to where the sand was softer and ended by plumping down in it to finish his chapter at his ease. The humble dependant, discouraged by his remoteness, wandered with a martyred droop of the head in another direction, and the exorbitant lady, watching the waves, offered a confused resemblance to a flying machine that had broken down.

When this drama began to fail Dencombe remembered that he had after all another pastime. Though such promptitude on the part of the publisher was rare he was already able to draw from its wrapper his 'latest,' perhaps his last. The cover of *The Middle Years* was duly meretricious, the smell of the fresh pages the very odour of sanctity; but for the moment he went no further —he had become conscious of a strange alienation. He had forgotten what his book was about. Had the assault of his old ailment, which he had so fallaciously come to Bournemouth to ward off, interposed utter blankness as to what had preceded it? He had finished the revision of proof before quitting London, but his subsequent fortnight in bed had passed the sponge over colour. He couldn't have chanted to himself a single sentence, couldn't have turned with curiosity or confidence to any particular page. His subject had already gone from him, leaving scarce a superstition behind. He uttered a low moan as he breathed the chill of this dark void, so desperately it seemed to represent the completion of a sinister process. The tears filled his mild eyes; something precious had passed away. This was the pang that had been sharpest during the last few years—the sense of ebbing time, of shrinking opportunity; and now he felt not so much that his last chance was going as that it was gone indeed. He had done all he should ever do, and yet hadn't done what he wanted. This was the laceration—that practically his career was over: it was as violent as a grip at his throat. He rose from his seat nervously—a creature hunted by a dread; then he fell back in his weakness and nervously opened his book. It was a single volume; he preferred single volumes and aimed at a rare compression. He began to read and, little by little, in this occupation, was pacified and reassured. Everything came back to him, but came back with a wonder, came back above all with a high and magnificent beauty. He read his own prose, he turned his own leaves, and had as he sat there with the spring sunshine on the page an emotion peculiar and intense. His career was over, no doubt, but it was over, when all was said, with *that*.

He had forgotten during his illness the work of the previous year; but what he had chiefly forgotten was that it was extraordinarily good. He dived once more into his story and was drawn down, as by a siren's hand, to where, in the dim underworld of fiction, the great glazed tank of art, strange silent subjects float. He recognised his motive and surrendered to his talent. Never probably had that talent, such as it was, been so fine. His difficulties were still there, but what was also there, to his perception, though probably, alas! to nobody's else, was the art that in most cases had surmounted them. In his surprised enjoyment of this ability he had a glimpse of a possible reprieve. Surely its force wasn't spent—there was life and service in it yet. It hadn't come to him easily, it had been backward and roundabout. It was the child of time, the nursling of delay; he had struggled and suffered for it, making sacrifices not to be counted, and now that it was really mature was it to cease to yield, to confess itself brutally beaten? There was an infinite charm for Dencombe in feeling as he had never felt before that diligence *vincit omnia*. The result produced in his little book was somehow a result beyond his conscious intention: it was as if he had planted his genius, had trusted his method, and they had grown up and flowered with this sweetness. If the achievement had been real, however, the process had been painful enough. What he saw so intensely today, what he felt as a nail driven in, was that only now, at the very last, had he come into possession. His development had been abnormally slow, almost grotesquely gradual. He had been hindered and retarded by experience, he had for long periods only groped his way. It had taken too much of his life to produce too little of his art. The art had come, but it had come after everything else. At such a rate a first existence was too short—long enough only to collect material; so that to fructify, to use the material, one should have a second age, an extension. This extension was what poor Dencombe sighed for. As he turned the last leaves of his volume he murmured 'Ah for another go, ah for a better chance!'

The three persons drawing his attention to the sands had vanished and then reappeared; they had now wandered up a path, an artificial and easy ascent, which led to the top of the cliff. Dencombe's bench was halfway down, on a sheltered ledge, and the large lady, a massive heterogeneous person with bold black eyes and kind red cheeks, now took a few moments to rest. She wore dirty gauntlets and immense diamond ear-rings; at first she looked vulgar, but she contradicted this announcement in an agreeable off-hand tone. While her companions stood waiting for her she spread her skirts on the end of Dencombe's seat. The young man had gold spectacles, through which, with his finger still in his red-covered book, he glanced at the volume, bound in the same shade of the same colour, lying on the lap of the original occupant of the bench. After an instant Dencombe felt him struck with a resemblance; he had recognised the gilt stamp on the crimson cloth, was reading *The Middle Years* and now noted that somebody else had kept pace with him. The stranger was startled, possibly even a little ruffled, to find himself not the only person favoured with an early copy. The eyes of the two proprietors met a moment, and Dencombe borrowed amusement from the expression of those of his competitor, those, it might even be inferred, of his admirer. They confessed to some resentment—they seemed to say: 'Hang it, has he got it *already*? Of course he's a brute of a reviewer!' Dencombe shuffled his copy out of sight while the opulent matron, rising from her repose, broke out: 'I feel already the good of this air!'

'I can't say I do,' said the angular lady. 'I feel myself quite let down.'

'I find myself horribly hungry. At what time did you order luncheon?' her protectress pursued.

The young person put the question by. 'Doctor Hugh always orders it.'

'I ordered nothing today—I'm going to make you diet,' said their comrade.

'Then I shall go home and sleep. *Qui dort dine!*'

'Can I trust you to Miss Vernham?' asked Doctor Hugh of his elder companion.

'Don't I trust *you*?' she archly inquired.

'Not too much!' Miss Vernham, with her eyes on the ground, permitted herself to declare. 'You must come with us at least to the house,' she went on while the personage on whom they appeared to be in attendance began to mount higher. She had got a little out of ear-shot; nevertheless Miss Vernham became, so far as Dencombe was concerned, less distinctly audible to murmur to the young men: 'I don't think you realise all you owe the Countess!'

Absently, a moment, Doctor Hugh caused his gold-rimmed spectacles to shine at her. 'Is that the way I strike you? I see—I see!'

'She's awfully good to us,' continued Miss Vernham, compelled by the lapse of the other's motion to stand there in spite of his discussion of private matters. Of what use would it have been that Dencombe should be sensitive to shades hadn't he detected in that arrest a strange influence from the quiet old convalescent in the great tweed cape? Miss Vernham appeared suddenly to become aware of some such connexion, for she added in a moment: 'If you want to sun yourself here you can come back after you've seen us home.'

Doctor Hugh, at this, hesitated, and Dencombe, in spite of a desire to pass for unconscious, risked a covert glance at him. What his eyes met this time, as happened, was, on the part of the young lady, a queer stare, naturally vitreous, which made her remind him of some figure—he couldn't name it—in a play or a novel, some sinister governess or tragic old maid. She seemed to scan him, to challenge him, to say out of general spite: 'What have you got to do with us?' At the same instant the rich humour of the Countess reached them from above: 'Come, come, my little lambs; you should follow your old *bergère!*' Miss Vernham turned away for it, pursing the ascent, and Doctor Hugh, after another mute appeal to Dencombe and a minute's evident demur, deposited his book on the bench is if to keep his place, or even a a gage of earnest return, and bounded without difficulty up the rougher part of the cliff.

Equally innocent and infinite are the pleasures of observation and the resources engendered by the trick of analysing life. It amused poor Dencombe, as he dawdled in his tepid air-bath, to believe himself awaiting a revelation of something at the back of a fine young mind. He looked hard at the book on the end of the bench, but wouldn't have touched it for the world. It served his purpose to have a theory that shouldn't be exposed to refutation. He already felt better of his melancholy; he had, according to his old formula, put his head at the window. A passing Countess could draw off the fancy when, like the elder of the ladies who had just retreated, she was as obvious as the giantess of a caravan. It was indeed general views that were terrible; short ones, contrary to an opinion sometimes expressed, were the refuge, were the remedy. Doctor Hugh couldn't possibly be anything but a reviewer who had understandings for early copies with publishers or with newspapers. He reappeared in a quarter of an hour with visible relief at finding Dencombe on the spot and the gleam of white teeth in an embarrassed but generous smile. He was perceptibly disappointed at the eclipse of the other copy of the book; it made a pretext the less for speaking to the quiet gentleman. But he spoke notwithstanding; he held up his own copy and broke out pleadingly: 'Do say, if you have occasion to speak of it, that it's the best thing he has done yet!

Dencombe responded with a laugh: 'Done yet' was so amusing to him, made such a grand avenue of the future. Better still, the young man took *him* for a reviewer. He pulled out *The Middle Years* from under his cape, but instinctively concealed any telltale look of fatherhood. This was partly because a person was always a fool for insisting to others on his work. 'Is that what you're going to say yourself?' he put to his visitor.

'I'm not quite sure I shall write anything. I don't, as a regular thing—I enjoy in peace. But it's awfully fine.'

Dencombe just debated. If the young man had begun to abuse him he would have confessed on the spot to his identity, but there was no harm in drawing out any impulse to praise. He drew it out with such success that in a few moments his new acquaintance, seated by his side, was confessing candidly that the works of the author of the volumes before them were the only ones he could read a second time. He had come the day before from London, where a friend of his, a journalist, had lent him his copy of the last, the copy sent to the office of the journal and already the subject of a 'notice' which, as was pretended there—but one had to allow for 'swagger'—it had taken a full quarter of an hour to prepare. He intimated that he was ashamed for his friend, and in the case of a work demanding and repaying study, of such inferior manners; and, with his fresh appreciation and his so irregular wish to express it, he speedily became for poor Dencombe a remarkable, a delightful apparition. Chance had brought the weary man of letters face to face with the greatest admirer in the new generation of whom it was supposable he might boast. The admirer in truth was mystifying, so rare a case was it to find a bristling young doctor—he looked like a German physiologist—enamoured of literary form. It was an accident, but happier that most accidents, so that Dencombe, exhilarated as well as confounded, spent half an hour in making his visitor talk while he kept himself quiet. He explained his premature possession of *The Middle Years* by an allusion to the friendship of the publisher, who, knowing he was at Bournemouth for his health, had paid him this graceful attention. He allowed he had been ill, for Doctor Hugh would infallibly have guessed it; he even went so far as to wonder if he mightn't look for some hygienic 'tip' from a personage combining so bright an enthusiasm with a presumable knowledge of the remedies now in vogue. It would shake his faith a little perhaps to have to take a doctor seriously who could take *him* so seriously, but he enjoyed this gushing modern youth and felt with an acute pang that there would still be work to do in a world in which such odd combinations were presented. It wasn't true, what he had tried for renunciation's sake to believe, that all the combinations were exhausted. They weren't by any means—they were infinite: the exhaustion was in the miserable artist.

Doctor Hugh, an ardent physiologist, was saturated with the spirit of the age in other words he had just taken his degree; but he was independent and various, he talked like a man who would have preferred to love literature best. He would fain have made fine phrases, but nature had denied him the trick. Some of the finest in *The Middle Years* had struck him inordinately, and he took the liberty of reading them to Dencombe in support of his plea. He grew vivid, in the balmy air, to his companion, for whose deep refreshment he seemed to have been sent; and was particularly ingenuous in describing how recently he had become acquainted, and how instantly infatuated, with the only man who had put flesh between the ribs of an art that was starving on superstitions. He hadn't yet written to him—he was deterred by a strain of respect. Dencombe at this moment rejoiced more inwardly than ever that he had never answered the photographers. His visitor's attitude promised him a luxury of intercourse, though he was sure a due freedom for Doctor Hugh would depend not a little on the Countess. He learned without delay what type of Countess was involved, mastering as well the nature of the tie that united the curious trio. The large lady, an Englishwoman by birth and the daughter of a celebrated baritone, whose taste *minus* his talent she had inherited, was the widow of a French nobleman and mistress of all that remained of the handsome fortune, the fruit of her father's earnings, that had constituted her dower. Miss Vernham, an odd creature but an accomplished pianist, was attached to her person at a salary. The Countess was generous, independent, eccentric; she travelled with her minstrel and her medical man. Ignorant and passionate, she had nevertheless moments in which she was almost irresistible. Dencombe saw her sit for her portrait in Doctor Hugh's free sketch, and felt the picture of his young friend's relation to her frame itself in his mind. This young friend, for a representative of the new psychology, was himself easily hypnotised, and if he became abnormally communicative it was only a sign of his real subjection. Dencombe did accordingly

what he wanted with him, even without being known as
Dencombe.

Taken ill on a journey in Switzerland the Countess had picked
him up at an hotel, and the accident of his happening to please
her had made her offer him, with her imperious liberality, terms
that couldn't fail to dazzle a practitioner without patients and
whose resources had been drained dry by his studies. It wasn't
the way he would have proposed to spend his time, but it was
time that would pass quickly, and meanwhile she was wonder-
fully kind. She exacted perpetual attention, but it was impossible
not to like her. He gave details about his queer patient, a 'type'
if there ever was one, who had in connexion with her flushed
obesity, and in addition to the morbid strain of violent and aim-
less will, a grave organic disorder; but he came back to his loved
novelist, whom he was so good as to pronounce more essentially
a poet than many of those who went in for verse, with a zeal
excited, as all his indiscretion had been excited, by the happy
chance of Dencombe's sympathy and the coincidence of their
occupation. Dencombe had confessed to a slight personal acquaintance with the author of *The Middle Years*, but had not felt
himself as ready as he could have wished when his companion,
who had never yet encountered a being so privileged, began to
be eager for particulars. He even divined in Doctor Hugh's eye
at that moment a glimmer of suspicion. But the young man was
too inflamed to be shrewd and repeatedly caught up the book
to exclaim: 'Did you notice this?' or 'Weren't you immensely
struck with that?' 'There's a beautiful passage toward the end,'
he broke out; and again he laid his hand on the volume. As he
turned the pages he came upon something else, while Dencombe
saw him suddenly change colour. He had taken up as it lay on
the bench Dencombe's copy instead of his own, and his neighbour at once guessed the reason of his start. Doctor Hugh looked
grave an instant; then he said: 'I see you've been altering the
text!' Dencombe was a passionate corrector, a fingerer of style;
the last thing he ever arrived at was a form final for himself. His
ideal would have been to publish secretly, and then, on the
published text, treat himself to the terrified revise, sacrificing
always a first edition and beginning for posterity and even for

the collectors, poor dears, with a second. This morning, in *The Middle Years*, his pencil had pricked a dozen lights. He was amused at the effect of the young man's reproach; for an instant it made him change colour. He stammered at any rate ambiguously, then through a blur of ebbing consciousness saw Doctor Hugh's mystified eyes. He only had time to feel he was about to be ill again—that emotion, excitement, fatigue, the heat of the sun, the solicitation of the air, had combined to play him a trick, before, stretching out a hand to his visitor with a plaintive cry, he lost his senses altogether.

Later he knew he had fainted and that Doctor Hugh had got him home in a Bath-chair, the conductor of which, prowling within hail for custom, had happened to remember seeing him in the garden of the hotel. He had recovered his perception on the way, and had, in bed that afternoon, a vague recollection of Doctor Hugh's young face, as they went together, bent over him in a comforting laugh and expressive of something more than a suspicion of his identity. That identity was ineffaceable now, and all the more that he was rueful and sore. He had been rash, been stupid, had gone out too soon, stayed out too long. He oughtn't to have exposed himself to strangers, he ought to have taken his servant. He felt as if he had fallen into a hole too deep to descry any little patch of heaven. He was confused about the time that had passed—he pieced the fragments together. He had seen his doctor, the real one, the one who had treated him from the first and who had again been very kind. His servant was in and out on tiptoe, looking very wise after the fact. He said more than once something about the sharp young gentleman. The rest was vagueness in so far as it wasn't despair. The vagueness, however, justified itself by dreams, dozing anxieties from which he finally emerged to the consciousness of a dark room and a shaded candle.

'You'll be all right again—I know all about you now,' said a voice near him that he felt to be young. Then his meeting with Doctor Hugh came back. He was too discouraged to joke about it yet, but made out after a little that the interest was intense for his visitor. 'Of course I can't attend you professionally— you've got your own man, with whom I've talked and who's excellent,' Doctor Hugh went on. 'But you must let me come and see you as a good friend. I've just looked in before going to bed. You're doing beautifully, but it's a good job I was with you on the cliff. I shall come in early tomorrow. I want to do something for you. I want to do everything. You've done a tremendous lot for me.' The young man held his hand, hanging over him, and poor Dencombe, weakly aware of this living pressure, simply lay there and accepted his devotion. He couldn't do anything less—he needed help too much.

The idea of the help he needed was very present to him that night, which he spent in a lucid stillness, an intensity of thought that constituted a reaction from his hours of stupor. He was lost, he was lost—he was lost, if he couldn't be saved. He wasn't afraid of suffering, of death, wasn't even in love with life; but he had had a deep demonstration of desire. It came over him in the long quiet hours that only with *The Middle Years* had he taken his flight; only on that day, visited by soundless processions, had he recognised his kingdom. He had had a revelation of his range. What he dreaded was the idea that his reputation should stand on the unfinished. It wasn't with his past but with his future that it should properly be concerned. Illness and age rose before him like spectres with pitiless eyes: how was he to bribe such fates to give him the second chance? He had had the one chance that all men have—he had had the chance of life. He went to sleep again very late, and when he awoke Doctor Hugh was sitting at hand. There was already by this time something beautifully familiar about him.

'Don't think I've turned out your physician,' he said: 'I'm acting with his consent. He has been here and seen you. Somehow he seems to trust me. I told him how we happened to come together yesterday, and he recognises that I've a peculiar right.'

Dencombe felt his own face pressing. 'How have you squared the Countess?'

The young man blushed a little, but turned it off. 'Oh never mind the Countess!'

'You told me she was very exacting.'

Doctor Hugh had a wait. 'So she is.'

'And Miss Vernham's an *intrigante*.'

'How do you know that?'

'I know everything. One *has* to, to write decently!'

'I think she's mad,' said limpid Doctor Hugh.

'Well, don't quarrel with the Countess—she's a present help to you.'

'I don't quarrel,' Doctor Hugh returned. 'But I don't get on with silly women.' Presently he added: 'You seem very much alone.'

'That often happens at my age. I've outlived, I've lost by the way.'

Doctor Hugh faltered; then surmounting a soft scruple: 'Whom have you lost?'

'Everyone.'

'Ah no,' the young man breathed, laying a hand on his arm.

'I once had a wife—I once had a son. My wife died when my child was born, and my boy, at school, was carried off by typhoid.'

'I wish I'd been there!' cried Doctor Hugh.

'Well—if you're here!' Dencombe answered with a smile that, in spite of dimness, showed how he valued being sure of his companion's whereabouts.

'You talk strangely of your age. You're not old.'

'Hypocrite—so early!'

'I speak physiologically.'

'That's the way I've been speaking for the last five years, and it's exactly what I've been saying to myself. It isn't till we *are* old that we begin to tell ourselves we're not.'

'Yet I know I myself am young,' Doctor Hugh returned.

'Not so well as I!' laughed his patient, whose visitor indeed would have established the truth in question by the honesty with which he changed the point of view, remarking that it must be one of the charms of age—at any rate in the case of high distinction—to feel that one has laboured and achieved. Doctor Hugh employed the common phrase about earning one's rest, and it made poor Dencombe for an instant almost angry. He recovered himself, however, to explain, lucidly enough, that if, ungraciously, he knew nothing of such a balm, it was doubtless because he had wasted inestimable years. He had followed literature from the first, but he had taken a lifetime to get abreast of her. Only today at last had he begun to *see,* so that all he had hitherto shown was a movement without a direction. He had ripened too late and was so clumsily constituted that he had had to teach himself by mistakes.

'I prefer your flowers then to other people's fruit, and your mistakes to other people's successes,' said gallant Doctor Hugh. 'It's for your mistakes I admire you.'

'You're happy—you don't know,' Dencombe answered.

Looking at his watch the young man had got up; he named the hour of the afternoon at which he would return. Dencombe warned him against committing himself too deeply, and expressed again all his dread of making him neglect the Countess—perhaps incur her displeasure.

'I want to be like you—I want to learn by mistakes!' Doctor Hugh laughed.

'Take care you don't make too grave a one! But do come back,' Dencombe added with the glimmer of a new idea.

'You should have had more vanity!' His friend spoke as if he knew the exact amount required to make a man of letters normal.

'No, no—I only should have had more time. I want another go.'

'Another go?'

'I want—an extension.'

'An extension?' Again Doctor Hugh repeated Dencombe's words, with which he seemed to have been struck.

'Don't you know?—I want to what they call "live." '

The young man, for good-bye, had taken his hand, which closed with a certain force. They looked at each other hard. 'You *will* live,' said Doctor Hugh.

'Don't be superficial. It's too serious!'

'You *shall* live!' Dencombe's visitor declared, turning pale.

'Ah that's better!' And as he retired the invalid, with a troubled laugh, sank gratefully back.

All that day and all the following night he wondered if it mightn't be arranged. His doctor came again, his servant was attentive, but it was to his confident young friend that he felt himself mentally appeal. His collapse on the cliff was plausibly explained and his liberation, on a better basis, promised for the morrow; meanwhile, however, the intensity of his meditations kept him tranquil and made him indifferent. The idea that occupied him was none the less absorbing because it was a morbid fancy. Here was a clever son of the age, ingenious and ardent, who happened to have set him up for connoisseurs to worship. This servant of his altar had all the new learning in science and all the old reverence in faith; wouldn't he therefore put his knowledge at the disposal of his sympathy, his craft at the disposal of his love? Couldn't he be trusted to invent a remedy for a poor artist to whose art he had paid a tribute? If he couldn't the alternative was hard: Dencombe would have to surrender to silence unvindicated and undivined. The rest of the day and all the next he toyed in secret with this sweet futility. Who would work the miracle for him but the young man who could combine such lucidity with such passion? He thought of the fairy-tales of science and charmed himself into forgetting that he looked for a magic that was not of this world. Doctor Hugh was an apparition, and that placed him above the law. He came and went while his patient, who now sat up, followed him with supplicating eyes. The interest of knowing the great author had made the young man begin *The Middle Years* afresh and would help him to find a richer sense between its covers. Dencombe had told him what he 'tried for'; with all his intelligence, on a first perusal, Doctor Hugh had failed to guess it. The baffled celebrity wondered then who in the world *would* guess it; he was amused once more at the diffused massive weight that could be thrown into the missing of an intention. Yet he wouldn't rail at the general mind today—consoling as that ever had been: the revelation of his own slowness had seemed to make all stupidity sacred.

Doctor Hugh, after a little, was visibly worried, confessing, on inquiry, to a source of embarrassment at home. 'Stick to the Countess—don't mind me,' Dencombe said repeatedly; for his companion was frank enough about the large lady's attitude. She was so jealous that she had fallen ill—she resented such a breach of allegiance. She paid so much for his fidelity that she must have it all: she refused him the right to other sympathies, charged him with scheming to make her die alone, for it was needless to point out how little Miss Vernham was a resource in trouble. When Doctor Hugh mentioned that the Countess would already have left Bournemouth if he hadn't kept her in bed, poor Dencombe held his arm tighter and said with decision: 'Take her straight away.' They had gone out together, walking back to the sheltered nook in which, the other day, they had met. The young man, who had given his companion a personal support, declared with emphasis that his conscience was clear—he could ride two horses at once. Didn't he dream for his future of a time when he should have to ride five hundred? Longing equally for virtue, Dencombe replied that in that golden age no patient would pretend to have contracted with him for his whole attention. On the part of the Countess wasn't such an avidity lawful? Doctor Hugh denied it, said there was no contract, but only a free understanding, and that a sordid servitude was impossible to a generous spirit; he liked moreover to talk about art, and that was the subject on which, this time, as they sat together on the sunny bench, he tried most to engage the author of *The Middle Years*. Dencombe, soaring again a little on the weak wings of convalescence and still haunted by that happy notion of an organised rescue, found another strain of eloquence to plead the cause of a certain splendid 'last manner,' the very citadel, as it would prove, of his reputation, the stronghold into which his real treasure would be gathered. While his listener gave up the morning and the great still sea ostensibly waited he had a wondrous explanatory hour. Even for himself he was inspired as he told what his treasure would consist of, the precious metals he would dig from the mine, the jewels rare, strings of pearls, he would hang between the columns of his temple. He was wondrous for himself, so thick his convictions crowded, but still more wondrous for Doctor Hugh, who assured him none the less that the very pages he had just published were already encrusted with gems. This admirer, however, panted for the combinations to come and, before the fact of the beautiful day, renewed to Dencombe his guarantee that his profession would hold itself responsible for such a life. Then he suddenly clapped his hand upon his watch-pocket and asked leave to absent himself for half an hour. Dencombe waited there for his return, but was at last recalled to the actual by the fall of a shadow across the ground. The shadow darkened into that of Miss Vernham, the young lady in attendance on the Countess; whom Dencombe, recognising her, perceived so clearly to have come to speak to him that he rose from his bench to acknowledge the civility. Miss Vernham indeed proved not particularly civil; she looked strangely agitated, and her type was now unmistakable.

'Excuse me if I do ask,' she said, 'whether it's too much to hope that you may be induced to leave Doctor Hugh alone;' Then before our poor friend, greatly disconcerted, could protest: 'You ought to be informed that you stand in his light—that you may do him a terrible injury.'

'Do you mean by causing the Countess to dispense with his services?'

'By causing her to disinherit him.' Dencombe stared at this, and Miss Vernham pursued, in the gratification of seeing she could produce an impression: 'It has depended on himself to come into something very handsome. He has had a grand prospect, but I think you've succeeded in spoiling it.'

'Not intentionally, I assure you. Is there no hope the accident may be repaired?' Dencombe asked.

'She was ready to do anything for him. She takes great fancies, she lets herself go—it's her way. She has no relations, she's free to dispose of her money, and she's very ill,' said Miss Vernham for a climax.

'I'm very sorry to hear it,' Dencombe stammered.

'Wouldn't it be possible for you to leave Bournemouth? That's what I've come to see about.'

He sank to his bench. 'I'm very ill myself, but I'll try!'

Miss Vernham still stood there with her colourless eyes and the brutality of her good conscience. 'Before it's too late, please!' she said; and with this she turned her back, in order, quickly, as if it had been a business to which she could spare but a precious moment, to pass out of his sight.

Oh yes, after this Dencombe was certainly very ill. Miss Vernham had upset him with her rough fierce news; it was the sharpest shock to him to discover what was at stake for a penniless young man of fine parts. He sat trembling on his bench, staring at the waste of waters, feeling sick with the directness of the blow. He was indeed too weak, too unsteady, too alarmed; but he would make the effort to get away, for he couldn't accept the guilt of interference and his honour was really involved. He would hobble home, at any rate, and then think what was to be done. He made his way back to the hotel and, as he went, had a characteristic vision of Miss Vernham's great motive. The Countess hated women of course—Dencombe was lucid about that; so the hungry pianist had no personal hopes and could only console herself with the bold conception of helping Doctor Hugh in order to marry him after he should get his money or else induce him to recognise her claim for compensation and buy her off. If she had befriended him at a fruitful crisis he would really, as a man of delicacy—and she knew what to think of that point—have to reckon with her.

At the hotel Dencombe's servant insisted on his going back to bed. The invalid had talked about catching a train and had begun with orders to pack; after which his racked nerves had yielded to a sense of sickness. He consented to see his physician, who immediately was sent for, but he wished it to be understood that his door was irrevocably closed to Doctor Hugh. He had his plan, which was so fine that he rejoiced in it after getting back to bed. Doctor Hugh, suddenly finding himself snubbed without mercy, would, in natural disgust and to the joy of Miss Vernham, renew his allegiance to the Countess. When his physician arrived Dencombe learned that he was feverish and that this was very wrong: he was to cultivate calmness and try, if possible, not to think. For the rest of the day he wooed stupidity; but there was an ache that kept him sentient, the probable sacrifice of his 'extension,' the limit of his course. His medical adviser was anything but pleased; his successive relapses were ominous. He charged this personage to put out a strong hand and take Doctor Hugh off his mind—it would contribute so much to his being quiet. The agitating name, in his room, was not mentioned again, but his security was a smothered fear, and it was not confirmed by the receipt, at ten o'clock that evening, of a telegram which his servant opened and read him and to which, with an address in London, the signature of

Miss Vernham was attached. 'Beseech you to use all influence to make our friend join us here in the morning. Countess much the worse for dreadful journey, but everything may still be saved.' The two ladies had gathered themselves up and had been capable in the afternoon of a spiteful revolution. They had started for the capital, and if the elder one, as Miss Vernham had announced, was every ill, she had wished to make it clear that she was proportionately reckless. Poor Dencombe, who was not reckless and who only desired that everything should indeed be 'saved,' sent this missive straight off to the young man's lodging and had on the morrow the pleasure of knowing that he had quitted Bournemouth by an early train.

Two days later he pressed in with a copy of a literary journal in his hand. He had returned because he was anxious and for the pleasure of flourishing the great review of *The Middle Years*, Here at least was something adequate—it rose to the occasion; it was an acclamation, a reparation, a critical attempt to place the author in the niche he had fairly won. Dencombe accepted and submitted; he made neither objection nor inquiry, for old complications had returned and he had had two dismal days. He was convinced not only that he should never again leave his bed, so that his young friend might pardonably remain, but that the demand he should make on the patience of beholders would be of the most moderate. Doctor Hugh had been to town, and he tried to find in his eyes some confession that the Countess was pacified and his legacy clinched; but all he could see there was the light of his juvenile joy in two or three of the phrases of the newspaper. Dencombe couldn't read them, but when his visitor had insisted on repeating them more than once he was able to shake an intoxicated head. 'Ah no—but they would have been true of what I *could* have done!'

'What people "could have done" is mainly what they've in fact done,' Doctor Hugh contended.

'Mainly, yes; but I've been an idiot!' Dencombe said.

Doctor Hugh did remain; the end was coming fast. Two days later his patient observed to him, by way of the feeblest of jokes, that there would now be no question whatever of a second chance. At this the young man stared; then he exclaimed : 'Why it has come to pass—it has come to pass! The second chance has been the public's—the chance to find the point of view, to pick up the pearl!'

'Oh the pearl!' poor Dencombe uneasily sighed. A smile as cold as a winter sunset flickered on his drawn lips as he added: 'The pearl is the unwritten—the pearl is the unalloyed, the *rest*, the lost!'"

From that hour he was less and less present, heedless to all appearance of what went on round him. His disease was definitely mortal, of an action as relentless, after the short arrest that had enabled him to fall in with Doctor Hugh, as a leak in a great ship. Sinking steadily, though this visitor, a man of rare resources, now cordially approved by his physician, showed endless art in guarding him from pain, poor Dencombe kept no reckoning of favour or neglect, betrayed no symptom of regret or speculation. Yet towards the last he gave a sign of having noticed how for two days Doctor Hugh hadn't been in his room, a sign that consisted of his suddenly opening his eyes to put a question. Had he spent those days with the Countess?

'The Countess is dead,' said Doctor Hugh. 'I knew that in a particular contingency she wouldn't resist. I went to her grave.'

Dencombe's eyes opened wider. 'She left you "something handsome"?'

The young man gave a laugh almost too light for a chamber of woe. 'Never a penny. She roundly cursed me.'

'Cursed you?' Dencombe wailed.

'For giving her up. I gave her up for *you*. I had to choose,' his companion explained.

'You chose to let a fortune go?'

'I chose to accept, whatever they might be, the consequences of my infatuation,' smiled Doctor Hugh. Then as a larger pleasantry: 'The fortune be hanged! It's your own fault if I can't get your things out of my head.'

The immediate tribute to his humour was a long bewildered moan; after which, for many hours, many days, Dencombe lay motionless and absent. A response so absolute, such a glimpse of a definite result and such a sense of credit, worked together in his mind and, producing a strange commotion, slowly altered and transfigured his despair. The sense of cold submersion left him—he seemed to float without an effort. The incident was extraordinary as evidence, and it shed an intenser light. At last he signed to Doctor Hugh to listen and, when he was down on his knees by the pillow, brought him very near. 'You've made me think it all a delusion.'

'Not your glory, my dear friend,' stammered the young man.

'Not my glory—what there is of it! It is glory—to have been tested, to have had our little quality and cast our little spell. The thing is to have made somebody care. You happen to be crazy, of course, but that doesn't affect the law.'

'You're a great success!' said Doctor Hugh, putting into his young voice the ring of a marriage-bell.

Dencombe lay taking this in; then he gathered strength to speak once more. 'A second chance—*that's* the delusion. There never was to be but one. We work in the dark—we do what we can—we give what we have. Our doubt is our passion and our passion is our task. The rest is the madness of art.'

'If you've doubted, if you've despaired, you've always "done" it,' his visitor subtly argued.

'We've done something or other,' Dencombe conceded.

'Something or other is everything. It's the feasible. It's *you!*'

'Comforter!' poor Dencombe ironically sighed.

'But it's true,' insisted his friend.

'It's true. It's frustration that doesn't count.'

'Frustration's only life,' said Doctor Hugh.

'Yes, it's what passes.' Poor Dencombe was barely audible, but he had marked with the words the virtual end of his first and only chance.

Fr. Rolfe ('Baron Corvo')
1860-1913

FREDERICK WILLIAM SERAFINO AUSTIN LEWIS MARY ROLFE, who referred to himself as 'Fr. [Father] Rolfe' and wrote under the name of 'Baron Corvo' was born on July 22, 1860, at 61, Cheapside, London. He was the eldest of five sons in a family of piano manufacturers. Rolfe's father was a Dissenter, but he himself became a convert to the Roman Church at the age of twenty-six.

Rolfe left school at fifteen, living for a while as an unattached student at Oxford.

Dearly loving a lord (with especial devotion to his powers of patronage), Rolfe became a master at a school for boy choristers run by the Marquis of Bute of Oban. In 1887 he entered the Catholic seminary at Oscott, but was soon discharged as unsuitable. Archbishop Smith of Edinburgh then sent him to the Scots College in Rome, but he was dismissed from there also as lacking the hallmark of genuine vocation.

Rolfe's life-long efforts to enter the priesthood—for other applications were to follow—caused him undying bitterness and frustration; and in his novel *Hadrian the Seventh* (1904), he features as the hero George Arthur Rose, rejected candidate for the priesthood who is raised to the papal throne only to be assassinated by a socialist agitator whose party doctrines Rose has been denying. Thus Rose, dying a martyr for his faith, provided Rolfe with his compensating dream. He certainly did not lack the outward shape of his desired calling, and has been described as 'slim, clean-shaven, bandy-legged and slightly clerical in appearance.'

After acting as tutor to the young Laird of Seton at Aberdeen, followed by two years at Holywell in Flintshire, painting ecclesiastical banners for Fr. Beauclerk—had charged ten pounds a head, and since the banners had a hundred figures, Rolfe sent in a bill for a thousand pounds, but finally, after much quarrelling, settled for the sum of fifty pounds—he came to London to see Henry Harland, editor of *The Yellow Book*, to whom he had mailed six stories from Wales.

These were the *Stories Toto told me*—folk tales concerning the saints narrated by a bright Italian boy to his English employer. Along with twenty-six new fables these appeared in volume form *In His Own Image* (1901), which Robert Hugh Benson (son of the Primate and an erstwhile friend) called 'The Fifth Gospel.'

The publisher Grant Richards was persuaded to finance Rolfe while he researched and worked upon his *Chronicles of the House of Borgia* (1901). 'He wrote like a genius and quarrelled like a madman,' states Katherine Lyon Mix, summing up the experience of the Harland circle who found that, as well as the peccadillo of leaving fleas in an upholstered armchair, Rolfe had the vindictive temper of a fiend.

Everything about Rolfe proclaimed his egomania plus a perse-cution-complex. D. H. Lawrence, who enjoyed both these traits, came out on his side, however, when writing of Rolfe's *Hadrian the Seventh* : 'If it is the book of a demon as [his] contemporaries said, it is the book of a man demon, not a mere *poseur*. And if some of it is caviare, at least it came out of the belly of a live fish.'

After many litigatory adventures, and many epistular passages-at-arms, Rolfe spent his last years in Venice, giving himself up fully to the homosexuality he had kept battened down. Passing the point of 'credit and excuses,' he died there in poverty aged fifty-three after a short riot of extravagant spending.

'A man with only the vaguest sense of realities,' such was the impression he left on Vincent O'Sullivan, who had been taught by him as a boy when Rolfe was a seminarist at Oscott. His title, like most of Rolfe's claims, seems suspect or unverifiable. Vincent O'Sullivan reports how 'In one of the few letters I wrote him after I left Oscott, I began as usual "Dear Mr. Rolfe." He replied "Baron Corvo, if you please—a designation I picked up in Italy." ' 'I was told,' O'Sullivan continued, 'that Rolfe went to Italy with [the Duc] Sforza [de Santafiore, who was a pupil at Oscott] as a tutor or something . . . I believe that Italian nobles have a right to bestow one of their minor titles on whom it suits them, and Corvo may have been one of Sforza's minor titles.' Rolfe's own account was that he received his title from an English lady, the Duchess Sforza-Cesarini, who bestowed it on him, with a small estate of land, when she adopted him as her grandson.

Other works by him include *Don Tarquino* (1905), *The Weird of the Wanderers* (1912), *The Desire and Pursuit of the Whole* (1934), *Hubert's Arthur* (1935).

Rolfe is an exotic among English novelists. One way of putting it would be to describe him as Pater plus fire and brimstone. Or, thinking forward, one can see a likeness between him and Ronald Firbank.

Rolfe is the subject of a brilliant and original biography by A. J. A. Symons entitled *The Quest of Corvo* (1934).

ABOUT SAMPIETRO AND SAMPAOLO

'Once upon a time, sir, the people in Rome were building two churches; the one for Sampietro on the Monte Vaticano, and the other for Sampaolo outside the walls of the city. The two gods used to spend all their spare time sitting on one of the balconies of heaven, and watching the builders; for they were very anxious about their churches. Sampietro desired to have His church finished before that of Sampaolo; wherefore, every night after it was dark outside, He used to leave the keys of heaven in the porch, and ask his brother, Santandrea, to give an eye to the gate while He went round the corner for a minute or two. Then He would slip down to the church of Sampaolo; and take to pieces the work which the builders had done during the day;

135

and if there were any carvings, or pillars, or things of that sort, which took His fancy, He would carry them away and build them into His own church, patching up the part, from which He had taken them, so well that no one could tell the difference. And so, while the builders of the church of Sampietro made a progress which was wonderful, the builders of the church of Sampaolo did not make any progress at all.

'This went on for a long while, and Sampaolo became more uneasy in his mind every day, and he could not take his food, and nothing gave him any pleasure. Santacecilia tried to amuse him with some new songs which she had made; but this drove him into anger, for he said that a woman ought to learn in silence with subjection.

'One day, while he was leaning over the balcony, he saw two pillars taken into his church, which were of yellow antique, most rare and precious, and had been sent from some foreign country; I do not know its name. He was altogether delighted; and he went down to the gate, and asked Sampietro to be so kind as to tell him whether He had ever seen finer pillars. But Sampietro only said that they were rather pretty; and then He asked Sampaolo to get out of the way, and to let Him shut the gate, in case that some improper souls should sneak in.

'That night, sir, when it was dark, Sampietro went and robbed those two pillars of yellow antique, and set them up in His own church. But in the morning, Sampaolo, having thought of nothing but his new pillars all through the night, said a black mass as being shorter; and then he went on to the balcony, to have the pleasure of looking at his church with its beautiful pillars of yellow antique. And when, he saw that they were not there, he became disturbed in his mind; and he went and sat down in a shady place to consider what he should do next. After much thought, it appeared to him that he had been robbed; and as he knew that a person, who has once committed a theft, will continue to steal as long as he remains free, he resolved to watch his church at night, that he might discover who had stolen his pillars.

'During the day the builders of the church of Sampaolo put up two fresh pillars of yellow antique, and two of porphyry, and two of green antique as well. Sampaolo gloated over these fine things from his seat on the balcony, for he knew them to be so beautiful that they would tempt the thief to make another raid, and then he would catch him.

'After Ave Maria, he made friends with one of the angels, who was putting on his armour in the guard-room before taking his place in the line of sentries who encircle the Città di Dio both by day and night. These, sir, are a hundred cubits high, and Sampaolo asked one of them, whose post would be near the gate, to hide him under his wings, so that he could watch for the robber without being seen. The angel said that he was most happy to oblige; for Sampaolo was a Roman of Rome, and very well-thought-of in heaven; and, when the night came on, he hid Sampaolo in the shadow of his feathers.

'Presently that Apostle saw Sampietro go out of the gate; and the light, of which the bodies of the gods are made, went with Him, so that, though the earth was in darkness, Sampaolo could see plainly all that He did. And He picked up the two fresh pillars of yelow antique, and the two of red porphyry, and also the two of green antique in His hand, just as you, sir, would pick up six paint-brushes; and He carried them to His own church on the Monte Vaticano, and set them up there. And when He had patched up the place from which He had taken the pillars so well that they could not be missed, He came back into heaven.

'Sampaolo met Him at the gate and accused Him of thieving; but Sampietro answered blusteringly that He was the Prince of the Apostles, and that He had a right to all the best pillars for His church. Sampaolo replied that, once before, he had had occasion to withstand Sampietro to the face because He was to be blamed (at Antioch, sir); and then high words arose, and the two gods quarrelled so loudly that the Padre Eterno, sitting on His Great White Throne, sent San Michele Arcangiolo to bring the disputants into The Presence.

'There, Sampaolo said :
' "O Re dej secolj, immortale at invisible,—The citizens of Rome are building two churches, the one for me and the other for Sampietro; and for some time I have noticed that while the builders of my church do not seem to make any progress in

their work, the church of Sampietro is nearly finished. The day before yesterday (and today is Saturday), two pillars of yellow antique were set up in my church, most beautiful pillars, O Signor Iddio; but somebody stole them away during the night. And yesterday six pillars were set up, two of yellow antique, two of green antique, and two of porphyry. Tonight I watched to see if they would be stolen; and I have seen Sampietro go down and take them to His own church on the Monte Vaticano."

'The Padre Eterno turned to Sampietro asking whether He had anything to say.

'And Sampietro answered:

' "O Re del Cielo,—We have long ago learnt the lesson that it is not well to deny that which La Sua Divina Maestà knows to be true; wherefore We acknowledge that We have taken the pillars, and many other decent things too, from the church of Sampaolo, and have set them up in Our Own. Nevertheless, We desire to represent that there can be no question of robbery here. O Dio Omnipotente, You have deigned to make Us the Prince of the Apostolic College, the Keeper of the Keys of Heaven, and the Head of Your Church on earth; and, We ask, is it fitting that the churches which men build in Our Honour should be less magnificent than those which they build for Sampaolo? There, in taking these paltry pillars, concerning which he chooses to make a fuss, We are simply within Our right—a right actually inherent in the dignity of the rank which Lo Splendore Immortale della Sua Maestà has been graciously pleased to confer upon Us."

'But this defence did not content the Padre Eterno. He said that the secret method in which Sampietro worked was a proof that He knew Himself to be doing what He ought not to do; and, further, that it was not fair to the men who were building the church of Sampaolo to take away the fine things for which they spent their money for the honour of Sampaolo. Wherefore He cautioned Sampietro not to allow it to occur again.

'On the next day there was a festa, when the builders did not work; but, on the Monday, they placed in the church of Sampaolo several slabs of lapis lazuli and malachite; and during the night Sampietro, who was the most bold and daring of men, had the hardihood to take them away and put them in His own church, right before the very eyes of Sampaolo, who stood at the gate to watch Him. By the time He was returned, Sampaolo had made a complaint before the Padre Eterno; and Sampietro found Himself most severely spoken to, and warned that, supposing Him to persist in His disobedience, not even His exalted rank, and general usefulness, and good conduct would save Him from punishment.

'The following day, which was Tuesday, a marvellous balda-chino of jasper and violet marble, being a gift from the Grand Turk, was put up in the church of Sampaolo; and at night Sam-pietro descended as usual and robbed it. For the third time Sampaolo complained to the Padre Eterno, and then all the Court of Heaven was summoned into The Presence to hear Judgment given.

'The Padre Eterno said—and His Voice, sir, was like rolling thunder—that as Sampietro had been guilty of disobedience to the Divine Decree, in that, urged on by vanity, He had taken the property of Sampaolo for His own church on the Monte Vaticano; and, by the act, had prevented the church of Sampaolo from becoming finished; it was an Order that, until the consummation of the world, the great church of Sampietro in Rome should never be completed. Also, the Padre Eterno added that, as He would give no encouragement to sneaks and tell-tale-tits, the church of Sampaolo Outside-The-Walls, though finished, should be subjected to destruction and demolition, and, as often as it was rebuilt, so often should it be destroyed.

'And you know, sir, that the church of Sampaolo is always being burned down or blown up, and that the church of Sam-pietro has never left the builders' hands.'

'George Egerton'
1860-1945

MARY CHEVALITA BRIGHT (*née* Dunne), who wrote under the *nomme-de-plume* of George Egerton, was born on December 14, 1860, in Melbourne, Australia. Her father was a sea captain and her mother's family came from Glamorgan.

Privately educated, Mary had much advantage and excitement in her girlhood years. She was in camp at Tauranga during the Maori War; and, on another occasion, arrived in a sailing vessel at Valparaiso (whence she had gone to see her great-uncle, an admiral) only to discover the port was being bombarded.

After travelling extensively in England, Ireland, and Wales, in 1888 she married her first husband H. H. W. Melville, who died the following year. In 1891 she married Egerton Clairmonte, who died ten years later. Her last marriage, to Reginald Golding Bright, occurred in 1901.

George Egerton once said that she had intended to be an artist, but became a writer when 'family affairs' prevented the necessary course of her studies. In 1893 there appeared her first volume of short stories, *Keynotes,* which dealt with the emotional intimacies of marriage and the psychology of sexual attraction as recorded by an intelligent woman. 'This volume,' Katherine Lyon Mix tells us, 'gained immediate recognition for its author, both laudatory and abusive. Lane [the publisher] was so pleased that he named after her book a projected series, the Keynote Series, each book in it having a cover design and keynote monogram of the author by Beardsley. To be included in this series was to be of Lane's élite.'

In 1894 came a second collection entitled *Discords* where, as La Gallienne wrote in his review of these new stories, 'George

Egerton appears more definitely as the advocate of the New Woman than in *Keynotes*. . . . In four of [the tales] she herself seems to appear under thin disguise as a sort of Pioneer Club Sister of Mercy, comforting the oppressed and disillusioned victims of man and destiny.' George Egerton's feminism has its monomaniacal side as brash as that upholding of the obvious superiority of the male. For all its feminist championship, however, the tale of *Wedlock*, from this book *Discords* has been chosen on account of its trenchant pathos.

Other volumes of short stories by her include *Symphonies* (1897) and *Fantasies* (1898). A gossip columnist in the June 1894 number of the *Bookbuyer* assured its readers that Mrs. Clairmonte (as she then was), proficient in five or six tongues, was busy compiling 'a vocabulary of fishing terms in four languages.' In 1911 she translated Henry Bernstein's play *The Whirlwind*, and in 1926 Knut Hansun's novel *Hunger*.

Henry James, who contributed to *The Yellow Book*, was not a friend of this new freedom in fiction—this 'larger latitude' in presenting sexual affairs, as one of his characters had christened it. It is thought that James satirized George Egerton (a libertarian lady boldly assuming the plumage of male nomenclature) in the character of Guy Walsingham—a latitudinarian—in his *Death of the Lion*.

George Egerton once went on record as saying that her recreations were languages, dialects, and needlework. She was said to have an attractive face with a decided chin.

The indispensable document for any personal study of her is *George Egerton. A leaf from the Yellow Book: Correspondence and Diaries edited by Terence de Vere White* (1958).

WEDLOCK

Two bricklayers are building a yellow brick wall to the rear of one of a terrace of new jerry-built houses in a genteel suburb. At their back is the remains of a grand old garden. Only the unexpired lease saves it from the clutch of the speculator. An apple-tree is in full blossom, and a fine elm is lying on the grass, sawn down, as it stood on the boundary of a 'desirable lot'; many fair shrubs crop up in unexpected places, a daphne-mezereum struggles to redden its berries amid a heap of refuse thrown out by the caretakers; a granite urn, portions of a deftly carven shield, a mailed hand and a knight's casque, relics of some fine old house demolished to accommodate the ever-increasing number of the genteel, lie in the trampled grass. The road in front is scarcely begun, and the smart butchers' carts sink into the soft mud and red brick-dust, broken glass, and shavings; yet many of the houses are occupied, and the unconquerable London soot has already made some of the cheap 'art' curtains look dingy. A brass plate of the 'Prudential Assurance Company' adorns the gate of Myrtle House; 'Collegiate School for Young Ladies' that of Evergreen Villa. Victoria, Albert, and Alexandra figure in ornamental letters over the stained-glass latticed square of three pretentious houses, facing Gladstone, Cleopatra, and Lobelia. The people move into 26 to the ring of carpenters' hammers in 27, and 'go carts,' perambulators, and half-bred fox terriers impede the movements of the men taking in the kitchen boiler to 28.

One of the men, a short, wiry-looking man of fifty, with grizzled sandy hair and a four days growth of foxy beard on his sharp chin, is whistling 'Barbara Allen' softly as he pats down a brick and scrapes the mortar neatly off the joinings. The other, tall and swarthy, a big man with a loose mouth and handsome wicked eyes and a musical voice, is looking down the laneway leading to a side street.

' 'Ere she comes, the lydy wot owns this 'ere desirable abode. I want 'er to lend me a jug. Wo-o-a hup, missis! Blind me tight if she ain't as boozed as they makes 'em! Look at 'er, Seltzer; ain't she a beauty, ain't she a sample of a decent bloke's wife! She's a fair sickener, she is. Hy, 'old 'ard! She dunno where she are!' with a grin.

But the woman, reeling and stumbling up the lane, neither hears nor sees; she is beyond that. She feels her way to the backyard door of the next house, and, rocking on her feet, tries to find the pocket of her gown. She is much under thirty, with a finely-developed figure. Her gown is torn from the gathers at the back and trails down, showing her striped petticoat; her jacket is of good material, trimmed with silk, but is dusty and lime-marked. Her face is flushed and dirty; and her light golden-brown fringe stands out straight over her white forehead; her bonnet is awry on the back of her head; her watch dangles from the end of a heavy gold chain, and the buttons of her jersey bodice gape open where the guard is passed through; she has a basket on her left arm. She clutches the wall and fumbles stupidly for the key, mumbling unintelligibly, and trying with all her might to keep her eyes open. The tall man watches her with ill-concealed disgust, and tosses a pretty coarse jest to her. The sandy man lays down his trowel and wipes his hands on his apron, and goes to her.

'Lookin' for yer key, missis? Let me 'elp yer; two 'eads is better nor one enny day!'

'Ca'an fin' it. M'm a bad wom—a bad wom—um,' she says, shaking her head solemnly at him, with heavy lids and distended pupils.

Meanwhile he has searched her pocket and opened the basket —nothing in it except a Family Novelette and a few gooseberries in a paper bag. He shakes his head, saying to himself: 'Dropped her marketing. It aint here, missis; sure you took it with ye?'

She nods stupidly and solemnly three times.

'Got the larchkey o' the fron' door?' queries the other.

She frowns, tries to pull up her skirt to get at her petticoat pocket, and lurches over.

'Old 'ard, missis, 'old 'ard. Throw them long legs o' yourn acrost the wall, maite, an' see if ye carn't let 'er in!' says the little man, catching her deftly. The other agrees, and the key grates in the lock inside and he opens the door.

'She took the key an' lorst it, that's wot she did. She's a nice ole cup o' tea; she's a 'ot member for a mile, she iz, an' no mistaike!' and he takes up his trowel and a brick, singing with a sweet tenor.

The little man helps her into the house through the hall into

144

the parlour. He unties her bonnet-strings, pulls off her jacket, and puts her into an arm-chair.

'Ye jist 'ave a sleep, an' ye'll be all right!'

She clutches at his hand in a foolish sort of way, and her eyes fill with tears.

''Ands orf, missis, 'ands orf, ye jist go to sleep!'

He halts in the kitchen and looks about him. It is very well furnished; the table is littered with unwashed breakfast things on trays—handsome china, plate, and table-napkins, all in confusion. He shakes his head, puts some coal in the range, closes the door carefully, and goes back to his work.

'Well, did ye put beauty to bed?' laughs the big man. 'I'd rather Jones owned 'er nor me. 'E picked a nice mother fur iz kids, 'e did! Yes, them three little nippers wot come out a wile ago is iz.'

''E must be pretty tidy orf,' says the little man; 'it looks very nice in there, an' seemin'ly the 'ole 'ouse is fitted up alike—pianner an' chiffoneers.'

'Oh, Jones is all right. 'E's a cute chap iz Jones. 'E's got a 'ell of a temper, that's all. 'E's bin barman at the Buckin'am for close twenty year; makes a book an' keeps iz eyes peeled. Bless ye, I know Jones since I woz a lad; iz first wife woz a sort o' cousin o' my missis—clever woman too. 'E took this 'un 'cos 'e thort e'd maike a bit out o' gentlemen lorgers, she bein' a prize cook an' 'e 'avin' the 'ouse out of a buildin' society, an' be a mother to the kids as well. She'll keep no lorgers she won't, an' she's a fair beauty for the kids. If she woz mine'—tapping a brick—'I'd bash 'er 'ed in!'

'Maybe ye wouldn't!' says the little man; 'thet iz if ye understood. Wot if it ain't 'er fault?'

'Ain't 'er fault! Ooze iz it then?'

'That I ain't prepared to say, not knowin' circumstances; but it might be as it runs in 'er family.'

'Well, I'm blowed, I often 'eerd' (with a grin, showing all his white teeth) 'o' wooden legs runnin' that way, but I never 'eerd tell o' gin!'

'Ye ain't a readin' man, I take it,' says the little man, with a touch of superiority, 'I thought that way onst meself. My ole woman drinks.' (He says it as if stating a casual fact that calls for no comment.) 'It woz then I came acrorst a book on " 'ereditty," wot comes down from parents to children, ye know, an' I set to findin' all about 'er family. I took a 'eap o' trouble about it, I did, I wanted to do fair by 'er. An' then sez I to meself: "Sam, she carn't 'elp it no more nor the colour of 'er 'air, an' that woz like a pine shavin' in sunshine. 'Er gran'father 'e drunk 'isself dead, an' then iz wife she reared my girl's mother for service—she woz cook at an 'otel in Aylesbury. Well, she married the boots; they 'ad a tidy bit saved, an' they took a country public with land an' orchard an' such like an' they did well for a long time. Then 'e took to liquor. I never could find out iz family 'istory; maybe as 'ow 'e couldn't 'elp it neither. 'E woz a Weller, an' she jined 'im arter a bit, which considerin' 'er father woz to be expected. My ole woman often told me 'ow she an' 'er brother used to 'ide out many a night in the orchard. Well they bust up an' 'e got notice to quit, an' wot does 'e do but goes an' 'angs 'isself to a willer next the well, an' she goes out to git a pail o' water an' finds 'im. That set 'er orf wuss nor ever, an' then she went orf sudden like with a parrylittic stroke. Some laidies took the children an' put 'em to school.' (He works steadily as he speaks.) 'Well, one bank 'olliday twenty-eight year come Whitsun' same date izzackly, I went down with a mate o' mine to an uncle of 'iz in Aylesbury; 'e 'ad a duck farm, an' I seed 'er. She woz as pretty as paint, an' there woz as much difference atween 'er an' city girls as new milk an' chalk an' water. I woz doin' well, times woz better; I 'ave three trades, when one iz slack I works at another. I got work down there an' we kep' company, an' got our 'ome together, an' woz married, an' woz az 'appy az might be for six year. Then our eldest little lad 'e set 'isself afire one day she woz out, an' they took 'im to the infirmary, but 'e died in a 'our, a' wen we went to fetch 'im 'ome 'e woz rolled in wite bandages most like one o' them mummies in the British Museum. It went to my girl's 'eart like, for she couldn't seem to recognise 'im nohow. An' 'twoz arter that I begin to notice she took a drop. At fust I woz real mad, I gave 'er a black eye onst; but then I came acrorst that book— I woz allus a man for readin'—an' I found out about 'er folk, an' I see az 'ow she couldn't 'elp it. It got worser an' worser an' arter two years we come up to town; I couldn't stand the shame of it. Then I went down to my ole mother; she woz livin' with a widowed sister in Kent, an' I up an' told 'er: I sez, "Mother, ye got to take the kids. I ain't goin' to 'ave no more with the curse on 'em, an I ain't goin' to 'ave 'em spoiled," an' I took 'em down an' sent 'er money regular, bad times same az good. She went on dreadful at first; I gave 'er a fair chance, I took 'er down to see 'em, and sez I: "Knock off the drink, ole girl, an' ye 'az 'em back!" She tried it; I really believe she did, but bless ye she couldn't, it woz in 'er blood same az the colourin' of 'er skin. I gave up 'ome then, wen she gets right mad she'd pawn everything in the show; I allus put my own things in a Monday morning an' takes 'em out a Saturday night, it keeps 'em safe. The landlady looks arter 'er own, an' so she ain't got much to dispose on. I carn't abide liquor meself, though I don't 'old with preachin' about it; an' that's wy they call me Seltzer Sam, and wy I gets my dinner in a cookshop.'

The little man is laying his bricks carefully one on top of the other.

'You spoke sort o' sharp to your missis today, coz she woz a bit laite, an' I thort as 'ow ye woz uncommon lucky to 'ave 'er come nice and tidy with it—it's been twenty years since I woz brought me dinner in a basin.'

There's a silence. The big man looks thoughtful, then he says suddenly:

'Well I couldn't do it, I couldn't do it, that's all I sez. Wy don't ye put 'er away someweres?'

'I did, but lor, it woz no matter o' good. I allus fancied she'd set 'erself o' fire or fall in the street or somethink an' get took to the station on a stretcher with the boys a' callin' "meat" arter 'er, an' I couldn't sleep for thinkin' of it, so I fetched 'er back. We woz very 'appy for six year, an' thet's more nor some folk az in all their lives, an' '—with a quaint embarrassment—'she were the only woman as ever I keered for, right from the fust minute I seed 'er 'oldin' a big bunch o' poppies an' that grass they call "wag wantons" down there, in 'er 'and, as pretty as a picture—an' I *didn't marry 'er cos she could cook*, that's no

147

wearin' reason to marry a woman for, leastwise not for me. An'
I wouldn't 'ave the children—I call 'em children, though, lor
bless yer, they're grown up and doin' well—I wouldn't 'ave 'em
think I'd turned their mother out o' doors—no'—with an
emphatic dab of mortar—'no, 'er fate's my fate, an' I ain't the
kind o' chap to turn the ole woman out for what she can by no
manner o' means 'elp!' and he puts another brick neatly on the
top of the last and scrapes the oozing mortar.

The big man rubs the back of his hand across his eyes, and
says with a gulp:

'Shake 'ands, mate, damme if I know wot to call yer, a
bloomin' archangel or a blasted softy.'

The woman lay as he left her, with her feet thrust out in
her half-buttoned boots, and her hands hanging straight down.
The sun crept round the room, and at length a clock chimed
four strokes up on the drawing-room floor. A woman sitting
writing at a table between the window looks up with a sigh of
relief, and moistens her lips; they are dry. A pile of closely
written manuscript lies on the floor beside her; she drops each
sheet as she finishes it.

She is writing for money, writing because she must, because
it is the tool given to her wherewith to carve her way; she is
nervous, overwrought, every one of her fingers seems as if it had
a burning nerve-knot in its tip; she has thrust her slippers aside,
for her feet twitch; she is writing feverishly now, for she has
been undergoing the agony of a barren period for some weeks,
her brain has seemed arid as a sand plain, not a flower of fancy
has sprung up in it; she has felt in her despair as if she were
hollowed out, honeycombed by her emotions, and she has cried
over her mental sterility. Her measure of success has come to her,
her public waits, what if she have nothing to give them? The
thought has worn her, whispered to her in dreams at night,
taken the savour out of her food by day. But this morning a little
idea came and grew, grew so blessedly, and she has been working since early day. Her landlady has forgotten her luncheon;
she never noticed the omission, but now she feels her frail body
give way under the strain; she will finish this chapter and have

some tea. She has heard steps below. She writes until the half-hour strikes, then drops the last sheet of paper with a sobbing sigh of relief. She pulls the bell sharply and sits waiting patiently. No one answers it. She rings again; there is a crash downstairs as of china falling with a heavy body, and a smothered groan. She trembles, listens, and then goes down.

The woman is lying in the doorway of the sitting-room, a small table with broken glass and wax flowers on the floor near her. She hides her face as she hears the light step.

'Did you hurt yourself? Can I help you?'

She drags her up, supports her into the bedroom and on to the unmade bed, and goes out into the kitchen. A look of weary disgust crosses her face as she sees the litter on the table. There is a knock at the back door, she opens it; three children peer cautiously in, keen-eyed London children with precocious know-ledge of the darker sides of life. They enter holding one another's hands. The eldest signs to the others to sit down, steals up the passage, peers through the slit of the door, and returns with a satisfied look and nods to the others.

'Your mother is not well, I am afraid,' the woman says timidly, she is nervous with children. The three pairs of eyes examine her slowly to see if she is honest.

'Our mother is in heaven!' says the boy as if repeating a formula. 'That's our stepmother, and she's boozed!'

'Johnny!' calls the woman from the inner room. The boy's face hardens into a sullen scowl, and she notices that he raises his hand involuntarily as if to ward off a blow, and that the smaller ones change colour and creep closer to one another. He goes to her—there is a murmur of voices.

'She sez I'm to get your tea!' he remarks as he comes out, and stirs up the dying fire. 'Ain't you 'ad nothin' since mornin'?'

She evades the question by asking: 'Have you children had anything?'

'We had some bread with us.' He opens a purse.

'There's nothin' in it, an' father gave' er 'arf a sovereign this mornin'!'

'I will give you some money if you come upstairs, and then you can get my tea.'

149

The boy is deft-handed, prematurely cute, with a trick of peering under his lashes. It annoys her, and she is relieved when she has had her tea and got rid of him. She is restless, upset, she feels this means moving again. What a weary round a working woman's life is! She is so utterly alone. The silence oppresses her, the house seems filled with whispers; she cannot shake off this odd feeling, she felt it the first time she entered it; the rooms were pretty, and she took them, but this idea is always with her.

She puts on her hat and goes out, down the half-finished road and into a lighted thoroughfare. Costers' carts are drawn up alongside the pavement; husbands and wives with the inevitable perambulator are pricing commodities; girls are walking arm in arm, tossing back a look or a jest to the youths as they pass. The accents of the passers-by, the vociferous call of the vendors, the jostling of the people jar on her; she turns back with tears in her eyes. Her loneliness strikes doubly home to her, and she resolves to join a woman's club; anything to escape it. She pauses near the door to get her latchkey, and notices the boy at the side entrance. He draws back into the shade as he sees her. She stands at her window and looks out into the murky summer night; a man comes whistling down the street; the boy runs to meet him, she sees him bend his head to catch the words better and then they turn back. She lights the gas and tries to read, she dreads the scenes she feels will follow, and she trembles when the door slams below and steps echo down the passage.

There is the low growl of the man's voice and the answers of the woman's, then both rise discordantly—a stifled scream and a heavy fall, footsteps down the passage, the bang of a door, and both voices raised in altercation, with the boy's voice striking shrilly in between—a blow, a crash of china and glass, then stillness. She is breathless with excitement; the quiet is broken by a sound of scuffling in the passage; he is going to put her out. Drag, and shove, and the scraping of feet, and the sullen 'you dare, you dare' of the woman, in reply to his muttered threats. She goes to the top of the stairs and cries:

'Don't hurt her, wait until morning to reason with her, don't hurt her!'

'Reason with 'er, miss! There ain't no way of reasoning with the likes of 'er, chuck 'er out is the only way. Would ye, would ye? Ye drunken beast?——'

The woman and the man sway together in the passage and her bodice is torn open at the breast and her hair is loose, and she loses her footing and falls as he drags her towards the door. She clutches at the chairs and brass umbrella-stand and drags them down; and the woman, watching, rushes upstairs and buries her face in the sofa cushions. Then the door bangs to and the woman outside rings and knocks and screams; windows open and heads peer out; then the boy lets her in and there seems to be a truce.

A charwoman brings her breakfast next morning, and it is tea-time before she sees *her*. She has on a clean pink cotton gown and her hair is nicely done and her skin looks very pink and white; but her eyes are swollen, and there is a bruise on one temple and a bad scratch on her cheek. She hangs her head sullenly and loiters with the tea-things; then she goes over to her and stands with her eyes on the ground and her hair glittering like golden down on the nape of her thick neck in the light from the window at her back.

'I am sorry for yesterday, miss, it was bad of me, but you won't go away? I won't do it again. Take it off the rent, only forgive me, won't you, miss?'

She is flushing painfully; her face is working, perhaps it seems worse because it is a heavily moulded face and it does not easily express emotions. It has the attractive freshness of youth and vivid colouring.

'We won't say anything more about it. I am so sorry; I am not used to scenes and it made me quite ill; I was frightened, I thought you would be hurt.'

The woman's face changes and as she raises her heavy white lids her eyes seem to look crosswise with a curious gleam in them and her voice is hoarse.

'That little beast told him, the little sneak! But I'll pay him for it, I'll pay him!'

An uneasy dislike stirs in the woman; she says very quietly.

'But you can't expect a man to come home and find you so and then be pleased.'

'No, but he shouldn't——' she checks herself and passes her hand across her forehead. The other woman observes her closely as she does most things—as material. It is not that her sympathies are less keen since she took to writing, but that the habit of analysis is always uppermost. She sees a voluptuously made woman, with a massive milk-white throat rising out of the neck of her pink gown; her jaw is square and prominent, her nose short and straight, her brows traced distinctly; she is attractive and repellent in a singular way.

'You don't know what works in me, miss——' She says no more, but it is evident that something is troubling her and that she is putting restraint on herself. Late in the evening, when the children are in bed, she hears her go up to their room; there is a sound of quick blows and a frightened whimper; and the next morning she is roused from her sleep by a child's scream and the woman's voice uttering low threats:

'Will you be quiet?' (whimper) 'will you be quiet? I'll teach you to make a row' (more stifled, frightened cries), and she feels in some subtle way that the woman is smothering the child in the bed-clothes. It worries her, and she never looks up at her when she brings in her breakfast. The latter feels it and watches her furtively. At lunch time it strikes her that she has been drinking again; she musters heart of grace and says to her:

'You promised to be good, Mrs. Jones. It seems to me to be such a pity that you should drink; why do you? You are very young!'

Her voice is naturally tender, and her words have an unexpected effect; the woman covers her face with her hands and rocks her shoulders. Suddenly she cries:

'I don't know; I get thinkin'; I 'ave 'ad a trouble. I never knew a woman drink for the love of it like men, there's most always a cause. Don't think I be a bad woman, miss, I ain't really, only I 'ave a trouble.' She talks hurriedly as if she can't help herself, as if the very telling is a necessity. 'I 'ad a little girl' (dropping her voice) 'before I was married—she's turned three, she's such a dear little thing, you never seen such 'air, miss, it's like floss silk an' 'er eyes are china blue, an' 'er lashes are that long'—measuring a good inch on her finger—'an' 'er skin is milk-white. I keep wantin' 'er all the time——' The tears fill her eyes and splash out. 'I was cook in a big business house, an' 'e was the 'ead of it—I was cruel fond of 'im. Then when my time came I went 'ome to my step-sister an' she nursed me. I paid 'er, an' then when I went out to service again she took 'er. I used to see 'er onst or twice a week. But she was fonder of 'er nor me, an' I couldn't bear it, it made me mad, I was jealous of everyone as touches 'er. Then Jones, 'e woz always after me, 'e knew about it, an' 'e promised me that I could 'ave 'er if I married 'im. I didn't want to marry, I only wanted 'er, an' I couldn't 'ave' er with me, an' 'e promised'—with resentful emphasis—' 'e swore as 'ow I could 'ave 'er. I took 'im on that an' 'e kep' puttin' me off, an' when I went to see 'er, 'e quarrelled, an' once when she was ill 'e wouldn't let me send 'er any money though 'e 'ad wot I saved when I married 'im—it just made me 'ate 'im—I see 'er so seldom, an' she calls '*er* mammy, it most kills me—I feel my 'ead burstin'—an' 'e laughed when I told 'im I wouldn't 'ave married 'im only for 'er sake!'

'Poor thing, it is hard, he ought to have kept his promise to you when he made it. Haven't you told him you wouldn't drink if you had her with you?'

'Where's the good? 'E says 'e never meant to keep it; as a man ain't such a fool as to keep a promise 'e makes a woman just to get 'er. 'E knows it sets me off, but 'e's that jealous that 'e can't abear 'er name. 'E says I would neglect 'is children, an' 'e called 'er names an' says 'e won't 'ave no bastard round with 'is children. That made me 'ate 'em first, nasty yellow things——'

'Yes, but the poor children are not to blame for it?'

'No, but they remind me of 'er, an' I 'ate the very sight of 'em.' There is such concentrated hatred in her voice that the woman shrinks. 'I ain't 'ad any money to send 'er this long time, but my sister's 'usband is as fond of 'er as 'is own; they 'ave seven of their own. I 'ate to see things in the shop windows, I used to keep 'er so pretty. I got a letter a while ago sayin' she wasn't very well, an' that set me off. You've spoken kind to me since you've been here, that's w'y I tell you, you won't think worse of me now than I deserve.'

She clears away the things sullenly, with her jaw set, and

the strange oblique light flickering in her eyes. It oppresses the other woman; she feels as if she is facing one of the lurid tragedies that outsiders are powerless to prevent. This woman with her fierce devotion to the child of the man who betrayed her; her marriage, into which she has been cheated by a promise never meant to be kept; and the step-children fanning her fierce dislike by the very childish attributes that waken love in other circumstances. She stays a week longer, but every whimper of the children, every fresh outburst wears upon her, and she leaves, not without speaking with all the earnestness and sympathy of her nature to the woman of whose fate she has an oppressive, inexplicable presentiment.

The tears in her eyes at leaving have touched the girl, for she is little more, and she has promised to try and be better, as she childishly puts it. Things have gone pleasantly for some days, and she has been patient with the children. One of them has been ill and she has nursed it, and today she has made them an apple-cake and sent them to the park, and she is singing to herself over her work; she is cleaning out her bedroom. It is Derby Day. He has the day off, and has gone to the races. He gave her five shillings before he started in the morning, telling her she might send it to the 'young 'un.'

It touched her, and she brushed his coat and kissed him of her own accord. She has felt kindly to him all the morning for it. She notices a button dangling off his working coat and takes it out to the kitchen to sew it on; he seldom brings it home. There is nothing in the pockets except a slip of 'events' cut out of some sporting paper; but the lining of the breast-pocket is torn, and as she examines it, the rustle of paper catches her ear. She smiles; what if it is a 'fiver'? She knows all about his betting. She slips two fingers down between the lining and works it up—a telegram. She still smiles, for she thinks she will find a clue to some of his winnings. She opens it, and reads, and her face changes; the blood rushes to it, until a triangular vein stands out on her forehead like a purple whipcord. Her throat looks as if it would burst; a pulse beats in her neck; her upper lip is completely sucked in by the set line of her under one, and her eyes positively squint. A fly that keeps buzzing on the pane rouses her to such a pitch that she seizes a boot off the table and sends it crashing through the pane of glass into the yard, liberating the fly at the same time. Then she tries to reread it, but there is a red blaze before her eyes. She goes out, up the lane, towards the unfinished houses, to where the bricklayers are at work, and hands it to the little man, saying hoarsely:

'Read it, I'm dazed, I can't see it rightly.'

The big man stops whistling and looks curiously at her. She is perfectly sober; the flush has ceded to a lead-white pallor, and her face twitches convulsively. She stands absolutely still, with her hands hanging heavily down, though she is devoured with impatience. The little man wipes his hands, and takes out his spectacles, and reads slowly:

'Susie dying, come at once, no hope. Expecting you since Saturday, wrote twice.'

A minute's silence—then a hoarse scream that seems to come from the depths of her chest; it frightens both men, so that the big man drops a brick, and a carpenter in the house comes to the window and looks out.

'Since Saturday!' she cries, 'today is Wednesday. When was it sent, tell me!' she shakes the little man in her excitement, and he scans the form slowly, with the deliberation of his class:

'Stratford, 7.45.'

'But the date! the date, man!'

'The 20th.'

'Today,' with a groan, 'is the 22nd. So it come Monday, and today is Wednesday, an' they wrote twice. It must 'ave come when I fetched 'is beer, an' 'e kept it. But the letters?—that little cub, that sneak of 'ell! Aah, wait!' She calls down curses with such ferocity of expression that the men shiver; then crushing the fateful paper inside the bosom of her gown, she rushes back, and in a few minutes they see her come out, tying on her bonnet as she runs.

'Well, this 'ere's a rum go, eh?' says the big man, regaining his colour, 'an' ooze Susie?'

The little man says nothing, only balances a brick in the palm of his hand before he fits it into its place, but his lips move silently.

155

In the parlour of one of a row of stiff two-storied houses, with narrow hall-doors in a poor street in Stratford, a little coffin painted white is laid on the table that is covered with a new white sheet.

There are plenty of flowers, from the white wreath sent by the grocer's wife, with a card bearing 'From a Sympathiser' in big silver letters, to the penny bunch of cornflowers of a playmate.

Susie has her tiny hands folded, and the little waxen face looks grey and pinched amongst the elaborately pinked-out glazed calico frills of her coffin lining. There is the unavoidable air of festivity that every holiday, even a sad one, imparts to a working-man's home. The children have their hair crimped and their Sunday clothes on, for they are going to the burial-ground in a grand coach with black horses and long tails, and they sit on the stairs and talk it over in whispers.

The men have come in at dinner-hour silently and stolidly, and looked at her, and gone out to the 'Dog and Jug' for a glass of beer to wash down whatever of sadness the sight of dead Susie may have roused in them.

Every woman in the row has had a cup of tea, and told of her own sorrows; related the death of every relative she has ever possessed, to the third and fourth degree, with the minuteness of irrelevant detail peculiar to her class. Every incident of Susie's death-struggle has been described with such morbid or picturesque addition as frequent rehearsals, or the fancy of the narrator, may suggest. Every corner of the house is crammed with people, for the funeral is to leave at three o'clock.

'Looks like satin it do, it's as pretty as ever I see!' pointing to the pinking, says one woman.

'Yes, Mr. Triggs thought a 'eap o' Susie, an' 'e took extry pains. 'E's a beautiful undertaker, an' 'e's goin' to send the 'earse with the wite plumes! Don't she just look a little hangel?'

So they stream in and out, and in the kitchen a circle of matrons hold a Vehmgericht over the mother.

'She's an unfeelin' brute, even if she iz yer arf sister, Mrs. Waters,' says a fat matron, 'to let that pretty, hinnocent hangel die without sein' 'er, not to speak o' buryin'. I 'ave no patience with sich ways!'

The roll of wheels and the jingle of tyres cuts short her speech, and the knocker bangs dully. Heads crane out in every direction, and one of the children opens the door, and the woman steps in.

In her pink gown! when everyone knows that not to pawn your bed or the washings-tubs, or anything available, to get a black skirt or crape bonnet, or at least a straw with bugles, is the greatest breach of propriety known to the poor, the greatest sticklers for mourning etiquette outside a German court. The half-sister is a quiet woman with smoothly-parted hair and tender eyes, and a strong likeness to her about the underhung chin. She goes forward and leads her to the room; the women fall back and talk in whispers.

'W'y didn't you send?' she asks fiercely, turning from the coffin.

'We wrote Friday, an' then, when you didn't come, we wrote Sunday. Jim couldn't go, an' I never left 'er a minute, an' Tiny an' little Jim 'ad the measles, an' Katie 'ad to mind 'em; but a mate o' Jim's went to the 'Buckin'am' on Monday mornin' an' told 'im, an' then we sent a tellygram, an, we couldn't do more, not if she were our own.'

There is a settled resignation in her voice; she has repeated it so often.

' 'E kep' the letters an' 'e never told me, an' I only found the tellygram this mornin' by accidin'. When's she to be buried?'

'At three o'clock,'—with a puzzled look at the set face.

'Leave me along of 'er then; go on!'—roughly.

The woman goes out, closes the door, and listens. Not a sound comes from the room, not one, not a sob nor cry. The women listen in silence when she tells them; they are used to the fierce passions of humanity, and jealousy is common amongst their men. After a while one of the children says, with an awe-struck face, 'Ma, she's singin'.' They go to the door and listen; she is crooning a nonsense song she used to sing to her when she was quite a baby, and the listening women pale, but fear to go in. For a long hour they hear her talking and singing to it; then the man comes to screw down the lid, and they find her on the sofa with the dead child on her lap, its feet, in their white cotton socks, sticking out like the legs of a great wax doll.

She lets them take it from her without a word, and watches them place it amongst the white frills, and lets them lead her out of the room. She sits bolt upright in the kitchen, with the same odd smile upon her lips and her hands hanging straight down. They go without her. When they return she is still sitting with her hands hanging, as if she has never stirred.

'Mother, w'y did they plant Susie in the ground? Mother, carn't you answer; will she grow?' queries one of the children, and something in the question rouses her. She starts up with a cry and a wild glare, and stares about as if in search of something—stands trembling in every limb, with the ugly flush on her face and the purple triangle on her forehead, and the pulse beating in her throat. The children cower away from her, and the sister watches her with frightened, pitying eyes.

'Sit down, Susan, there's a dear, sit down an' 'ave some tea!'

'No, I've got to go—I've got to go—I've got t——' she mutters, swaying unsteadily on her feet. The words come thickly, and the end of the sentence is lost.

'She'd be better if she could cry, poor thing!' says the fat matron.

'Give 'er somethink belonged to the young 'un!' says a little woman with a black eye. The sister goes to a drawer in the dresser and turns over some odds and ends and finds a necklet of blue beads with a brass clasp, and hands it to her. She takes it with a hoarse cry as of an animal in dire pain, and rocks and moans and kisses it, but no tears come; and then, before they can realise it, she is out through the passage and the door slams. When they get to it and look out, she is hurrying wildly down the street, with her pink gown fluttering, and the roses nodding in her bonnet, through a drizzle of soft rain.

Six o'clock rings; the rain still falls steadily, and, through its dull beat, the splash of big drops on to the new boards in a roofless house, and the blows of a hammer, strike sharply.

'Comin' mate?' queries the big man. 'No? Well, so long!' He shoulders his straw kit and turns up the collar of his coat and goes off whistling. The little man puts his tools away, fastens a sack about his shoulders and creeps into a square of bricks—they had thrown some loose planks across the top earlier in the day as a sort of protection against the rain; he lights his pipe and sits patiently waiting for her return. He is hungry, and his wizened face looks pinched in the light of the match as he strikes it, but he waits patiently.

The shadows have closed in when she gets back, for she has walked all the way from Liverpool Street, unheeding the steady rain that has come with the south-west wind. The people maddened her. She felt inclined to strike them. A fierce anger surged up in her against each girl who laughed, each man who talked of the winner. She felt inclined to spit at them, make faces, or call them names. Her dress is bedrabbled, the dye of the roses has soaked through the gold of her fringe and runs down her forehead as if she has a bleeding wound there. The gas is lit in the kitchen, and her tea is laid and the kettle in singing on the stove; a yellow envelope is lying on the top of the cup; she opens it and turns up the gas and reads it:

'Been in luck today, going home with Johnson, back early tomorrow evening.'

She puts it down with a peculiar smile. She has the string of beads in her hand; she keeps turning them round her finger; then she steals to the foot of the stairs and listens.

The little man has watched her go in, and stands in the laneway looking up at the house. A light appears in the top back window, but it must come from the stairs, it is too faint to be in the room itself. He bends his head as if to listen, but the steady fall of the rain and the drip of the roof on to some loose sheets of zinc dominate everything. He walk away a bit and watches a shadow cross the blinds; his step crunches on the loose bricks and stones; a woman rushes down the flagged path of the next house and opens the door.

'Is that Mr. Sims?'

'No, ma'am, I'm one of the workmen.'

She has left her kitchen door open, and as the light streams out he can see she is a thin woman with an anxious look.

'I thought it was Mr. Sims, the watchman. My baby is

threatened with convulsions. I wanted him to run for the doctor at the end of the terrace; I daren't leave him, and my sister's lame. Will you go? It isn't far!'

She is listening, and though he hears nothing, she darts off calling, 'There he's off, do go, *do go*. Say Mrs. Rogers's baby, Hawthorn House, No. 23.'

He stands a moment irresolute; the shadow moves across the blind, and a second smaller shadow seems to wave across it; or was it only the rising wind flicking the blind? and is it fancy, or did not a stifled cry reach him; and was it from that room it came or from Mrs. Rogers's baby? The little man is shaking with anxiety; he feels as if some malignant fate in the shape of Mrs. Rogers's baby is playing tricks with him, to bring about a catastrophe he has stayed to avert. He is torn both ways; he can offer no excuse for not going; he dare not explain the secret dread that has kept him here supperless in the rain watching the house where the three motherless children sleep. He turns and runs stumbling over the rubbish into the side street and arrives breathless at the corner house where the red lamp burns at the gate—rings—what a time they keep him—it seems ages, and visions keep tumbling kaleidoscopically through his brain; the very red of the light adds colour to the horrid tragedy he sees enacted in excited fury.

'The doctor is out; won't be back for some time; there's a Dr. Phillips round the corner,' explains the smart maid—the door slams to.

'Yes, Dr. Phillips is in; you must wait a minute,' ushering him into a waiting-room. He sits on the edge of the chair with his wet hat in his hand. Two other people are waiting: a girl with a swelled face, and a sickly-looking man.

A door opens, someone beckons, the man goes in. He looks at the clock—five minutes pass, seven, ten—each seems an hour—fifteen—and the woman's face as she went in, and the frightened children (his mate questioned them at tea-time), and the shadow on the blind of the room they slept in! Why should Mrs. Rogers's baby go and get convulsions just this particular night? seems as though it were to be—seventeen; no, he won't wait any longer. The strange, inexplicable fear clutching the little man's soul gives him courage, though the well-furnished house awes him; he slips out into the hall, opens the door, and rings the bell. The same girl answers it.

'Well I never! W'y, I just let you in. Carn't you wait yer turn—the *idea!*'

A pale young man with spectacles coming down the stairs asks:

'What is it you want, my man?' The girl tosses her head and goes downstairs.

'I can't wait, sir; Mrs. Rogers's baby, 'Awthorn 'Ouse, No. 23 Pelham Road, round the corner, got the convulsions. She wants the doctor as soon as 'e can.'

'All right, I'll be round in a second.'

The little man hurries back, trying to add up the time he has been away—twenty-five minutes, it must be twenty-five, perhaps twenty-seven. The yard door of Mrs. Rogers's house is open, and a girl peers out as he runs up the lane.

'The doctor woz out; Dr. Phillips is comin' at onst!' His eyes rest on the window of the next house as he speaks. It is dark up there and silent. He pays no heed to the thanks of the girl, and he hears the tap of her crutch up the flagged path with a gasp of relief.

What has happened whilst he has been away on his errand of mercy? Has anything happened? After all, why should this ghastly idea of a tragedy possess him? He climbs on to a heap of loose bricks and peers over the wall—darkness and silence. He goes down the lane and round to the front of the house. A dim light shines through the stained glass over the door showing up the name 'Ladas,' that is all, yet the little man shivers. The rain has soaked through his coat and is trickling down his neck; he scratches his head in perplexity, muttering to himself, 'I'm afear'd, an' I dunno wot I'm afear'd on. I meant to wotch; maybe arsk 'er for a light. It ain't my fault if Mrs. Rogers's baby came atween—but twarn't no wearin' reason to marry for,' and he goes down the road and faces home. The rain ceases, and a tearful moon appears, and the water drips off the roof with a clucking sound. Upstairs in a back room in the silent house a pale strip of moonlight flickers over a dark streak on

F   161

the floor, that trickles slowly from the pool at the bedside out under the door, making a second ghastly pool on the top step of the stairs—a thick sorghum red, blackening as it thickens, with a sickly serous border. Downstairs the woman sits in a chair with her arms hanging down. Her hands are crimson as if she has dipped them in dye. A string of blue beads lies on her lap, and she is fast asleep; and she smiles as she sleeps, for Susie is playing in a meadow, a great meadow crimson with poppies, and her blue eyes smile with glee, and her golden curls are poppy-crowned, and her little white feet twinkle as they dance, and her pinked-out grave frock flutters, and her tiny waxen hands scatter poppies, blood-red poppies, in handfuls over three open graves.

Arthur Machen
1863-1947

ARTHUR MACHEN, the only son of a clergyman, was born at Caerleon-on-Usk in 1863.

A dreamy introspective boy, whose literary idols were De Quincey and Scott, he found that the private schools he attended made little or no impression on him. At eighteen he obtained a post as clerk in a publishing office in Paddington. From office work he turned to badly-paid teaching and when this failed he attempted free-lancing until all his money was gone.

It was during this period that he wrote *The Anatomy of Tobacco* (1884) under the pseudonym of Leolinus Siluriensis, kindly described by a reviewer as 'a second-rate imitation of Stevenson.' After the failure of his first London adventure, he returned to Wales, whose landscape of ancient peace had haunted him as he trod the city pavements. Here he sufficed to keep himself alive by translating such works as *L'Heptameron* and *Le Moyen de Parvenir*. Later, in 1930, he completed *Casanova's Memoirs* in twelve volumes.

Machen belongs to the 'nineties by reason of three weird works of fiction: *The Great God Pan* (1894), *The Three Imposters* (1895), and *The Hill of Dreams*, published in 1907 but written ten years earlier. He classified the last work as being the first of his 'long picaresque romance[s] of the soul;' but there is much in the two previous books by him which is covered by his description. Machen is in the tradition of Sheridan Le Fanu as a writer of supernatural fiction. There is the same combination of the esoteric, the occult, and the horrific which are to be discovered in G. K. Chesterton and Charles Williams.

Machen's stories are aesthetic propaganda in aid of the

163

proposition that 'man is made a mystery for mysteries and visions.' In keeping with such greater minds as Matthew Arnold and John Henry Newman, he was opposed to the two 'paper theories' of materialism: 'sixpenny science' and 'useful knowledge'. The typical 'English City clerk, "flourishing" towards the end of the nineteenth century,' he describes as 'a member of a most hopeless class, living in the most hopeless surroundings that the world has ever seen.'

If the 'nineties was the Age of Maupassant in fiction, it was also the Age of Madame Blavatsky in terms of fashionable *avant-garde* thought; and the diatribe of W. B. Yeats against 'Huxley and Tyndall, whom I detested' was to be echoed by Machen in his fiction.

Appropriately, he was the creator of the myth of 'The Angels of Mons'—contributed to the *Evening News*—which thousands of soldiers believed in devoutly during the First World War.

In 1902 he joined the Benson Shakespearean Repertoire Company, and John Gunter described the old ex-actor, a little while before his death in 1947, with his thick white hair 'in a horizontal bob,' his 'clouded blue eyes,' and 'his waxen hand.'

Machen left two autobiographical portraits: *Far Off Things* (1922) and *Things Near and Far* (1923). An outside assessment of the man is to be found in *Arthur Machen: A Biography* by A. Reynolds and W. Charlton (1963).

NOVEL OF THE IRON MAID

I think the most extraordinary event which I can recall took place about five years ago. I was then feeling my way; I had declared for business, and attended regularly at my office; but I had not succeeded in establishing a really profitable connection, and consequently I had a good deal of leisure time on my hands. I have never thought fit to trouble you with the details of my private life; they would be entirely devoid of interest. I must briefly say, however, that I had a numerous circle of acquaintance, and was never at a loss as how to spend my evenings. I was so fortunate as to have friends in most of the ranks of the social order; there is nothing so unfortunate, to my mind, as a specialised circle, wherein a certain round of ideas is continually traversed and retraversed. I have always tried to find out new types and persons whose brains contained something fresh to me; one may chance to gain information even from the conversation of city men on an omnibus. Amongst my acquaintance I knew a young doctor, who lived in a far outlying suburb, and I used often to brave the intolerably slow railway journey to have the pleasure of listening to his talk. One night we conversed so eagerly together over our pipes and whisky that the clock passed unnoticed; and when I glanced up, I realised with a shock that I had just five minutes in which to catch the last train. I made a dash for my hat and stick, jumped out of the house and down the steps, and tore at full speed up the street. It was no good, however; there was a shriek of the engine-whistle, and I stood there at the station door and saw far on the long dark line of the embankment a red light shine and vanish, and a porter came down and shut the door with a bang.

'How far to London?' I asked him.

'A good nine miles to Waterloo Bridge.' And with that he went off.

Before me was the long suburban street, its dreary distance marked by rows of twinkling lamps, and the air was poisoned by the faint, sickly smell of burning bricks; it was not a cheerful prospect by any means, and I had to walk through nine miles of such streets, deserted as those of Pompeii. I knew pretty well what direction to take, so I set out wearily, looking at the stretch of lamps vanishing in perspective; and as I walked, street after street branched off to right and left, some far-reaching, to distances that seemed endless, communicating with other systems of thoroughfare, and some mere protoplasmic streets, beginning in orderly fashion with serried two-storied houses, and ending suddenly in waste, and pits, and rubbish-heaps, and fields whence the magic had departed. I have spoken of systems of thoroughfare, and I assure you that walking alone through these silent places I felt fantasy growing on me, and some glamour of the infinite. There was here, I felt, an immensity as in the outer void of the universe; I passed from unknown to unknown, my way marked by lamps like stars, and on either hand was an world where myriads of men dwelt and slept, street leading into street, as it seemed to world's end. At first the road by which I was travelling was lined with houses of unutterable monotony, a wall of grey brick pierced by two stories of windows, drawn close to the very pavement; but by degrees I noticed an improvement, there were gardens, and these grew larger; the suburban builder began to allow himself a wider scope; and for a certain distance each flight of steps was guarded by twin lions of plaster, and scents of flowers prevailed over the fume of heated bricks. The road began to climb a hill, and looking up a side street I saw the half moon rise over plane-trees, and there on the other side was as if a white cloud had fallen, and the air around it was sweetened as with incense; it was a may-tree in full blcom. I pressed on stubbornly, listening for the wheels and the clatter of some belated hansom; but into that land of men who go to the city in the morning and return in the evening the hansom rarely enters, and I had resigned myself once more to the walk, when I suddenly became aware that someone was advancing to meet me along the sidewalk. The man was strolling rather aimlessly; and though the time and the place would have allowed an unconventional style of dress, he was vested in the ordinary frockcoat, black tie, and silk hat of civilisation. We met each other under the lamp, and, as often happens in this great town, two casual passengers brought face to face found each in the other an acquaintance.

'Mr. Mathias, I think?' I said.

'Quite so. And you are Frank Burton. You know you are a man with a Christian name, so I won't apologise for my familiarity. But may I ask where you are going?'

I explained the situation to him, saying I had traversed a region as unknown to me as the darkest recesses of Africa. 'I think I have only about five miles further,' I concluded.

'Nonsense! you must come home with me. My house is close by; in fact, I was just taking my evening walk when we met.

Come along; I dare say you will find a makeshift bed easier than a five-mile walk.'

I let him take my arm and lead me along, though I was a good deal surprised at so much geniality from a man who was, after all, a mere casual club acquaintance. I suppose I had not spoken to Mr. Mathias half a dozen times; he was a man who would sit silent in an arm-chair for hours, neither reading nor smoking, but now and again moistening his lips with his tongue and smiling queerly to himself. I confess he had never attracted me, and on the whole I should have preferred to continue my walk. But he took my arm and led me up a side street, and stopped at a door in a high wall. We passed through the still, moonlit garden, beneath the black shadow of an old cedar, and into an old red-brick house with many gables. I was tired enough, and I sighed with relief as I let myself fall into a great leather arm-chair. You know the infernal grit with which they strew the sidewalk in those suburban districts; it makes walking a penance, and I felt my four-mile tramp had made me more weary than ten miles on an honest country road. I looked about the room with some curiosity; there was a shaded lamp, which threw a circle of brilliant light on a heap of papers lying on an old brass-bound secretaire of the last century, but the room was all vague and shadowy, and I could only see that it was long and low, and that it was filled with indistinct objects which might be furniture. Mr. Mathias sat down in a second arm-chair, and looked about him with that odd smile of his. He was a queer-looking man, clean shaven, and white to the lips. I should think his age was something between fifty and sixty.

'Now I have got you here,' he began, 'I must inflict my hobby on you. You knew I was a collector? Oh yes, I have devoted many years to collecting curiosities, which I think are really curious. But we must have a better light.'

He advanced into the middle of the room, and lit a lamp which hung from the ceiling; and as the bright light flashed round the wick, from every corner and space there seemed to start a horror. Great wooden frames, with complicated apparatus of ropes and pulleys, stood against the wall; a wheel of strange shape had a place beside a thing that looked like a gigantic gridiron; little tables glittered with bright steel instruments carelessly put down as if ready for use; a screw and vice loomed out, casting ugly shadows, and in another nook was a saw with cruel jagged teeth.

'Yes,' said Mr. Mathias, 'they are, as you suggest, instruments of torture—of torture and death. Some—many, I may say—have been used; a few are reproductions after ancient examples. Those knives were used for flaying; that frame is a rack, and a very fine specimen. Look at this; it comes from Venice. You see that sort of collar, something like a big horse-shoe? Well, the patient, let us call him, sat down quite comfortably, and the horse-shoe was neatly fitted round his neck. Then the two ends were joined with a silken band, and the executioner began to turn a handle connected with the band. The horse-shoe contracted very gradually as the band tightened, and the turning continued till the man was strangled. It all took place quietly, in one of those queer garrets under the leads. But these things are all European; the Orientals are, of course, much more ingenious. These are the Chinese contrivances; you have heard of the "Heavy Death"? It is my hobby, this sort of thing. Do you know, I often sit here, hour after hour, and meditate over the collection. I fancy I see the faces of the men who have suffered, faces lean with agony, and wet with sweats of death growing distinct out of the gloom, and I hear the echoes of their cries for mercy. But I must show you my latest acquisition. Come into the next room.'

I followed Mr. Mathias out. The weariness of the walk, the late hour, and the strangeness of it all made me feel like a man in a dream; nothing would have surprised me very much. The second room was as the first, crowded with ghastly instruments; but beneath the lamp was a wooden platform, and a figure stood on it. It was a large statue of a naked woman, fashioned in green bronze, the arms were stretched out, and there was a smile on the lips; it might well have been intended for a Venus, and yet there was about the thing an evil and deadly look.

Mr. Mathias looked at it complacently. 'Quite a work of art, isn't it?' he said 'It's made of bronze, as you see, but it has long had the name of the Iron Maid. I got it from Germany, and it was only unpacked this afternoon; indeed, I have not yet had time to open the letter of advice. You see that very small knob between the breasts? Well, the victim was bound to the Maid, the knob was pressed, and the arms slowly tightened round the neck. You can imagine the result.'

As Mr. Mathias talked, he patted the figure affectionately. I had turned away, for I sickened at the sight of the man and his loathsome treasure. There was a slight click, of which I took no notice; it was not much louder than the tick of a clock; and then I heard a sudden whirr, the noise of machinery in motion, and faced round. I have never forgotten the hideous agony on Mathias's face as those relentless arms tightened about his neck; there was a wild struggle as of a beast in the toils, and then a shriek that ended in a choking drone. The whirring noise had suddenly changed into a heavy droning. I tore with all my might at the bronze arms, and strove to wrench them apart, but I could do nothing. The head had slowly bent down, and the green lips were on the lips of Mathias.

Of course, I had to attend at the inquest. The letter which had accompanied the figure was found unopened on the study table. The German firm of dealers cautioned their client to be most careful in touching the Iron Maid, as the machinery had been put in thorough working order.

Richard Le Gallienne
1866-1947

RICHARD LE GALLIENNE, was born in Liverpool on January 20, 1866. His forebears were of Breton descent by way of the Channel Islands; but it is said that he owned the full French flavour of his name to Oscar Wilde. 'At least it was Oscar,' as Ella d'Arcy told Katherine Lyon Mix, 'who had suggested placing the masculine article before the obviously feminine form. "It'll be the making of you, Dick," he had prophesied, and though Henley protested peevishly, "Even his name is ungrammatical," Le Gallienne had done well in London as poet, publisher's reader, and critic.'

Katherine Lyon Mix goes on to remark (in her work on *The Yellow Book: A Study in Yellow*, 1960) how 'At twenty-eight, his finely chiselled profile, pale skin, and raven hair curling over his velvet coat collar set him off from more mundane figures at the Bodley Head, [and] William Archer thought "such a name and such a physiognomy . . . hard to live up to.'

If Symons was the impresario of *fin-de-siècle* literature at periodical level, it was Le Gallienne who sought to popularize the *'nineties* idea with the newspaper reader. Much as one may feel that the two volumes of his *Retrospective Reviews 1891-1895* (1896) are an elegant exercise in log-rolling, one notes the positive generosity of the critic when he declares that 'Praise is more important than judgment. It is only at agricultural societies that men dare sit in judgment on the rose.'

Le Gallienne might, as Lionel Johnson stated, feel 'the *sentiment* of beautiful things in art and life, not their *truth*,' but along with critical generosity, as a reviewer his manners were always exemplary. As he himself maintained : 'A gentleman is always a gentleman—even when he writes anonymous criticism.'

Essentially a man of letters, Le Gallienne concerned himself with fiction, verse, and criticism, but this interest and attention were almost exclusively literary. It was style and posture not story, thought, or poem that all his writings consciously proclaimed.

This being so, what one gets in his fiction—a couple or so of novels, notably *The Quest of the Golden Girl* (1896) and *The Romance of Zion Chapel* (1898); and a few odd puff-pastry fantasies scattered throughout the pages of his two *Prose Fancies*, *First Series* (1895) and *Second Series* (1896)—is the ' 'nineties attitude', parodied with or without intention, and exaggerated always without a becoming sense of shame. Sentimental though he was, he could be original. *The Romance of Zion Chapel* is based on the novel notion of selling aestheticism to the Nonconformists. ('How they brought the good news of a Morris wallpaper to Coalchester' is one of the chapter headings.) All told, it reads much as if Pater had attempted to write for the women's magazines, but with a sprightliness of wit lacking from the Master's exquisite *gravitas*.

In 1898 he left England for New York. One is surprised to learn that he never found his way to Hollywood. As with Dame Edith Sitwell—much venerated in that cinematic Mecca—his prose has a similar self-conscious panache.

THE WOMAN'S HALF-PROFITS
O ma pauvre Muse! est-ce toi?

Fame in Athens and Florence took the form of laurel; in London it is represented by 'Romeikes.' Hyacinth Rondel, the very latest new poet, sat one evening not long ago in his elegant new chambers, with a cloud of those pleasant witnesses about him, as charmed by 'the rustle' of their 'loved Apollian leaves' as though they had been veritable laurel or veritable bank-notes. His rooms

were provided with all those distinguished comforts and elegan-
cies proper to a success that may any moment be interviewed.
Needless to say, the walls had been decorated by Mr. Whistler,
and there was not a piece of furniture in the room that had not
belonged to this or that poet deceased. Priceless autograph
portraits of all the leading actors and actresses littered the
mantelshelf with a reckless prodigality; the two or three choice
etchings were, of course, no less conspicuously inscribed to their
illustrious confrère by the artists—naturally, the very latest
hatched in Paris. There was hardly a volume in the elegant
Chippendale bookcases not similarly inscribed. Mr. Rondel would
as soon have thought of buying a book as of paying for a stall.
To the eye of imagination, therefore, there was not an article
in the room which did not carry a little trumpet to the distinguished poet's honour and glory. Hidden from view in his
buhl cabinet, but none the less vivid to his sensitive egoism, were
those tenderer trophies of his power, spoils of the chase, which
the adoring feminine had offered up at his shrine: all his love-
letters sorted in periods, neatly ribboned and snugly ensconced
in various sandalwood niches—much as urns are ranged at the
Crematorium, Woking—with locks of hair of many hues. He
loved most to think of those letters in which the women had
gladly sought a spiritual suttee, and begged him to cement the
stones of his temple of fame with the blood of their devoted
hearts. To have had a share in building so distinguished a life—
that was enough for them! They asked no such inconvenient
reward as marriage: indeed, one or two of them had already
obtained that boon from others. To serve their purpose, and then,
if it must be, to be forgotten, or—wild hope—to be embalmed
in a sonnet sequence: that was reward enough.

In the midst of this silent and yet so eloquent orchestra, which
from morn to night was continually crying 'Glory, glory, glory'
in the ear of the self-enamoured poet, Hyacinth Rondel was
sitting one evening. The last post had brought him the above-
mentioned leaves of the Romeike laurel, and he sat in his easiest
chair by the bright fire, adjusting them, metaphorically, upon
his high brow, a decanter at his right hand and cigarette smoke
curling up from his left. At last he had drained all the honey

from the last paragraph, and, with rustling shining head, he turned a sweeping triumphant gaze around his room. But, to his surprise, he found himself no longer alone. Was it the Muse in dainty modern costume and delicately tinted cheek? Yes! It was one of those discarded Muses who sometimes remain upon the poet's hands as Fates.

When she raised her veil she certainly looked more of a Fate than a Muse. Her expression was not agreeable. The poet, afterwards describing the incident and remembering his Dante, spoke of her in an allegorical sonnet as 'lady of terrible aspect,' and symbolised her as Nemesis.

He now addressed her as 'Annette,' and in his voice were four notes of exclamation. She came closer to him, and very quietly, but with an accent that was the very quintessence of Ibsenism, made the somewhat mercantile statement: 'I have come for my half-profits!'

'Half-profits! What do you mean? Are you mad?'

'Not in the least! I want my share in the profits of all this pretty poetry,' and she contemptuously ran her fingers over the several slim volumes on the poet's shelves which represented his own contribution to English literature.

Rondel began to comprehend, but he was as yet too surprised to answer.

'Don't you understand?' she went on. 'It takes two to make poetry like yours—

> "They steal their song the lips that sing
> From lips that only kiss and cling."

Do you remember? Have I quoted correctly? Yes, here it is!' taking down a volume entitled *Liber Amoris*, the passionate confession which had first brought the poet to fame. As a matter of fact, several ladies had 'stood' for this series, but the poet had artfully generalised them into one supreme Madonna, whom Annette believed to be herself. Indeed, she had furnished the warmest and the most tragic colouring. Rondel, however, had for some time kept his address a secret from Annette. But the candle set upon a hill cannot be hid: fame has its disadvantages. To a man with creditors or any other form of 'a past,' it is no little dangerous to have his portrait in the *Review of Reviews*. A well-known publisher is an ever-present danger. By some such means Annette had found her poet. The papers could not be decorated with reviews of his verse, and she not come across some of them. Indeed she had, with burning cheek and stormy bosom, recognised herself in many an intimate confession. It was her hair, her face, all her beauty, he sang, though the poems were dedicated to another.

She turned to another passage as she stood there—'How pretty it sounds *in poetry!*' she said, and began to read:

' "There in the odorous meadowsweet afternoon,
    With the lark like the dream of a song in the dreamy blue.
  All the air abeat with the wing and buzz of June,
    We met—she and I, I and she," [You and I, I and you.]
  'And there, while the wild rose and woodbine deliciousness
    blended,
  We kissed and we kissed and we kissed, till the afternoon
    ended. . . . " '

Here Rondel at last interrupted—

'Woman!' he said, 'are your cheeks so painted that you have lost all sense of shame?' But she had her answer—

'Man! are you so *great* that you have lost the sense of pity? And which is the greater shame: to publish your sins in large paper and take royalties for them, or to speak of them, just you and I together, you and I, as "there in the odorous meadowsweet afternoon"?'

'Look you,' she continued, 'an artist pays his model at least a shilling an hour, and it is only her body he paints: but you use body and soul, and offer her nothing. Your blues and reds are the colours you have stolen from her eyes and her heart—stolen, I say, for the painter pays so much a tube for his colours, so much an hour for his model, but you——'

'I give you immortality. Poor fly, I give you amber,' modestly suggested the poet.

But Annette repeated the word 'Immortality!' with a scorn that almost shook the poet's conceit, and thereupon produced an account, which ran as follows:

'Mr. Hyacinth Rondel

Dr. to Miss Annette Jones,

For moiety of the following royalties:

Moonshine and Meadowsweet . . .	500	copies
Coral and Bells, ...	750	,,
Liber Amoris, 3 editions, ...	3,000	,,
Forbidden Fruit, 5 editions, . . .	5,000	,,

9,250 copies at 1s.
=£462, 10s.

Moiety of same due to Miss Jones, £231, 5s.'

'I don't mind receipting it for two hundred and thirty,' she said, as she handed it to him.

Hyacinth was completely awakened by this: the joke was growing serious. So he at once roused up the bully in him, and ordered her out of his rooms. But she smiled at his threats, and still held out her account. At last he tried coaxing: he even had the insolence to beg her, by the memory of the past they had shared together, to spare him. He assured her that she had vastly overrated his profits, that fame meant far more cry than wool: that, in short, he was up to the neck in difficulties as it was, and really had nothing like that sum in his possession.

'Very well, then,' she replied at last, 'you must marry me instead. Either the money or the marriage. Personally, I prefer the money'—Rondel's egoism twinged like a hollow tooth—'and if you think you can escape me and do neither, look at this!' and she drew a revolver from her pocket.

'They are all loaded,' she added. 'Now, which is it to be?'

Rondel made a movement as if to snatch the weapon from her, but she sprang back and pointed it at his head.

'If you move, I fire.'

Now one would not need to be a minor poet to be a coward under such circumstances. Rondel could see that Annette meant what she said. She was clearly a desperate woman, with no great passion for life. To shoot him and then herself would be a little thing in the present state of her feelings. Like most poets, he was a prudent man—he hesitated, leaning with closed fist upon the table. She stood firm.

'Come,' she said at length, 'which is it to be—the revolver, marriage, or the money?' She ominously clicked the trigger, 'I give you five minutes.'

It was five minutes to eleven. The clock ticked on while the two still stood in their absurdly tragic attitudes—he still hesitating, she with her pistol in line with the brain that laid the golden verse. The clock whirred before striking the hour. Annette made a determined movement. Hyacinth looked up; he saw she meant it, all the more for the mocking indifference of her expression.

'Once more—death, marriage, or the money?'

The clock struck.

'The money,' gasped the poet.

But Annette still kept her weapon in line.

'Your cheque-book!' she said. Rondel obeyed.

'Pay Miss Annette Jones, or order, the sum of two hundred and thirty pounds. No, don't cross it!'

Rondel obeyed.

'Now, toss it over to me. You observe I still hold the pistol.'

Rondel once more obeyed. Then, still keeping him under cover of the ugly-looking tube, she backed towards the door.

'Good-bye,' she said. 'Be sure I shall look out for your next volume."

Rondel, bewildered as one who had lived through a fairy-tale, sank into his chair. Did such ridiculous things happen? He turned to his cheque-book. Yes, there was the counterfoil, fresh as a new wound, from which indeed his bank account was profusely bleeding.

Then he turned to his laurels: but, behold, they were all withered.

So, after a while, he donned hat and coat, and went forth to seek a flatterer as a pick-me-up.

Henry Harland
1861–1905

HENRY HARLAND, son of a lawyer, was born on March 1, 1861, in New York. He was educated at Harvard, where he read Divinity, but shortly afterwards became a clerk and wrote a series of novels under the pseudonym of Sidney Luska.

Arriving in England in 1889, he set about transforming his style and *persona*. Quite blithely he re-slanted his early years to be more in keeping with his ideal of an aristocratic bohemian cosmopolite. He suggested that he was the natural son of the Emperor Franz Joseph, and gaily tossed off the following information to the *Dictionary of National Biography*: 'Born at St. Petersburg . . . brought up mainly in Rome . . . studied at the University of Paris.' It only remained to find a style in which this Old-World eclecticism could be gaily or vividly conveyed with the maximum of sophistication; and Le Gallienne in *The Romantic '90's* has left us the endearing image of Harland cultivating his literary p's and q's. 'The polishing of his prose was for him his being's end and aim, and I have often seen him at that sacred task of a forenoon, in his study-bedroom, still in pyjamas and dressing-gown, with a coffee-pot on the hearth, bending over an exquisite piece of handwriting, like a goldsmith at his bench. It was his theory that the brain was freshest immediately after rising, and he was jealous of dissipating that morning energy by any activities of the toilet, leaving his bath and his breakfast, which with him, of course, was *déjeuner*, till the real business of the day, a page of "perfect prose," was accomplished.'

By 1893, with the publication of the stories in *Mademoiselle Miss*, he was thought of as a coming man; and when John Lane

179

started *The Yellow Book* in 1894, he chose Harland as his literary editor. Though a feeble phalanx of the *avant-garde* compared with the later and shorter-lived *Savoy*, its first four numbers (with Beardsley covers) caused a flattering conflagration in the press. With the Wilde scandal in 1895, and the immediate dismissal of Beardsley as art-editor, *The Yellow Book* opted for respectability, and enjoyed the innocuous existence which that sterling virtue confers, deceasing only with its thirteenth number.

Max Beerbohm roundly declared that 'Henry Harland was a very enlightened and fine editor.' This is certainly true as to his choice of fiction, but for verse and criticism he showed no flair; though he himself wrote engagingly on new books of the day under the pseudonym of 'The Yellow Dwarf.'

In 1895 he published his second book *Grey Roses*, which was well reviewed by Le Gallienne, who, not uncharacteristically, preferred the tinselled and meretricious tales to those of Harland in more sober vein. With *Comedies and Errors* in 1898, his career as a short-storyist was over. 'Later,' remarks Bernard Muddiman in *The Men of the 'Nineties*, 'he opened up a new vein of dainty comedy fiction is almost rose-leaf prose whose happy delicacy of thought and style he never equalled again.' The book which marked this new phase was his novel *The Cardinal's Snuff Box* (1900), to be followed by *The Lady Paramount* (1902) and *My Friend Prospero* (1904).

A delicate valetudinarian all his life, Harland has recalled how he completed *The Cardinal's Snuff Box* during the 'monstrous dark and dour and sour London winter' of 1897-8. The book proved a best-seller and Harland betook himself to Italy, dying of consumption at San Remo.

Though Harland lacked the artist's fuller vision, he possessed the craftsman's true dedication, the professional's obsessive love for his calling. When he was too weak to take up his pen, his one hope was for a brief turn in his disease so that he could 'sit up and work, sit down and flog.' The last novel on which he was engaged was finished by his wife's hand after his death. Appropriately its title was *The Royal End* (1909).

A BROKEN LOOKING-GLASS

He climbed the three flights of stone stairs, and put his key into the lock; but before he turned it, he stopped—to rest, to take breath. On the door his name was painted in big white letters, Mr. Richard Dane. It is always silent in the Temple at midnight; tonight the silence was dense, like a fog. It was Sunday night; and on Sunday night, even within the hushed precincts of the Temple, one is conscious of a deeper hush.

When he had lighted the lamp in his sitting-room, he let himself drop into an armchair before the empty fireplace. He was tired, he was exhausted. Yet nothing had happened to tire him. He had dined, as he always dined on Sundays, with the Rodericks, in Cheyne Walk; he had driven home in a hansom. There was no reason why he should be tired. But he was tired. A deadly lassitude penetrated his body and his spirit, like a fluid. He was too tired to go to bed.

'I suppose I am getting old,' he thought.

To a second person the matter would have appeared, not one of supposition, but of certainty, not of progression, but of accomplishment. Getting old indeed? But he *was* old. It was an old man, grey and wrinkled and wasted, who sat there, limp, sunken upon himself in his easy-chair. In years, to be sure, he was under sixty; but looked like a man of seventy-five.

'I am getting old, I suppose I am getting old.'

And vaguely, dully, he contemplated his life, spread out behind him like a misty landscape, and thought what a failure it had been. What had it come to? What had it brought him? What had he done or won? Nothing, nothing. It had brought him nothing but old age, solitude, disappointment, and, tonight especially, a sense of fatigue and apathy that weighed upon him like a suffocating blanket. On a table, a yard or two away, stood a decanter of whisky, with some soda-water bottles and tumblers; he looked at it with heavy eyes, and he knew that there was what he needed. A little whisky would strengthen him, revive him, and make it possible for him to bestir himself and undress and

181

go to bed. But when he thought of rising and moving to pour the whisky out, he shrank from that effort as from an Herculean labour; no—he was too tired. Then his mind went back to the friends he had left in Chelsea half an hour ago; it seemed an indefinably long time ago, years and years ago; they were like blurred Phantoms, dimly remembered from a remote past.

Yes, his life had been a failure; total, miserable, abject. It had come to nothing; its harvest was a harvest of ashes. If it had been a useful life, he could have accepted its unhappiness; if it had been a happy life, he could have forgiven its uselessness; but it had been both useless and unhappy. He had done nothing for others, he had won nothing for himself. Oh, but he had tried, he had tried. When he had left Oxford people expected great things of himself. He was admitted to be clever, to be gifted; he was ambitious, he was in earnest. He wished to make a name, he wished to justify his existence by fruitful work. And he had worked hard. He had put all his knowledge, all his talent, all his energy, into his work; he had not spared himself; he had passed laborious days and studious nights. And what remained to show for it? Three or four volumes upon Political Economy, that had been read in their day a little, discussed a little, and then quite forgotten—superseded by the books of newer men. 'Pulped, pulped,' he reflected bitterly. Except for a stray dozen of copies scattered here and there—in the British Museum, in his College library, on his own bookshelves—his published writings had by this time (he could not doubt) met with the common fate of unappreciated literature, and been 'pulped.'

'Pulped—pulped; pulped—pulped.' The hateful word beat rhythmically again and again in his tired brain; and for a little while that was all he was conscious of.

So much for the work of his life. And for the rest? The play? The living? Oh, he had nothing to recall but failure. It had sufficed that he should desire a thing, for him to miss it; that he should set his heart upon a thing, for it to be removed beyond the sphere of his possible acquisition. It had been so from the beginning; it had been so always. He sat motionless as a stone, and allowed his thoughts to drift listlessly hither and thither in the current of memory. Everywhere they encountered wreckage, derelicts; defeated aspirations, broken hopes. Languidly he envisaged these. He was too tired to resent, to rebel. He even found a certain sluggish satisfaction in recognising with what unvarying harshnes destiny had treated him, in resigning himself to the unmerited.

He caught sight of his hand, lying flat and inert upon the brown leather of his chair. His eyes rested on it, and for the moment he forgot everything else in a sort of torpid study of it. How white it was, how thin, how withered; the nails were parched into minute corrugations; the veins stood out like dark wires; the skin hung loosely on it, and had a dry lustre: an old man's hand. He gazed at it fixedly, till his eyes closed and his head fell forward. But he was not sleepy, he was only tired and weak.

He raised his head with a start and changed his position. He felt cold; but to endure the cold was easier than to get up, and put something on, or go to bed.

How silent the world was; how empty his room. An immense feeling of solitude, of isolation, fell upon him. He was quite cut off from the rest of humanity here. If anything should happen to him, if he should need help of any sort, what could he do? Call out? But who would hear? At nine in the morning the porter's wife would come with his tea. But if anything should happen to him in the meantime? There would be nothing for it but to wait till nine o'clock.

Ah, if he had married, if he had had children, a wife, a home of his own, instead of these desolate bachelor chambers!

If he had married, indeed! It was his sorrow's crown of sorrow that he had not married, that he had not been able to marry, that the girl he had wished to marry wouldn't have him. Failure? Success? He could have accounted failure in other things a trifle, he could have laughed at what the world calls failure, if Elinor Lynd had become his wife. But that was the heart of his misfortune, she wouldn't have him.

He had met her for the first time when he was a lad of twenty, and she a girl of eighteen. He could see her palpable before him now: her slender girlish figure, her bright eyes, her laughing mouth, her warm brown hair curling round her forehead. Oh, how he had loved her. For twelve years he had waited upon her, wooed her, hoped to win her. But she had always said, 'No—I don't love you. I am very fond of you; I love you as a friend; we all love you that way—my mother, my father, my sisters. But I can't marry you.' However, she married no one else, she loved no one else: and for twelve years he was an ever-welcome guest in her father's house; and she would talk with him, play to him, pity him; and he could hope. Then she died. He called one day, and they said she was ill. After that there came a blank in his memory—a gulf, full of blackness and redness, anguish and confusion; and then a sort of dreadful sudden calm, when they told him she was dead.

He remembered standing in her room, after the funeral, with her father, her mother, her sister Elizabeth. He remembered the pale daylight that filled it, and how orderly and cold and forsaken it all looked. And there was her bed, the bed she had died in; and there her dressing-table, with her combs and brushes; and there her writing-desk, her bookcase. He remembered a row of medicine bottles on the mantelpiece; he remembered the fierce anger, the hatred of them, as if they were animate, that had welled up in his heart as he looked at them, because they had failed to do their work.

'You will wish to have something that was hers, Richard,' her mother said. 'What would you like?'

On her dressing-table there was a small looking-glass, in an ivory frame. He asked if he might have that, and carried it away with him. She had looked into it a thousand times, no doubt; she had done her hair in it; it had reflected her, enclosed her, contained her. He could almost persuade himself that something of her must remain in it. To own it was like owning something of herself. He carried it home with him, hugging it to his side with a kind of passion.

He had prized it, he prized it still, as his dearest treasure; the looking-glass in which her face had been reflected a thousand times; the glass that had contained her, known her; in which something of herself, he felt, must linger. To handle it, look at it, into it, behind it, was like holding a mystic communion with her; it gave him an emotion that was infinitely sweet and bitter, a pain that was dissolved in joy.

The glass lay now, folded in its ivory case, on the chimney-shelf in front of him. That was its place; he always kept it on his chimney-shelf, so that he could see it whenever he glanced round his room. He leaned back in his chair, and looked at it; for a long time his eyes remained fixed upon it. 'If she had married me, she wouldn't have died. My love, my care, would have healed her. She could not have died.' Monotonously, automatically, the phrase repeated itself over and over again in his mind, while his eyes remained fixed on the ivory case into which her looking-glass was folded. It was an effect of his fatigue, no doubt, that his eyes, once directed upon an object, were slow to leave it for another; that a phrase once pronounced in his thought had this tendency to repeat itself over and over again.

But at last he roused himself a little, and leaning forward, put his hand out and up, to take the glass from the shelf. He wished to hold it, to touch it and look into it. As he lifted it towards him, it fell open, the mirror proper being fastened to a leather back, which was glued to the ivory, and formed a hinge. It fell open; and his grasp had been insecure; and the jerk as it opened was enough. It slipped from his fingers, and dropped with a crash upon the hearthstone.

The sound went through him like a physical pain. He sank back in his chair, and closed his eyes. His heart was beating as after a mighty physical exertion. He knew vaguely that a calamity had befallen him; he could vaguely imagine the splinters of broken glass at his feet. But his physical prostration was so great as to obliterate, to neutralise, emotion. He felt very cold. He felt that he was being hurried along with terrible speed through darkness and cold air. There was the continuous roar of rapid motion in his ears, a faint, dizzy bewilderment in his head. He felt that he was trying to catch hold of things, to stop his progress, but his hands closed upon emptiness; that he was trying to call out for help, but he could make no sound. On—on—on, he was being whirled through some immeasurable abyss of space.

'Ah, yes, he's dead, quite dead,' the doctor said. 'He has been dead some hours. He must have passed away peacefully, sitting here in his chair.'

'Poor gentleman,' said the porter's wife. 'And a broken looking-glass beside him. Oh, it's a sure sign, a broken looking-glass.'

Arthur Symons
1865-1945

ARTHUR WILLIAM SYMONS, the son of a Methodist minister and a mother whom he alleged was unstable, was born at Milford Haven on February 21, 1865.

Christianity and the chapel ethos never had any meaning for him, unless they were answerable for a deep unconscious fear of life and the hereafter. Although his formal education was of a broken and patchy order, he early became a fine linguist, and acted as the leading cultural importer of French art and letters in the 'nineties.

Living till his marriage in 1901 in chambers in the Temple off Fountain Court, he shared a first floor flat, at different times, with Havelock Ellis and W. B. Yeats. It was Ellis who first accompanied Symons on one of his numerous pilgrimages to Paris, but it was Yeats who confirmed him in his own temperamental and eclectic conclusions. His best-known critical work, *The Symbolist Movement in Literature* (1899), is dedicated to Yeats, 'both as an expression of deep personal friendship and because you, more than anyone else, will sympathize with what I say in it, being yourself the chief representative of that movement in your country.'

As a writer of short stories, Yeats was, in fact, a good deal more of a Symbolist than his friend Symons, whose volumes of tales, *Spiritual Adventures,* collected and published in 1905, belongs more to an earlier so-called Decadent phase. The distinction is largely academic; but Symons' book, when first announced, was to have been entitled *The Decadent Movement in Literature,* and Impressionism and Symbolism were—he told the reader in 1893—the 'two main branches' of that movement.

Behind the Symbolism of Yeats lay his Rosicrucian occultist

187

studies, whereas the only symbol of the timeless—of escape from the wheel of necessity—in Symons is an escapist image of art. This is not to say that *Spiritual Adventures* is a book without an air all its own. Symons, with Pater's volume in mind, spoke of them as 'a book of *Imaginary Portraits;*' and this is, in truth, what they are—a gallery of studies in morbid psychology, the morbidity which is an integral part of the abnormal thinking-patterns of the artist.

There are autobiographical clues in these tales to the enigma of Symons the man. A *Prelude to Life* tells us what an essential 'solitudinarian' he was. *An Autumn City*, descriptive of Arles, offers hints on his disharmony in marriage; *Seaward Lackland* speaks of the religious sense of damnation which Symons may have understood, in a personal sense, in purely secular terms. Lastly, there is *Extracts from the Journal of Henry Luxulyan* which strangely foresees the madness which overtook Symons in 1908—an account of which he himself published twenty-two years afterwards under the title *Confession: A Study in Pathology.*

Ian Fletcher has well summed up Symons when he speaks of him as 'a good minor poet, an excellent translator, a major critic.' Perhaps it merely remains to add 'and an editor of courage, taste, and distinction.' Certainly the eight numbers of the Beardsley-Symons-Smithers periodical *The Savoy* (1896-7) make the proclamatory *Yellow Book* look mild and insipid as most parish magazines.

The fullest work, to date, on his life is *Arthur Symons: A Critical Biography* by Roger Lhombreaud (1963). One will clearly know more of this ambiguous man when Karl Beckson publishes the long-awaited edition of Symons' letters.

ESTHER KAHN

Esther Kahn was born in one of those dark, evil-smelling streets with strange corners which lie about the Docks. It was a quiet street, which seemed to lead nowhere, but to stand aside, for some not quite honest purpose of its own. The blinds of some of these houses were always drawn; shutters were nailed over some of the windows. Few people passed; there were never many children playing in the road; the women did not stand talking at their open doors. The doors opened and shut quietly; dark faces looked out from behind the windows; the Jews who lived there seemed always to be at work, bending over their tables, sewing and cutting, or else hurrying in and out with bundles of clothes under their arms, going and coming from the tailors for whom they worked. The Kahns all worked at tailoring: Esther's father and mother and grandmother, her elder brother and her two elder sisters. One did seaming, another button-holing, another sewed on buttons; and, on the poor pay they got for that, seven had to live.

As a child Esther had a strange terror of the street in which she lived. She was never sure whether something dreadful had just happened there, or whether it was just going to happen. But she was always in suspense. She was tormented with the fear of knowing what went on behind those nailed shutters. She made up stories about the houses, but the stories never satisfied her. She imagined some great, vague gesture; not an incident, but a gesture; and it hung in the air suspended like a shadow. The gestures of people always meant more to her than their words; they seemed to have a secret meaning of their own, which the words never quite interpreted. She was always unconsciously on the watch for their meaning.

At night, after supper, the others used to sit around the table, talking eagerly. Esther would get up and draw her chair into the corner by the door, and for a time she would watch them, as if she were looking on at something, something with which she had no concern, but which interested her for its outline and movement. She saw her father's keen profile, the great, hooked nose, the black, prominent shifty eye, the tangled black hair straggling over the shirt-collar; her mother, large, placid, with masses of black, straight hair coiled low over her sallow cheeks; the two sisters, sharp and voluble, never at rest for a moment; the brother, with his air of insolent assurance, an immense self-satisfaction hooded under his beautifully curved eyelids; the grandmother,

with her bent and mountainous shoulders, the vivid malice of
her eyes, her hundreds of wrinkles. All these people, who had so
many interests in common, who thought of the same things,
cared for the same things, seemed so fond of one another in an
instinctive way, with so much hostility for other people who
were not belonging to them, sat there night after night, in the
same attitudes, always as eager for the events of today as they
had been for the events of yesterday. Everything mattered to
them immensely, and especially their part in things; and no one
thing seemed to matter more than any other thing. Esther cared
only to look on; nothing mattered to her; she had no interest
in their interests; she was not sure that she cared for them
more than she would care for other people; they were what she
supposed real life was, and that was a thing in which she had
only a disinterested curiosity.

Sometimes, when she had been watching them until they had
all seemed to fade away and form again in a kind of vision more
precise than the reality, she would lose sight of them altogether
and sit gazing straight before her, her eyes wide open, her lips
parted. Her hands would make an unconscious movement, as if
she were accompanying some grave words with an appropriate
gesture; and Becky would generally see it, and burst into a
mocking laugh, and ask her whom she was mimicking.

'Don't notice her,' the mother said once; 'she's not a human
child, she's a monkey; she's clutching out after a soul, as they do.
They look like little men, but they know they're not men, and
they try to be; that's why they mimic us.'

Esther was very angry; she said to herself that she would be
more careful in future not to show anything that she was feeling.

At thirteen Esther looked a woman. She was large-boned, with
very small hands and feet, and her body seemed to be generally
asleep, in a kind of brooding lethargy. She had her mother's hair,
masses of it, but softer, with a faint natural wave in it. Her face
was oval, smooth in outline, with a nose just Jewish enough for
the beauty of suave curves and unemphatic outlines. The lips
were thick, red, strung like a bow. The whole face seemed to
await, with an infinite patience, some moulding and awakening
force, which might have its way with it. It wanted nothing,

anticipated nothing; it waited. Only the eyes put life into the mask, and the eyes were the eyes of the tribe; they had no personal meaning in what seemed to be their mystery; they were ready to fascinate innocently, to be intolerably ambiguous without intention; they were fathomless with mere sleep, the unconscious dream which is in the eyes of animals.

Esther was neither clever nor stupid; she was inert. She did as little in the house as she could, but when she had to take her share in the stitching she stitched more neatly than any of the others, though very slowly. She hated it, in her languid smouldering way, partly because it was work and partly because it made her prick her fingers, and the skin grew hard and ragged where the point of the needle had scratched it. She liked her skin to be quite smooth, but all the glycerine she rubbed into it at night would not take out the mark of the needle. It seemed to her like the badge of her slavery.

She would rather not have been a Jewess; that, too, was a kind of badge, marking her out from other people; she wanted to be let alone, to have her own way without other people's help or hindrance. She had no definite consciousness of what her own way was to be; she was only conscious, as yet, of the ways that would certainly not be hers.

She would not think only of making money, like her mother, nor of being thought clever, like Becky, nor of being admired because she had good looks and dressed smartly, like Mina. All these things required an effort, and Esther was lazy. She wanted to be admired, and to have money, of course, and she did not want people to think her stupid; but all this was to come to her, she knew, because of some fortunate quality in herself, as yet undiscovered. Then she would shake off everything that now clung to her, like a worn-out garment that one keeps only until one can replace it. She saw herself rolling away in a carriage towards the west; she would never come back. And it would be like a revenge on whatever it was that kept her stifling in this mean street; she wanted to be cruelly revenged.

As it was, her only very keen pleasure was in going to the theatre with her brother or her sisters; she cared nothing for the music-halls, and preferred staying at home to going with the others when they went to the Pavilion or the Foresters. But when there was a melodrama at the Standard, or at the Elephant and Castle, she would wait and struggle outside the door and up the narrow, winding stairs, for a place as near the front of the gallery as she could get. Once inside, she would never speak, but she would sit staring at the people on the stage as if they hypnotised her. She never criticised the play, as the others did; the play did not seem to matter; she lived in it without will or choice, merely because it was there and her eyes were on it.

But after it was over and they were at home again, she would become suddenly voluble as she discussed the merits of the acting. She had no hesitations, was certain that she was always in the right, and became furious if anyone contradicted her. She saw each part as a whole, and she blamed the actors for not being consistent with themselves. She could not understand how they could make a mistake. It was so simple, there were no two ways of doing anything. To go wrong was as if you said no when you meant yes; it must be wilful.

'You ought to do it yourself, Esther,' said her sisters, when they were tired of her criticisms. They meant to be satirical, but Esther said, seriously enough: 'Yes, I could do it; but so could that woman if she would let herself alone. Why did she try to be something else all the time?'

Time went slowly with Esther; but when she was seventeen she was still sewing at home and still waiting. Nothing had come to her of all that she had expected. Two of her cousins, and a neighbour or two, had wanted to marry her; but she had refused them contemptuously. To her sluggish instinct men seemed only good for making money, or, perhaps, children; they had not come to have any definite personal meaning for her. A little man called Joel, who had talked to her passionately about love, and had cried when she refused him, seemed to her an unintelligible and ridiculous kind of animal. When she dreamed of the future, there was never anyone of that sort making fine speeches to her.

But, gradually, her own real purpose in life had become clear. She was to be an actress. She said nothing about it at home, but she began to go round to the managers of the small theatres in

v. ARTHUR SYMONS
From a photograph taken about 1900

VI. ARTHUR MORRISON
*(Reproduced by permission of the Trustees of the British
Museum)*

the neighbourhood, asking for an engagement. After a long time the manager gave her a small part. The piece was called 'The Wages of Sin,' and she was to be the servant who opens the door in the first act to the man who is going to be the murderer in the second act, and then identifies him in the fourth act.

Esther went home quietly and said nothing until supper-time. Then she said to her mother: 'I am going on the stage.'

'That's very likely,' said her mother, with a sarcastic smile; 'and when do you go on, pray?'

'On Monday night,' said Esther.

'You don't mean it!' said her mother.

'Indeed I mean it,' said Esther, 'and I've got my part. I'm to be the servant in "The Wages of Sin." '

Her brother laughed. 'I know,' he said, 'she speaks two words twice.'

'You are right,' said Esther; 'will you come on Monday, and hear how I say them?'

When Esther had made up her mind to do anything, they all knew that she always did it. Her father talked to her seriously. Her mother said: 'You are much too lazy, Esther; you will never get on.' They told her that she was taking the bread out of their mouths, and it was certain she would never put it back again. 'If I get on,' said Esther, 'I will pay you back exactly what I would have earned, as long as you keep me. Is that a bargain? I know I shall get on, and you won't repent of it. You had better let me do as I want. It will pay.'

They shook their heads, looked at Esther, who sat there with her lips tight shut, and a queer, hard look in her eyes, which were trying not to seem exultant; they looked at one another, shook their heads again, and consented. The old grandmother mumbled something fiercely, but as it sounded like bad words, and they never knew what Old Testament language she would use, they did not ask her what she was meaning.

On Monday Esther made her first appearance on the stage. Her mother said to her afterwards: 'I thought nothing of you, Esther; you were just like any ordinary servant.' Becky asked her if she had felt nervous. She shook her head; it had seemed quite natural to her, she said. She did not tell them that a great

wave of triumph had swept over her as she felt the heat of the
gas footlights come up into her eyes, and saw the floating cluster
of white faces rising out of a solid mass of indistinguishable darkness. In that moment she drew into her nostrils the breath of life.

Esther had a small part to understudy, and before long she
had the chance of playing it. The manager said nothing to her,
but soon afterwards he told her to understudy a more important
part. She never had the chance to play it, but, when the next
piece was put on at the theatre, she was given a part of her
own. She began to make a little money, and, as she had promised,
she paid so much a week to her parents for keeping her. They
gained by the bargain, so they did not ask her to come back
to the stitching. Mrs. Kahn sometimes spoke of her daughter to
the neighbours with a certain languid pride; Esther was making
her way.

Esther made her way rapidly. One day the manager of a West
End theatre came down to see her; he engaged her at once to
play a small, but difficult part in an ambitious kind of melodrama that he was bringing out. She did it well, satisfied the
manager, was given a better part, did that well, too, was engaged
by another manager, and, in short, began to be looked upon
as a promising actress. The papers praised her with moderation;
some of the younger critics, who admired her type, praised her
more than she deserved. She was making money; she had come
to live in rooms of her own, off the Strand; at twenty-one she
had done, in a measure what she wanted to do; but she was not
satisfied with herself. She had always known that she could act,
but how well could she act? Would she never be able to act any
better than this? She had drifted into the life of the stage as
naturally as if she had never known anything else; she was at
home, comfortable, able to do what many others could not do.
But she wanted to be a great actress.

An old actor, a Jew, Nathan Quellen, who had taken a kind
of paternal interest in her, and who helped her with all the good
advice that he had never taken to himself, was fond of saying
that the remedy was in her own hands.

'My dear Esther,' he would tell her, smoothing his long grey
hair down over his forehead, 'you must take a lover; you must

fall in love; there's no other way. You think you can act, and you have never felt anything worse than a cut finger. Why it's an absurdity! Wait till you know the only thing worth knowing; till then you're in short frocks and a pinafore.'

He cited examples, he condensed the biographies of the great actresses for her benefit. He found one lesson in them all, and he was sincere in his reading of history as he saw it. He talked, argued, protested; the matter seriously troubled him. He felt he was giving Esther good advice; he wanted her to be the thing she wanted to be. Esther knew it and thanked him, without smiling; she sat brooding over his words; she never argued against them. She believed much of what he said; but was the remedy, as he said, in her own hands? It did not seem so.

As yet no man had spoken to her blood. She had the sluggish blood of a really profound animal nature. She saw men calmly, as calmly as when little Joel had cried because she would not marry him. Joel still came to see her sometimes, with the same entreaty in his eyes, not daring to speak it. Other men, very different men, had made love to her in very different ways. They had seemed to be trying to drive a hard bargain, to get the better of her in a matter of business; and her native cunning had kept her easily on the better side of the bargain. She was resolved to be a business woman in the old trade of the affections; no one should buy or sell her except at her own price, and she set the price vastly high.

Yet Quellen's words set her thinking. Was there, after all, but one way to study for the stage? All the examples pointed to it, and, what was worse, she felt it might be true. She saw exactly where her acting stopped short.

She looked around her with practical eyes, not seeming to herself to be doing anything unusual or unlikely to succeed in its purpose. She thought deliberately over all the men she knew; but who was there whom it would be possible to take seriously? She could think of only one man : Philip Haygarth.

Philip Haygarth was a man of five-and-thirty, who had been writing plays and having them acted, with only a moderate success for nearly ten years. He was one of the accepted men, a man whose plays were treated respectfully, and he had the reputation of being much cleverer than his plays. He was short, dark, neat, very worldly-looking, with thin lips and reflective, not quite honest eyes. His manner was cold, restrained, with a mingling of insolence and diffidence. He was a hard worker and a somewhat deliberately hard liver. He avoided society and preferred to find his relaxation among people with whom one did not need to keep up appearances, or talk sentiment, or pay afternoon calls. He admired Esther Kahn as an actress, though with many reservations; and he admired her as a woman, more than he ever admired anybody else. She appealed to all his tastes; she ended by absorbing almost the whole of those interests and those hours which he set apart, in his carefully arranged life, for such matters.

He made love to Esther much more skilfully than any of her other lovers, and, though she saw through his plans as clearly as he wished her to see through them, she was grateful to him for a certain finesse in his manner of approach. He never mentioned the word 'love,' except to jest at it; he concealed even the extent to which he was really disturbed by her presence; his words spoke only of friendship and of general topics. And yet there could never be any doubt as to his meaning; his whole attitude was a patient waiting. He interested her; frankly, he interested her : here, then, was the man for her purpose. With his admirable tact, he spared her the least difficulty in making her meaning clear. He congratulated himself on a prize; she congratulated herself on the accomplishment of a duty.

Days and weeks passed, and Esther scrutinised herself with a distinct sense of disappointment. She had no moral feeling in the matter; she was her own property, it has always seemed to her, free to dispose of as she pleased. The business element in her nature persisted. This bargain, this infinitely important bargain, had been concluded, with open eyes, with a full sense of responsibility, for a purpose, the purpose for which she lived. What was the result?

She could see no result. The world had in no sense changed for her, as she had been supposing it would change; a new excitement had come into her life, and that was all. She wondered what it was that a woman was expected to feel under the circumstances, and why she had not felt it. How different had been her feelings when she walked across the stage for the first time! That had really been a new life, or the very beginning of life. But this was no more than a delightful episode, hardly to be disentangled from the visit to Paris which had accompanied it. She had, so to speak, fallen into a new habit, which was so agreeable, and seemed so natural, that she could not understand why she had not fallen into it before; it was a habit she would certainly persist in, for its own sake. The world remained just the same.

And her art: she had learned nothing. No new thrill came into the words she spoke; her eyes, as they looked across the footlights, remembered nothing, had nothing new to tell.

And so she turned, with all the more interest, an interest almost impersonal, to Philip Haygarth when he talked to her about acting and the drama, when he elaborated his theories which, she was aware, occupied him more then she occupied him. He was one of those creative critics who can do every man's work but their own. When he sat down to write his own plays, something dry and hard came into the words, the life ebbed out of those imaginary people who had been so real to him, whom he had made so real to others as he talked. He constructed admirably and was an unerring judge of the construction of plays. And he had a sense of acting which was like the sense that a fine actor might have, if he could be himself and also some-one looking on at himself. He not only knew what should be done, but exactly why it should be done. Little suspecting that he had been chosen for the purpose, though in so different a manner, he set himself to teach her art to Esther.

He made her go through the great parts with him; she was Juliet, Lady Macbeth, Cleopatra; he taught her how to speak verse and how to feel the accent of speech in verse, another kind of speech than prose speech; he trained her voice to take hold of the harmonies that lie in words themselves; and she caught them, by ear, as one born to speak many languages catches a foreign language. She went through Ibsen as she had gone through Shakespeare; and Haygarth showed her how to take hold of this very difficult subject-matter, so definite and so elusive.

And they studied good acting-plays together, worthless plays that gave the actress opportunities to create something out of nothing. Together they saw Duse and Sarah Bernhardt; and they had seen Réjane in Paris, in crudely tragic parts; and they studied the English stage, to find out why it maintained itself at so stiff a distance from nature. She went on acting all the time, always acting with more certainty; and at last she attempted more serious parts, which she learned with Haygarth at her elbow.

She had to be taught her part as a child is taught its lesson; word by word, intonation by intonation. She read it over, not really knowing what it was about; she learned it by heart mechanically, getting the words into her memory first. Then the meaning had to be explained to her, scene by scene, and she had to say the words over until she had found the right accent. Once found, she never forgot it; she could repeat it identically at any moment; there were no variations to allow for. Until that moment she was reaching out blindly in the dark, feeling about her with uncertain fingers.

And, with her, the understanding came with the power of expression, sometimes seeming really to proceed from the sound to the sense, from the gesture inward. Show her how it should be done, and she knew why it should be done; sound the right notes in her ears, arrest her at the moment when the note came right, and she understood, by a backward process, why the note should sound thus. Her mind worked, but it worked under suggestion, as the hypnotists say; the idea had to come to her through the instinct, or it would never come.

As Esther found herself, almost unconsciously, becoming what she had dreamed of becoming, what she had longed to become, and, after all, through Philip Haygarth, a more personal feeling began to grow up in her heart towards this lover who had found his way to her, not through the senses, but through the mind. A kind of domesticity had crept into their relations, and this drew Esther nearer to him. She began to feel that he belonged to her. He had never, she knew, been wholly absorbed in her, and she had delighted him by showing no jealousy, no anxiety to keep him. As long as she remained so, he felt that she had a sure hold on him. But now she began to change, to concern herself more with his doings, to assert her right to him, as she had never hitherto cared to do. He chafed a little at what seemed an unnecessary devotion.

Love, with Esther, had come slowly, taking his time on the journey; but he came to take possession. To work at her art was to please Philip Haygarth; she worked now with a double purpose. And she made surprising advances as an actress. People began to speculate : had she genius, or was this only an astonishingly developed talent, which could go so far and no farther?

For, in this finished method, which seemed so spontaneous and yet at the same time so deliberate, there seemed still to be something, some slight, essential thing, almost unaccountably lacking. What was it? Was it a fundamental lack, that could never be supplied? Or would that slight, essential thing, as her admirers prophesied, one day be supplied? They waited.

Esther was now really happy, for the first time in her life; and as she looked back over those years, in the street by the Docks, when she had lived alone in the midst of her family, and since then, when she had lived alone, working, not finding the time long, nor wishing it to go more slowly, she felt a kind a surprise at herself. How could she have gone through it all? She had not even been bored. She had had a purpose, and now that she was achieving that purpose, the thing itself seemed hardly to matter. Her art kept pace with her life; she was giving up nothing in return for happiness; but she had come to prize the happiness, her love, beyond all things.

She knew that Haygarth was proud of her, that he looked upon her talent, genius, whatever it was, as partly the work of his hands. It pleased her that this should be so; it seemed to bind him to her more tightly.

In this she was mistaken, as most women are mistaken when they ask themselves what it is in them that holds their lovers. The actress interested Haygarth greatly, but the actress interested him as a problem, as something quite apart from his feelings as a man, as a lover. He had been attracted by the woman, by what was sombre and unexplained in her eyes, by the sleepy grace of her movements, by the magnetism that seemed to

drowse in her. He had made love to her precisely as he would
have made love to an ignorant, beautiful creature who walked on
in some corner of a Drury Lane melodrama. On principle, he
did not like clever women. Esther, it is true, was not clever, in
the ordinary, tiresome sense; and her startling intuitions, in
matters of acting, had not repelled him, as an exhibition of the
capabilities of woman, while they preoccupied him for a long
time in that part of his brain which worked critically upon any
interesting material. But nothing that she could do as an artist
made the least difference to his feeling about her as a woman; his
pride in her was like his pride in a play that he had written
finely, and put aside; to be glanced at from time to time, with
cool satisfaction. He had his own very deliberate theory of values,
and one value was never allowed to interfere with another. A
devoted, discreet amateur of woman, he appreciated women
really for their own sakes, with an unflattering simplicity. And
for a time Esther absorbed him almost wholly.

He had been quite content with their relations as they were
before she fell seriously in love with him, and this new, profound
feeling, which he had never even dreaded, somewhat disturbed
him. She was adopting almost the attitude of a wife, and he had
no ambition to play the part of a husband. The affections were
always rather a strain upon him; he liked something a little less
serious and a little more exciting.

Esther understood nothing that was going on in Philip Haygarth's mind, and when he began to seem colder to her, when
she saw less of him, and then less, it seemed to her that she could
still appeal to him by art and still touch him by her devotion. As
her warmth seemed more and more to threaten his liberty, the
impulse to tug at his chain became harder to resist. He continued,
unvarying interest in her acting, his patience to helping her, in
working with her, kept for for some time from realising how little
was left now of the more personal feeling. It was a sharp surprise,
as well as with a blinding rage, that she discovered one day,
beyond possibility of mistake, that she had a rival, and that Haygarth was only doling out to her the time left over from her rival.

It was an Italian, a young girl who had come over to London
with an organ grinder, and who posed for sculptors when she

could get a sitting. It was a girl who could barely read and write, an insignificant creature, a peasant from the Campagna, who had nothing but her good looks and the distinction of her attitude. Esther was beside herself with rage, jealousy, mortification; she loved, and she could not pardon. There was a scene of un-measured violence. Haygarth was cruel, almost with intention; and they parted, Esther feeling as if her life had been broken sharply in two.

She was at the last rehearsals of a new play by Haygarth, a play in which he had tried for once to be tragic in the bare straightforward way of the things that really happen. She went through the rehearsals absentmindedly, repeating her words, which he had taught her how to say, but scarcely attending to their meaning. Another thought was at work behind this mechanical speech, a continual throb of remembrance, going on monotonously. Her mind was full of other words, which she heard as if an inner voice were repeating them; her mind made up pictures, which seemed to pass slowly before her eyes : Hay-garth and the other woman. At the last rehearsal Quellen came round to her, and, ironically as she thought, complimented her on her performance. She meant, when the night came, not to fail : that was all.

When the night came, she said to herself that she was calm, that she would be able to concentrate herself on her acting and act just as usual. But, as she stood in the wings, waiting for her moment to appear, her eyes went straight to the eyes of the other woman, the Italian model, the organ-grinder's girl, who sat, smiling contentedly, in the front of a box, turning her head sometimes to speak to someone behind her, hidden by the cur-tain. She was dressed in black, with a rose in her hair : you could have taken her for a lady; she was triumphantly beautiful. Esther shuddered as if she had been struck; the blood rushed into her forehead and swelled and beat against her eyes. Then, with an immense effort, she cleared her mind of everything but the task before her. Every nerve in her body lived with a separate life as she opened the door at the back of the stage, and stood waiting for the applause to subside, motionless under the eyes of the audience. There was something in the manner of her entrance that seemed to strike the fatal note of the play. She had never been more restrained, more effortless; she seemed scarcely to be acting; only, a magnetic current seemed to have been set in motion between her and those who were watching her. They held their breaths, as if they were assisting at a real tragedy; as if, at any moment, this acting might give place to some horrible, naked passion of mere nature. The curtain rose and rose again at the end of the first act; and she stood there, bowing gravely, in what seemed a deliberate continuation, into that interval, of the sentiment of the piece. Her dresses were taken off her and put on her, for each act, as if she had been a lay-figure. Once, in the second act, she looked up at the box; the Italian woman was smiling emptily, but Haygarth, taking no notice of her, was leaning forward with his eyes fixed on the stage. After the third act he sent to Esther's dressing-room a fervent note, begging to be allowed to see her. She had made his play, he said, and she had made herself a great actress. She crumpled the note fiercely, put it carefully into her jewel-box, and refused to see him. In the last act she had to die, after the manner of the Lady of the Camellias, waiting for the lover who, in this case, never came. The pathos of her acting was almost unbearable, and, still, it seemed not like acting at all. The curtain went down on a great actress.

Esther went home stunned, only partly realising what she had done, or how she had done it. She read over the note from Haygarth, unforgivingly; and the long letter that came from him in the morning. As reflection returned, through all the confused suffering and excitement, to her deliberate, automatic nature, in which a great shock had brought about a kind of release, she realised that all she had wanted, during most of her life, had at last come about. The note had been struck, she had responded to it, as she responded to every suggestion, faultlessly; she knew that she could repeat the note, whenever she wished, now that she had once found it. There would be no variation to allow for, the actress was made at last. She might take back her lover, or never see him again, it would make no difference. It would make no difference, she repeated, over and over again, weeping uncontrollable tears.

Ernest Dowson
1867-1900

ERNEST CHRISTOPHER DOWSON was born at The Grove, Belmont Hill, Lee, Kent, on August 2, 1867, the son of an East End dry-dock owner.

Due to his father's defective health, he spent much of his boyhood in Frence whence his parent repaired to seek the sun. As a result of this Gallic upbringing, he won a mastery of the French tongue and kept himself in his bleak years by the labour of translation finely performed.

A year at Queen's College, Oxford, left him without a degree but, as Desmond Flower remarks, 'a love for Catallus, Propertius, Flaubert, Balzac, Verlaine, and Henry James.' He had already contributed his first short story to the magazine *Temple Bar* before he came down from Oxford, and thought of himself as a prose author of fiction rather than a master of elegaic verse (as he was to feature for future generations). In his Introduction to *The Stories of Ernest Dowson* (1949), Mark Longaker states that an Oxford contemporary of the poet 'reported that his chief literary ambitions were in prose, that "poetry, when it came, was an outburst, a digression";' and Yeats declared that it was his desire to hold, in durable form in his hand, the few verses of Dowson's he had heard read out in an upstairs room of the Cheshire Cheese, Fleet Street, that led him to suggest publishing 'the first book of the Rhymers' Club.'

Many of his poems derived their inspiration from his unhappy passion for Adelaide Faltinowicz—or, Missie, as he called her— the daughter of a Soho restaurant-keeper. With his early friend Victor Plarr (author of the charming memoir *Ernest Dowson, Reminiscences 1887-98*, 1914) he planned a joint collection of verse to be entitled *Vine Leaf and Violet*. This project, which dated from 1891, unfortunately miscarried and it was not till 1896 that his first book of poems, *Verses*, appeared with the Leonard Smithers imprint, to be followed the next year by a mannered elegy in dramatic form, *The Pierrot of the Minute*.

These verse-works had been pre-dated by two books of fiction: A *Comedy of Masks*, in collaboration with Arthur Moore (1893), and his own first book, *Dilemmas, Stories and Studies in Sentiment*, published by John Lane in 1895.

As a reader to John Lane, Le Gallienne had advised his employer to publish this collection on the grounds of 'the general delicacy of the treatment.' Although reviews were favourable, royalties after six months amounted only to seven pounds ten shillings. The remaining stories published by him were never gathered together in book form during his lifetime. As Mark Longaker has remarked: "All the tales are subdued in colour . . . even when springtime provides the setting. They are chosen chaste restrained records of suffering, of devotion to an ideal, and unselfishness." This is substantially true, but perhaps it overlooks the strength of that grim authentic *tour-de-force*, *The Dying of Francis Donne* (contributed to the fourth number of *The Savoy*, August 1896, and included in this selection). Two further works barely preceded his death: The novel *Adrian Rime* (1899), a second collaboration with Arthur Moore, and a verse book with five prose-poems, *Decorations* (1899).

After long emotional exile in Brittany, where he fled to avoid the ghost of Adelaide and nurse the remnants of a lung, he returned to England and died at Catford in the small labourer's cottage of his friend Robert Sherard. Collapsing with only a shilling in his pocket, he was none the less given—as Edgar Jepson remarked—'a good funeral—quite a good funeral.'

The main sources of knowledge on his life and work are *The Letters of Ernest Dowson*, edited by Desmond Flower and Henry Maas (1967), and *Ernest Dowson* by Mark Longaker (1945).

THE DYING OF FRANCIS DONNE
A STUDY
Memento homo, quia pulvis es et in pulverem reverteris

I

He had lived so long in the meditation of death, visited it so often in others, studied it with such persistency, with a sentiment in which horror and fascination mingled; but it had always been, as it were, an objective, alien fact, remote from himself and his own life. So that it was in a sudden flash, quite too stupefying to admit in the first instance of terror, that knowledge of his mortality dawned on him. There was absurdity in the idea too.

"I, Francis Donne, thirty-five and some months old, am going to die,' he said to himself; and fantastically he looked at his image in the glass, and sought, but quite vainly, to find some change in it which should account for this incongruity, just as, searching in his analytical habit into the recesses of his own mind, he could find no such alteration of his inner consciousness as would explain or justify his plain conviction. And quickly, with reason and casuistry, he sought to rebut that conviction.

The quickness of his mind—it had never seemed to him so nimble, so exquisite a mechanism of syllogism and deduction—was contraposed against his blind instinct of the would-be self-deceiver, in a conflict to which the latter brought something of desperation, the fierce, agonised desperation of a hunted animal at bay. But piece by piece the chain of evidence was strengthened. The subtle and agile mind of his, with its special knowledge, cut clean through the shrinking protests of instinct, removing them as surely and as remorselessly, he reflected in the image most natural to him, as the keen blade of his surgical knives had removed malignant ulcers.

'I, Francis Donne, am going to die,' he repeated, and, presently, 'I *am going to die soon*; in a few months, in six perhaps, certainly in a year.'

Once more, curiously, but this time with a sense of neutrality, as he had often diagnosed a patient, he turned to the mirror.

Was it his fancy, or, perhaps, only for the vague light that he seemed to discover a strange grey tone about his face?

But he had always been a man of very sallow complexion.

There were a great many little lines, like pen-scratches, scarring the parchment-like skin beneath the keen eyes: doubtless, of late, these had multiplied, become more noticeable, even when his face was in repose.

But, of late, what with his growing practice, his lectures, his writing; all the unceasing labour, which his ambitions entailed, might well have aged him somewhat. That dull, immutable pain, which had first directed his attention from his studies, his investigations, his profession, to his corporal self, the actual Francis Donne, that pain which he would so gladly have called inexplicable, but could explain so precisely, had ceased for the moment. Nerves, fancies! How long it was since he had taken any rest! He had often intended to give himself a holiday, but something had always intervened. But he would do so now, yes, almost immediately; a long, long holiday—he would grudge nothing—somewhere quite out of the way, somewhere, where there was fishing, in Wales, or perhaps in Brittany; that would surely set him right.

And even while he promised himself this necessary relaxation in the immediate future, as he started on his afternoon round, in the background of his mind there lurked the knowledge of its futility; rest, relaxation, all that, at this date, was, as it were, some tardy sacrifice, almost hypocritical, which he offered to powers who might not be propitiated.

Once in his neat brougham, the dull pain began again; but by an effort of will he put it away from him. In the brief interval from house to house—he had some dozen visits to make—he occupied himself with a medical paper, glanced at the notes of a lecture he was giving that evening at a certain Institute on the 'Limitations of Medicine.'

He was very late for dinner, and his man, Bromgrove, greeted him with a certain reproachfulness, in which he traced, or seemed to trace, a half-patronising sense of pity. He reminded himself that on more than one occasion, of late, Bromgrove's manner had perplexed him. He was glad to rebuke the man irritably on some pretext, to dismiss him from the room, and he hurried, without appetite, through the cold or overdone food which was the reward of his tardiness.

His lecture over, he drove out to South Kensington, to attend a reception at the house of a great man—great not only in the scientific world, but also in the world of letters. There was some of the excitement of success in his eyes as he made his way, with smiles and bows, in acknowledgment of many compliments, through the crowded rooms. For Francis Donne's lectures—those of them which were not entirely for the initiated—had grown into the importance of a social function. They had almost succeeded in making science fashionable, clothing its dry bones in a garment of so elegantly literary a pattern. But even in the ranks of the profession it was only the envious, the unsuccessful, who ventured to say that Donne had sacrificed doctrine to popularity, that his science was, in their contemptuous parlance, 'mere literature.'

Yes, he had been very successful, as the world counts success, and his consciousness of this fact, and the influence of the lights, the crowd, the voices, was like absinthe on his tired spirit. He had forgotten, or thought he had forgotten, the phantom of the last few days, the phantom which was surely waiting for him at home.

But he was reminded by a certain piece of news which late in the evening fluttered the now diminished assembly; the quite sudden death of an eminent surgeon, expected there that night, an acquaintance of his own, and more or less of each one of the little, intimate group which tarried to discuss it. With sympathy, with a certain awe, they spoke of him, Donne and others; and both the awe and the sympathy were genuine.

But as he drove home, leaning back in his carriage, in a discouragement, in a lethargy, which was only partly due to physical reaction, he saw visibly underneath their regret—theirs and his own—the triumphant assertion of life, the egoism of instinct. They were sorry, but oh, they were glad! royally glad, that it was another, and not they themselves whom something mysterious had of a sudden snatched away from his busy career, his interests, perhaps from all intelligence; at least, from all the pleasant sensuousness of life, the joy of the visible world, into darkness. And honestly dared not to blame it. How many times had not he, Francis Donne himself, experienced it, that egoistic assertion of life in the presence of the dead—the poor, irremediable dead? . . . And now, he was only good to give it to others.

Latterly, he had been in the habit of subduing sleeplessness with injections of morphia, indeed in infinitesimal quantities. But tonight, although he was more than usually restless and awake, by a strong effort of reasonableness he resisted his impulse to take out the little syringe. The pain was at him again with the same dull and stupid insistence; in its monotony, losing some of the nature of pain and becoming a mere nervous irritation. But he was aware that it would not continue like that. Daily, almost hourly, it would gather strength and cruelty; the moments of respite from it would become rarer, would cease. From a dull pain it would become an acute pain, and then a torture, and then an agony, and then a madness. And in those last days, what peace might be his would be the peace of morphia, so that it was essentian that, for the moment, he should not abuse the drug.

And as he knew that sleep was far away from him, he propped himself up with two pillows, and by the light of a strong reading lamp settled himself to read. He had selected the work of a distinguished German savant upon the cardiac functions, and a short treatise of his own, which was covered with recent annotations, in his crabbed handwriting, upon 'Aneurism of the Heart.' He read avidly, and against his own deductions, once more his instinct raised a vain protest. At last he threw the volumes aside, and lay with his eyes shut, without, however, extinguishing the light. A terrible sense of helplessness overwhelmed him; he was seized with an immense and heartbreaking pity for poor humanity as personified in himself; and for the first time since he had ceased to be a child, he shed puerile tears.

II

The faces of his acquaintance, the faces of the students at his lectures, the faces of Francis Donne's colleagues at the hospital, were altered; were, at least, sensibly altered to his morbid self-consciousness. In everyone whom he encountered, he detected or fancied that he detected, an attitude of evasion, a hypocritical air of ignoring a fact that was obvious and unpleasant. Was it so obvious, then, the hidden horror which he carried incessantly about him? Was his secret, which he would still guard so jealously, become a by-word and an anecdote in his little world? And a great rage consumed him against the inexorable and inscrutable forces which had made him to destroy him; against himself, because of his proper impotence; and, above all, against the living, the millions who would remain when he was no longer, the living, of whom many would regret him (some of them his personality, and more, his skill), because he could see under all the unconscious hypocrisy of their sorrow, the exultant self-satisfaction of their survival.

And with his burning sense of helplessness, of a certain bitter injustice in things, a sense of shame mingled; all the merely physical dishonour of death shaping itself to his sick and morbid fancy into a violent symbol of what was, as it were, an actual *moral* or intellectual dishonour. Was not death, too, inevitable and natural an operation as it was, essentially a process to undergo apart and hide jealously, as much as other natural and ignoble processes of the body?

And the animal, who steals away to an uttermost place in the forest, who gives up his breath in a solitude and hides his dying like a shameful thing,—might he not offer an example that it would be well for the dignity of poor humanity to follow?

Since Death is coming to me, said Francis Donne to himself, let me meet it, a stranger in a strange land, with only strange faces round me and the kind indifference of strangers, instead of the intolerable pity of friends.

III

On the bleak and wave-tormented coast of Finisterre, somewhere between Quiberon and Fouesnant, he reminded himself of a little fishing-village: a few scattered houses (one of them being an *auberge* at which ten years ago he had spent a night), collected round a poor little grey church. Thither Francis Donne went, without leave-takings or explanation, almost secretly, giving but the vaguest indications of the length or direction of his absence. And there for many days he dwelt, in the cottage which he had hired, with one old Breton woman for his sole attendant, in a state of mind which, after all the years of energy, of ambitious labour, was almost peace.

Bleak and grey it had been, when he had visited it of old, in the late autumn; but now the character, the whole colour of the country was changed. It was brilliant with the promise of summer, and the blue Atlantic, which in winter churned with its long crested waves so boisterously below the little white light-house, which warned mariners (alas! so vainly), against the shark-like cruelty of the rocks, now danced and glittered in the sunshine, rippled with feline caresses round the hulls of the fishing-boats whose brown sails floated so idly in the faint air.

Above the village, on a grassy slope, whose green was almost lurid, Francis Donne lay, for many silent hours, looking out at the placid sea, which could yet be so ferocious, at the low violet line of the Island of Groix, which alone interrupted the monotony of sky and ocean.

He had brought many books with him but he read in them rarely; and when physical pain gave him a respite for thought, he thought almost of nothing. His thought was for a long time a lethargy and a blank.

Now and again he spoke with some of the inhabitants. They were a poor and hardy, but a kindly race: fishers and the wives of fishers, whose children would grow up and become fishermen and the wives of fishermen in their turn. Most of them had wrestled with death; it was always so near to them that hardly one of them feared it; they were fatalists, with the grim and resigned fatalism of the poor, of the poor who live with the treachery of the sea.

Francis Donne visited the little cemetery, and counted the innumerable crosses which testified to the havoc which the sea had wrought. Some of the graves were nameless; holding the bodies of strange seamen which the waves had tossed ashore.

'And in a little time I shall lie here,' he said to himself; 'and here as well as elsewhere,' he added with a shrug, assuming, and, for once, almost sincerely, the stoicism of his surroundings, 'and as lief today as tomorrow.'

On the whole, the days were placid; there were even moments when, as though he had actually drunk in renewed vigour from that salt sea air, the creative force of the sun, he was tempted to doubt his grievous knowledge, to make fresh plans for life. But these were fleeting moments, and the reaction from them was terrible. Each day his hold on life was visibly more slender, and the people of the village saw, and with a rough sympathy, which did not offend him, allowed him to perceive that they saw, the rapid growth and the inevitableness of his end.

IV

But if the days were not without their pleasantness, the nights were always horrible—a torture of the body and an agony of the spirit. Sleep was far away, and the brain, which had been lulled till the evening, would awake, would grow electric with life and take strange and abominable flights into the darkness of the pit, into the black night of the unknowable and the unknown.

And interminably, during those nights which seemed eternity, Francis Donne questioned and examined into the nature of that Thing, which stood, a hooded figure beside his bed, with a menacing hand raised to beckon him so peremptorily from all that lay within his consciousness.

He had been all his life absorbed in science; he had dissected, how many bodies; and in what anatomy had he ever found a soul? Yet if his avocations, his absorbing interest in physical phenomena, had made him somewhat a materialist, it had been almost without his consciousness. The sensible, visible world of matter had loomed so large to him, that merely to know that had seemed to him sufficient. All that might conceivably lie outside it, he had, without negation, been content to regard as outside his province.

And now, in his weakness, in the imminence of approaching

dissolution, his purely physical knowledge seemed but a vain possession, and he turned with a passionate interest to what had been said and believed from time immemorial by those who had concentrated their intelligence on that strange essence, which might after all be the essence of one's personality, which might be that sublimated consciousness—the Soul—actually surviving the infamy of the grave?

> Animula, vagula, blandula!
> Hospes comesque corporis,
> Quae nunc abibis in loca?
> Pallidula, rigida, nudula.

Ah, the question! It was a harmony, perhaps (as, who had maintained? whom the Platonic Socrates in the 'Phaedo' had not too successfully refuted), a harmony of life, which was dissolved when life was over? Or, perhaps, as how many metaphysicians had held both before and after a sudden great hope, perhaps too generous to be true, had changed and illuminated, to count-less millions, the inexorable figure of Death—a principle, indeed, immortal, which came and went, passing through many corporal conditions until it was ultimately resolved into the great mind, pervading all things? Perhaps? . . . But what scanty consolation, in all such theories, to the poor body, racked with pain and craving peace, to the tortured spirit of self-consciousness so achingly anxious not to be lost.

And he turned from these speculations to what was, after all, a possibility like the others; the faith of the simple, of these fishers with whom he lived, which was also the faith of his own childhood, which indeed, he had never repudiated, whose practices he had simply discarded, as one discards puerile gar-ments when one comes to man's estate. And he remembered, with the vividness with which, in moments of great anguish, one remembers things long ago familiar, forgotten though they may have been for years, the triumphant declarations of the Church:

Omnes quidem resurgemus, sed nom omnes immutabimur. In momento, in ictu oculi, in novissima tuba: canet enim tuba: et mortui resurgent incorrupti, et nos immutabimur. Oportet enim corruptibile hoc induere immortalitatem. Cum autem mortale hoc induerit immortalitatem tunc fiet sermo qui scriptus est: Absorpta est mors in victoria. Ubi est, mors, victoria tua? Ubi est, mors, stimulus tuus?

Ah, for the certitude of that! of that victorious confutation of the apparent destruction of sense and spirit in a common ruin . . . But it was a possibility like the rest: and had it not more need than the rest to be more than a possibility, if it would be a consolation, in that it promised more? And he gave it up, turning his face to the wall, lay very still, imagining himself already stark and cold, his eyes close, his jaw closely tied (lest the ignoble changes which had come to him should be too ignoble), while he waited until the narrow boards, within which he should lie, had been nailed together, and the bearers were ready to convey him into the corruption which was to be his part.

And as the window-pane grew light with morning, he sank into a drugged, unrestful sleep, from which he would awake some hours later with eyes more sunken and more haggard cheeks. And that was the pattern of many nights.

V

One day he seemed to wake from a night longer and more troubled than usual, a night which had, perhaps, been many nights and days, perhaps even weeks; a night of an ever-increasing agony, in which he was only dimly conscious at rare intervals of what was happening, or of the figures coming and going around his bed: the doctor from a neighbouring town, who had stayed by him unceasingly, easing his paroxysms with the little merciful syringe; the soft, practised hands of a sister of charity about his pillow; even the face of Bromgrove, for whom doubtless he had sent, when he had foreseen the utter helplessness which was at hand.

He opened his eyes, and seemed to discern a few blurred figures against the darkness of the closed shutters through which one broad ray filtered in; but he could not distinguish their faces, and he closed his eyes once more. An immense and ineffable tiredness had come over him that this—*this* was Death; this was the thing against which he had cried and revolted; the horror from which he would have escaped; this utter luxury of physical exhaustion, this calm, this release.

The corporal capacity of smiling had passed from him, but he would fain have smiled.

And for a few minutes of singular mental lucidity, all his life flashed before him in a new relief; his childhood, his adolescence, the people whom he had known; his mother, who had died when he was a boy, of a malady from which, perhaps, a few years later, his skill had saved her; the friend of his youth who had shot himself for so little reason; the girl whom he had loved, but who had not loved him . . . All that was distorted in life was adjusted and justified in the light of his sudden knowledge. *Beati mortui* . . . and then the great tiredness swept over him once more, and a fainter consciousness, in which he could yet just dimly hear, as in a dream, the sound of Latin prayers, and feel the application of the oils upon all the issues and approaches of his wearied sense; then utter unconsciousness, while pulse and heart gradually grew fainter until both ceased. And that was all.

Arthur Morrison
1863-1945

ARTHUR MORRISON was born in the county of Kent, near to the London borders, in 1863.

He began writing as a journalist in the eighteen-eighties and was one of the distinguished team of W. E. Henley's 'young men' (Kipling, Barrie, Stevenson—and even, from time to time, W. B. Yeats) who appeared in the pages of the *National Observer*.

Most of the stories in *Tales of Mean Streets* (1894)—dedicated 'To William Ernest Henley'—had, in fact, appeared in the latter's journal. It was with this collection that Morrison made his name. A Zola-esque exploration of how the other half lives, *Tales of Mean Streets* is not the work of a *Yellow Book* aesthete. Its prose is neither precious nor choice, but has the sterling virtues of speed and strength associated with the writing of what Henry Harland called 'Mr. Henley's truculent Fifth Form.' Provided we are prepared to turn a blind eye to the passing cliché, Morrison is, indeed, a powerful writer. Sociologically, *Tales of Mean Streets* is a work of signal importance; and the author's Introduction to the East End of London ethos, with its 'dismal lack of accent, its sordid uniformity, its utter remoteness from delight,' is full of fascinating 'period' features no longer observable in the nineteen-thirties when the Socialist Realist writers once more took up the proletarian theme.

Tales of Means Streets and *A Child of the Jago* (1898)—Morrison's full-length 'slum' novel—belong to that early pioneering in 'kitchen-sink' fiction which includes Richard Whiting's *No. 5 John Street* (1899), H. W. Nevinson's *Neighbours of*

Ours (1895), and Somerset Maugham's best-seller *Liza of Lambeth* (1897).

Outside his fiction Morrison yielded to at least one aspect of greenery-yallery fashion. He developed a passion for the *japonais* and in 1911 published a comprehensive work in two folio volumes entitled *The Painters of Japan*, and two years later his fine collection of Chinese and Japanese art was acquired by the British Museum.

He was also celebrated in the 'nineties for his detective stories —*Martin Hewitt, Investigator* (1894), *Chronicles of Martin Hewitt* (1895) and *Adventures of Martin Hewitt* (1896)—the leading character of which stories has been described as 'the first detective of conspicuous note to follow in the footsteps of Sherlock Holmes.'

LIZERUNT

I

Lizer's Wooing

Somewhere in the register was written the name Elizabeth Hunt; but seventeen years after the entry the spoken name was Lizerunt. Lizerunt worked at a pickle factory, and appeared abroad in an elaborate and shabby costume, usually supplemented by a white apron. Withal she was something of a beauty. That is to say, her cheeks were very red, her teeth were very large and white, her nose was small and snub, and her fringe was long and shiny; while her face, new-washed, was susceptible of a high polish. Many such girls are married at sixteen, but Lizerunt was belated, and had never a bloke at all.

Billy Chope was a year older than Lizerunt. He wore a billy-cock with a thin brim and a permanent dent in the crown; he had a bobtail coat, with the collar turned up at one side and down at the other as an expression of independence; between his meals he carried his hands in his breeches pockets; and he lived with his mother, who mangled. His conversation with Lizerunt consisted long of perfunctory nods; but great things happened this especial Thursday evening, as Lizerunt, making for home, followed the fading red beyond the furthermost end of Commercial Road. For Billy Chope, slouching in the opposite direction, lurched across the pavement as they met, and taking the nearer hand from his pocket, caught and twisted her arm, bumping her against the wall.

'Garn,' said Lizerunt, greatly pleased: 'le' go!' For she knew that this was love.

'Where yer auf to, Lizer?'

' 'Ome, o' course, cheeky. Le' go'; and she snatched—in vain—at Billy's hat.

Billy let go, and capered in front of her. She feigned to dodge by him, careful not to be too quick, because affairs were developing.

'I say, Lizer,' said Billy, stopping his dance and becoming business-like, 'goin' anywhere Monday?'

'Not along o' you, cheeky: you go 'long o' Beller Dawson, like wot you did Easter.'

'Blow Beller Dawson; she ain't no good. I'm goin' on the Flats. Come?'

Lizerunt, delighted but derisive, ended with a promise to 'see.' The bloke had come at last, and she walked home with the feeling of having taken her degree. She had half assured herself of it two days before, when Sam Cardew threw an orange peel at her, but went away after a little prancing on the pavement. Sam was a smarter fellow than Billy, and earned his own living; probably his attentions were serious; but one must prefer the bird in hand. As for Billy Chope, he went his way, resolved himself to take home what mangling he should find his mother had finished, and stick to the money; also, to get all he could from her by blandishing and bullying: that the jaunt to Wanstead Flats might be adequately done.

There is no other fair like Whit Monday's on Wanstead Flats. Here is a square mile and more of open land where you may howl at large; here is no danger of losing yourself as in Epping Forest; the public-houses are always with you; shows, shies, swings, merry-go-rounds, fried-fish stalls, donkeys are packed closer than on Hampstead Heath; the ladies' tormentors are larger, and their contents smell worse than at any other fair. Also, you may be drunk and disorderly without being locked up —for the stations won't hold everybody—and when all else has palled, you may set fire to the turf. Hereinto Billy and Lizerunt projected themselves from the doors of the Holly Tree on Whit Monday morning. But through hours on hours of fried fish and half-pints both were conscious of a deficiency. For the hat of Lizerunt was brown and old; plush it was not, and its feather was a mere foot long and of a very rusty black. Now, it is not decent for a factory girl from Limehouse to go bank-holidaying under any but a hat of plush, very high in the crown, of a wild blue or a wilder green, and carrying withal an ostrich feather, pink or scarlet or what not; a feather that springs from the fore-part, climbs the crown, and drops as far down the shoulders as may be. Lizerunt knew this, and, had she had no bloke, would have stayed at home. But a chance is a chance. As it was, only another such hapless girl could measure her bitter envy of the feathers about her, or would so joyfully have given an ear for the proper splendour. Billy, too, had a vague impression, muddled by but not drowned in half-pints, that some degree of plush was condign to the occasion and to his own expenditure. Still, there was no quarrel; and the pair walked and ran with arms about each other's necks; and Lizerunt thumped her bloke on the back at proper intervals; so that the affair went regularly on the whole : although, in view of Lizerunt's shortcomings, Billy did not insist on the customary exchange of hats.

Everything, I say, went well and well enough until Billy bought a ladies' tormentor and began to squirt it at Lizerunt. For then Lizerunt went scampering madly, with piercing shrieks, until her bloke was left some little way behind, and Sam Cardew, turning up at that moment and seeing her running alone in the crowd, threw his arms about her waist and swung her round him again and again, as he floundered gallantly this way and that, among the shies and the hokey-pokey barrows.

' 'Ullo, Lizer! Where *are* y' a-comin' to? If I 'adn't laid 'old o' ye—!' But here Billy Chope arrived to demand what the 'ell Sam Cardew was doing with his gal. Now Sam was ever readier for a fight than Billy was; but the sum of Billy's half-pints was large: wherefore the fight began. On the skirt of an hilarious ring Lizerunt, after some small outcry, triumphed aloud. Four days before, she had no bloke; and here she stood with two, and those two fighting for her! Here in the public gaze, on the Flats! For almost five minutes she was Helen of Troy.

And in much less time Billy tasted repentance. The haze of half-pints was dispelled, and some teeth went with it. Presently, whimpering and with a bloody muzzle, he rose and made a running kick at the other. Then, being thwarted in a bolt, he flung himself down; and it was like to go hard with him at the hands of the crowd. Punch you may on Wanstead Flats, but execration and worse is your portion if you kick anybody except your wife. But, as the ring closed, the helmets of two policemen were seen to be working in over the surrounding heads, and Sam Cardew, quickly assuming his coat, turned away with such an air of blamelessness as is practicable with a damaged eye; while Billy went off unheeded in an opposite direction.

Lizerunt and her new bloke went the routine of half-pints and merry-go-rounds, and were soon on right thumping terms; and Lizerunt was as well satisfied with the issue as she was proud of the adventure. Billy was all very well; but Sam was better. She resolved to draw him for a feathered hat before next bank holiday. So the sun went down on her and her bloke hanging on each other's necks and straggling towards the Romford Road with shouts and choruses. The rest was tram-car, Bow Music Hall, half-pints, and darkness.

Billy took home his wounds, and his mother, having moved his wrath by asking their origin, sought refuge with a neighbour. He accomplished his revenge in two instalments. Two nights later Lizerunt was going with a jug of beer, when somebody sprang from a dark corner, landed her under the ear, knocked her sprawling; and made off to the sound of her lamentations. She did not see who it was, but she knew; and next day Sam Cardew was swearing he'd break Billy's back. He did not, however, for that same evening a gang of seven or eight fell on him with sticks and belts. (They were Causeway chaps, while Sam was a Brady's Laner, which would have been reason enough by itself, even if Billy Chope had not been one of them.) Sam did his best for a burst through and a run, but they pulled and battered him down; and they kicked him about the head, and they kicked him about the belly; and they took to their heels when he was speechless and still.

He lay at home for near four weeks, and when he stood up again it was in many bandages. Lizerunt came often to his bedside, and twice she brought an orange. On these occasions there was much talk of vengeance. But the weeks went on. It was a month since Sam had left his bed; and Lizerunt was getting a little tired of bandages. Also, she had begun to doubt and to consider bank holiday—scarce a fortnight off. For Sam was stone broke, and a plush hat was farther away than ever. And all through the later of these weeks Billy Chope was harder than ever on his mother, and she, well knowing that if he helped her by taking home he would pocket the money at the other end, had taken to finishing and delivering in his absence, and, threats failing to get at the money, Billy Chope was impelled to punch her head and gripe her by the throat.

There was a milliner's window, with a show of nothing but fashionable plush-and-feather hats, and Lizerunt was lingering hereabouts one evening; when someone took her by the waist, and someone said, 'Which d'ye like, Lizer? The yuller un?'

Lizerunt turned and saw that it was Billy. She pulled herself away, and backed off, sullen and distrustful. 'Garn,' she said.

'Straight,' said Billy, 'I'll sport ye one. . . . No kid, I will.'

'Garn,' said Lizerunt once more, 'Wot ye gittin' at now?'

But presently, being convinced that bashing wasn't in it, she approached less guardedly; and she went away with a paper bag and the reddest of all the plushes and the bluest of all the feathers; a hat that challenged all the Flats the next bank holiday, a hat for which no girl need have hesitated to sell her soul. As for Billy, why, he was as good as another; and you can't have everything; and Sam Cardew, with his bandages and his grunts and groans, was no great catch after all.

This was the wooing of Lizerunt: for in a few months she and

Billy married under the blessing of a benignant rector, who periodically set aside a day for free weddings, and, on principle, encouraged early matrimony. And they lived with Billy's mother.

II

Lizer's First

When Billy Chope married Lizerunt there was a small rejoicing. There was no wedding-party; because it was considered that what there might be to drink would be better in the family. Lizerunt's father was not, and her mother felt no interest in the affair; not having seen her daughter for a year, and happening, at the time, to have a month's engagement in respect of a drunk and disorderly. So that there were but three of them; and Billy Chope got exceedingly tipsy early in the day; and in the evening his bride bawled a continual chorus, while his mother, influenced by that unwonted quartern of gin the occasion sanctioned, wept dismally over her boy, who was much too far gone to resent it.

His was the chief reason for rejoicing. For Lizerunt had always been able to extract ten shillings a week from the pickle factory, and it was to be presumed that as Lizer Chope her earning capacity would not diminish; and the wages would make a very respectable addition to the precarious revenue, depending on the mangle, that Billy extorted from his mother. As for Lizer, she was married. That was the considerable thing; for she was but a few months short of eighteen, and that, as you know, is a little late.

Of course there were quarrels very soon; for the new Mrs. Chope, less submissive at first than her mother-in-law, took a little breaking in, and a liberal renewal of the manual treatment once applied in her courting days. But the quarrels between the women were comforting to Billy: a diversion and a source of better service.

As soon as might be Lizer took the way of womankind. This circumstance brought an unexpected half-crown from the evangelical rector who had married the couple gratis; for recognising Billy in the street by accident, and being told of Mrs.

Chope's prospects, as well as that Billy was out of work (a fact undeniable), he reflected that his principles did on occasion lead to discomfort of a material sort. And Billy, to whose comprehension the half-crown opened a new field of receipt, would doubtless have long remained a client of the rector, had not that zealot hastened to discover a vacancy for a warehouse porter, the offer of presentation whereunto alienated Billy Chope for ever. But there were meetings and demonstrations of the Unemployed; and it was said that shillings had been given away; and, as being at a meeting in a street was at least amusing as being in a street where there was no meeting, Billy often went, on the off chance. But his lot was chiefly disappointment: wherefore he became more especially careful to furnish himself ere he left home.

For certain weeks cash came less freely than ever from the two women. Lizer spoke of providing for the necessities of the expected child, a manifestly absurd procedure, as Billy pointed out, since, if they were unable to clothe or feed it, the duty would fall on its grandmother. That was law, and nobody could get over it. But even with this argument, a shilling cost him many more demands and threats than it had used, and a deal more general trouble.

At last Lizer ceased from going to the pickle factory, and could not even help Billy's mother at the mangle for long. This lasted for near a week, when Billy, rising at ten with a bad mouth, resolved to stand no nonsense, and demanded two shillings.

'Two bob? Wot for?' Lizer asked.

' 'Cos I want it. None o' yer lip.'

'Aint got it,' said Lizer sulkily.

'That's a bleed'n' lie.'

'Lie yerself.'

'I'll break y'in 'arves, ye blasted 'eifer!' He ran at her throat and forced her back over a chair. 'I'll pull yer face auf! If y' don't give me the money, gawblimy, I'll do for you!'

Lizer strained and squalled. 'Le' go! You'll kill me an' the kid too!' she grunted hoarsely. Billy's mother ran in and threw her arms about him, dragging him away. 'Don't Billy,' she said, in terror. 'Don't Billy—not now! You'll get in trouble. Come away! She might go auf, an' you'd get in trouble!'

Billy Chope flung his wife over and turned to his mother. 'Take yer 'ands auf me,' he said: 'go on, or I'll gi' ye somethin' for yerself.' And he punched her in the breast by way of illustration.

'You shall 'ave what I've got, Billy, if it's money,' the mother said. 'But don't go an' git yerself in trouble, don't. Will a shillin' do?'

'No, it won't. Think I'm a bloomin' kid? I mean 'avin two bob this mornin'.'

'I was a'keepin' it for the rent, Billy, but——'

'Yus; think o' the bleed'n' lan'lord 'fore me, don't ye?' And he pocketed the two shillings. 'I ain't settled with you yut, my gal,' he added to Lizer; 'mikin' about at 'ome an' 'idin' money. You wait a bit.'

Lizer climbed into an erect position, and, gravid and slow, had got as far as the passage. Mistaking this for a safe distance, she replied with defiant railings. Billy made for her with a kick that laid her on the lower stairs, and, swinging his legs round his mother as she obstructed him, entreating him not to get in trouble, he attempted to kick again in a more telling spot. But a movement among the family upstairs and a tap at the door hinted of interference, and he took himself off.

Lizer lay doubled up on the stairs, howling: but her only articulate cry was,—'Gawd 'elp me, it's comin'!'

Billy went to the meeting of the Unemployed, and cheered a proposal to storm the Tower of London. But he did not join the procession following a man with a handkerchief on a stick, who promised destruction to every policeman in his path: for he knew the fate of such processions.

III

A Change of Circumstances

Lizer was some months short of twenty-one when her third child was born. The pickle factory had discarded her some time before, and since that her trade had consisted in odd jobs of charing. Odd jobs of charing have a shade the better of a pickle factory in the matter of respectability, but they are precarious, and they are worse paid at that. In the East End they are sporadic and few. Moreover, it is in the household where paid help is a rarity that the bitterness of servitude is felt. Also, the uncertainty and irregularity of the returns were a trouble to Billy Chope. He was never sure of having got them all. It might be ninepence, or a shilling, or eighteenpence. Once or twice, to his knowledge, it had been half-a-crown, from a chance job at a doctor's or a parson's, and once it was three shillings. That it might be half-a-crown or three shillings again, and that some of it was being kept back, was ever the suspicion evoked by Lizer's evening homing. Plainly, with these fluctuating and uncertain revenues, more bashing than ever was needed to ensure the extraction of the last copper; empty-handedness called for bashing on its own account; so that it was often Lizer's hap to be refused a job because of a black eye.

Lizer's self was scarcely what it had been. The red of her cheeks, once bounded only by the eyes and the mouth, had shrunk to a spot in the depth of each hollow; gaps had been driven in her big white teeth; even the snub nose had run to a point, and the fringe hung dry and ragged, while the bodily outline was as a sack's. At home, the children lay in her arms or tumbled at her heels, puling and foul. Whenever she was near it, there was the mangle to be turned; for lately Billy's mother had exhibited a strange weakness, sometimes collapsing with a gasp in the act of brisk or prolonged exertion, and often leaning on whatever stood hard by and grasping at her side. This ailment she treated, when she had twopence, in such terms as made her smell of gin and peppermint; and more than once this circumstance had inflamed the breast of Billy her son, who was morally angered by this boozing away of money that should have been his.

Lizer's youngest, being seven or eight months old, was mostly taking care of itself, when Billy made a welcome discovery after a hard and pinching day. The night was full of blinding wet, and the rain beat on the window as on a drum. Billy sat over a small fire in the front room smoking his pipe, while his mother folded clothes for delivery. He stamped twice on the hearth, and then, drawing off his boot, he felt inside it. It was a nail. The

VII. HUBERT CRACKANTHORPE

poker-head made a good anvil, and, looking about for a hammer, Billy bethought him of a brick from the mangle. He rose, and, lifting the lid of the weight-box, groped about among the clinkers and the other ballast till he came upon a small but rather heavy paper parcel. ' 'Ere—wot's this?' he said, and pulled it out.

His mother, whose back had been turned, hastened across the room, hand to breast (it had got to be her habit). 'What is it, Billy?' she said. 'Not that: there's nothing there. I'll get anything you want, Billy.' And she made a nervous catch at the screw of paper. But Billy fended her off, and tore the package open. It was money, arranged in little columns of farthings, halfpence, and threepenny pieces, with a few sixpences, a shilling or two, and a single half-sovereign. 'O.' said Billy, 'this is the game, is it?—'idin' money in the mangle! Got any more?' And he hastily turned the brickbats.

'No, Billy, don't take that—don't!' implored his mother. 'There'll be some money for them things when they go 'ome—'ave that. I'm savin' it, Billy, for something partic'ler: s'elp me Gawd, I am, Billy."

'Yus,' replied Billy, raking diligently among the clinkers, 'savin' it for a good ol' booze. An' now you won't 'ave one. Bleedin' nice thing, 'idin' money away from yer own son!'

'It ain't for that, Billy—s'elp me, it ain't; it's case anythink 'appens to me. On'y to put me away decent, Billy, that's all. We never know, an' you'll be glad of it t'elp bury me if I should go any time——'

'I'll be glad of it now,' answered Billy, who had it in his pocket; an I've got it. You ain't a dyin' sort, *you* ain't; an' if you was, the parish 'ud soon tuck *you* up. P'raps you'll be straighter about money after this.'

'Let me 'ave *some*, then—you can't want it all. Give me some, an' then 'ave the money for the things. There's ten dozen and seven, and you can take 'em yerself if ye like.'

'Wot—in this 'ere rain? Not me? I bet I'd 'ave the money if I wanted it without that. 'Ere—change these 'ere fardens at the draper's wen you go out: there's two bob's worth an' a penn'orth; I don't want to bust my pockets wi' them.'

While they spoke Lizer had come in from the back room. But

she said nothing: she rather busied herself with a child she had in her arms. When Billy's mother, despondent and tearful, had tramped out into the rain with a pile of clothes in an oilcloth wrapper, she said sulkily, without looking up, 'You might 'a' let 'er kep' that; you git all you want.'

At another time this remonstrance would have provoked active hostilities; but now, with the money about him, Billy was complacently disposed. 'You shut yer 'ead,' he said, 'I got this, any'ow. She can make it up out o' my rent if she likes.' This last remark was a joke, and he chuckled as he made it. For Billy's rent was a simple fiction, devised, on the suggestion of a smart canvasser, to give him the parliamentary vote that made him one of the People.

That night Billy and Lizer slept, as usual, in the bed in the back room, where the two younger children also were. Billy's mother made a bedstead nightly with three chairs and an old trunk in the front room by the mangle, and the eldest child lay in a floor-bed near her. Early in the morning Lizer awoke at a sudden outcry of the little creature. He clawed at the handle till he opened the door, and came staggering and tumbling into the room with screams of terror. 'Wring 'is blasted neck,' his father grunted sleepily. 'Wot's the kid 'owlin' for?'

'I's 'f'aid o' g'anny—I's 'f'aid o' g'anny!' was all the child could say; and when he had said it, he fell to screaming once more.

Lizer rose and went to the next room; and straightway came a scream from her also. 'O—O—Billy! Billy! O my Gawd! Billy come 'ere!'

And Billy, fully startled, followed in Lizer's wake. He blundered in, rubbing his eyes, and saw.

Stark on her back in the huddled bed of old wrappers and shawls lay his mother. The outline of her poor face—strained in an upward stare of painful surprise—stood sharp and meagre against the black of the grate beyond. But the muddy old skin was white, and looked cleaner than its wont, and many of the wrinkles were gone.

Billy Chope, half-way across the floor, recoiled from the corpse, and glared at it pallidly from the doorway.

'Good Gawd!' he croaked faintly, 'is she dead?'

Seized by a fit of shuddering breaths, Lizer sank on the floor, and, with her head across the body, presently broke into a storm of hysterical blubbering, while Billy, white and dazed, dressed hurriedly and got out of the house.

He was at home as little as might be until the coroner's officer carried away the body two days later. When he came for his meals, he sat doubtful and querulous in the matter of the front room door's being shut. The dead once clear away, however, he resumed his faculties, and clearly saw that here was a bad change for the worse. There was the mangle, but who was to work it? If Lizer did, there would be no more charing jobs—a clear loss of one-third of his income. And it was not at all certain that the people who had given their mangling to his mother would give it to Lizer. Indeed, it was pretty sure that many would not, because mangling is a thing given by preference to widows, and many widows of the neighbourhood were perpetually competing for it. Widows, moreover, had the first call in most odd jobs whereunto Lizer might turn her hand: an injustice whereon Billy meditated with bitterness.

The inquest was formal and unremarked, the medical officer having no difficulty in certifying a natural death from heart disease. The bright idea of a collection among the jury, which Billy communicated, with pitiful representations, to the coroner's officer, was brutally swept aside by that functionary, made cunning by much experience. So the inquest brought him naught save disappointment and a sense of injury. . . .

The mangling orders fell away as suddenly and completely as he had feared: they were duly absorbed among the local widows. Neglect the children as Lizer might, she could no longer leave them as she had done. Things, then, were bad with Billy, and neither threats nor thumps could evoke a shilling now.

It was more than Billy could bear: so that, ' 'Ere,' he said one night, 'I've 'ad enough o' this. You go and get some money; go on.'

'Go an' git it?' replied Lizer. 'O yus. That's easy, ain't it? "Go an' git it," says you. 'Ow?'

'Any'ow—I don' care. Go on.'

'Wy,' replied Lizer, looking up with wide eyes, 'd'ye think I can go an' pick it up in the street?'

'Course you can. Plenty others does, don't they?'

'Gawd, Billy . . . wot d'ye mean?'

'Wot I say; plenty others does it. Go on—you ain't so bleed'n' innocent as all that. Go an' see Sam Cardew. Go on—'ook it.'

Lizer, who had been kneeling at the child's floor-bed, rose to her feet, pale faced and bright of eye.

'Stow kiddin', Billy,' she said. 'You don't mean that. I'll go round to the fact'ry in the mornin'; p'raps they'll take me on temp'ry.'

'Damn the fact'ry.'

He pushed her into the passage. 'Go on—you git me some money, if you don't want yer bleed'n' 'ead knocked auf.'

There was a scuffle in the dark passage, with certain blows, a few broken words, and a sob. Then, the door slammed and Lizer Chope was in the windy street.

George Gissing
1857-1903

GEORGE ROBERT GISSING was born at Wakefield in York-
shire on November 22, 1857, the son of a pharmaceutical
chemist who married a solicitor's daughter. Gissing was haunted
throughout his life by the demon respectability. He had been
born just a little higher, or a little lower in the social scale, he
might have eluded this devitalizing fetish.

At school he proved a brilliant scholar. After attending a
Quaker establishment in Worcestershire, he proceeded to Owen
College, Manchester, where prizes and scholarships showered
down upon him.

Unfortunately, he formed a relationship with a young woman
of the streets; and, seeking to set her up and reform her, he
appropriated certain college monies. After serving a prison sentence, he was sent to America by his friends. He worked as a
tutor and gas-fitter in Boston; and when his funds ran out, nearly
starved in Chicago. It was there, *faux de mieux,* that he turned
to writing, contributing to the *Chicago Tribune* a number of
tales only reprinted in book form as *Brownie* in 1931.

On his return from the States, he took up with the young
woman, Marianne Harrison, through whom he had ruined his
college career. Their marriage was not a success, and she died
drink-sodden and diseased. His second marriage with a servant
girl, Edith Underwood, whom he picked up in Regent's Park,
proved no more of a blessing. They were joined matrimonially
in 1891, but parted for good in 1897. It was then that Gissing
encountered the only woman who brought him happiness—
Gabrielle Fleury, a French woman of the intellectual bourgeoise,
who approached him on the question of translating his work.

Leaving England with her, he contracted a suppositious (since bigamous) marriage on the Continent.

His last years were fruitful ones for him in that he was doing the work he wished to do. Commissioned by a publisher, he wrote on the author who perhaps meant most to him. *Charles Dickens: A Critical Study* (1898) is a work of discriminating enthusiasm, suggesting that Gissing's literary roots—for all his admiration for Balzac—are indisputably, parochially English. There was one important exception to this. If English fiction was his choice when it came to the modern world, when it came to the world of the past it was Graeco-Roman culture which counted. 'Why, my dear fellow,' he once remarked to Morley Roberts, an old college friend, 'do you know there are actually miserable men who do not know—who have never heard of—the minuter differences between Dochmiacs and Antipasts!'

Nor was Gissing's zest for the Classical world limited to a nice sense of distinction between the Greek metres. A late holiday in the Mediterranean resulted in the travel book *By the Ionian Sea: Notes of a Ramble in Southern Italy* (1901), and when he died in 1903, he was 'past the middle' of his 'sixth-century story' *Veranilda*, published posthumously in 1904.

G. W. Stonier brilliantly christened him 'the English Gorky, with butterfly collar.' Both parts of this contradictory description are important. In pursuing the annals of the unlucky, deprived, dispossessed, and *déclassé*, Gissing is very much doing the work of the great Russian But, equally, in his fastidious idealism, his civil-service-like pendantry, his temperamental snobbishness ('I hate low, uneducated people! I hate them worse than the filthiest vermin! . . . They ought to be swept off the face of the earth!' he makes one of his characters expostulate), and in his narrow propriety, he is, indeed, the realist 'with butterfly collar.' His semi-autobiography, *The Private Papers of Henry Rycroft* (1908), is commonly held to be his best work yet readers, unbefogged by the maudlin zenophobia of the work as a whole, must surely smile at the following culinary dictum of prim grey Ryecroft : 'Talking of vegetables, can the inhabited globe offer anything to vie with the English potato just steamed?' That this dim grey bible of defeat, masquerading as a Gospel of

Moderation, should have been almost instantly elevated to the status of an English classic is an interesting reflection on the reading habits of our middle classes.

All of Gissing's significant work was done by him *against the grain* of his natural inclinations. As A. C. Ward well remarks, 'the dominant themes in his novels are Money, Marriage, and the Masses,' and these themes are to be met with most memorably in *New Grub Street* (1891) and *Odd Women* (1893).

Although he wrote and published many short stories in the 'nineties, only one book of them appeared in those years, *Human Odds and Ends* (1898). *The House of Cobwebs* (1906) and *A Victim of Circumstances* (1927) are two important posthumous collections.

The best brief pronouncement on Gissing is that which G. W. Stonier delivered in the World Classics edition *New Grub Street* (1958): 'He is the moralist of a rainy day. How ugly everything is, how dull, how it pours; and with what wretched patience do houses outstare one another and people pull their umbrellas lower!—and getting darker!—really we heardly know how we put up with it. It! There is the big, hopeless grudge.'

The three main sources of our knowledge on Gissing are *The Private Life of Henry Maitland* by Morley Richards (1912), a biography in the form of a novel; *George Gissing: A Critical Study* by Frank Swinnerton (1923); and *George Gissing: Grave Comedian* by M. C. Donnelly (1954).

COMRADES IN ARMS

Luncheon hour was past, and the tide of guests had begun to ebb. From his cushioned corner, his familiar seat in the restaurant, Wilfrid Langley kept an observant eye upon chatting groups and silent solitaries who still lingered at the tables near him. In this quiet half-hour, whilst smoking a cigarette and enjoying his modest claret, he caught the flitting suggestion of many a story, sketch, gossipy paper. A woman's laugh, a man's surly visage, couples oddly assorted, scraps of dialogue heard amid the confused noises—everywhere the elements of drama, to be fused and united in his brain. Success had multiplied his powers a hundredfold; success and the comforts that came with it—savoury meats, wine, companionship. No one was dependent upon him; no one restrained his liberty; he lived where he chose, and how he chose. And for all that—his age fell short of thirty—something seemed to him amiss in the bounty of the gods.

A figure was moving in his direction; he looked up from a moment's reverie, to see a woman seat herself at the opposite side of his table. A laugh of pleased recognition; a clasp of hands.

'Thought I might find you here,' said Miss Childerstone. She turned to the waiter. 'Roast mutton—potatoes—bread. And—soda-water.'

'Soda!' Langley exclaimed in surprise. 'That's where you women make a mistake. You need a stimulant.'

'Thanks, old man; I am better acquainted with my needs than you are. Here's something for you.'

She threw an evening paper at him saying, 'Page seven.' Langley opened it, and his eyes sparkled with pleasure. A notice of his new book; three-quarters of a column; high laudation, as he saw immediately.

'Yours?' he asked.

'Take it without questions, and be thankful you're not slated.'

'It is yours. Don't I know the fine Roman hand? Irony in the first sentence.' He read in silence for a few minutes, then gave his companion a look of warm gratitude. 'You're a good sort.'

Miss Childerstone was drinking deep of her soda-water. Neither plain nor pretty, she had noticeable features, a keen good-humoured eye, an air of self-possession and alertness. She dressed well, with a view to the fitness of things. Her years were in the fourth decade.

She began to eat, but, it seemed, with little appetite.

'I've had a headache since yesterday. I should like to go to bed and lie there for a week. But there's my stuff for Tomlinson. Don't feel like it, I tell you.'

'I see now that you look out of sorts. Yes, you look bad. I

tell you what—couldn't I scrawl something that would do for Tomlinson?'

She looked at him, and smiled.

'I dare say you could. Any rubbish you wanted to shoot somewhere. The truth is, I don't think I'm equal to it.—No, I can't eat. Thump! thump! on the back of the head.'

They discussed the literary business in question, and Langley undertook to supply the article due from his friend to a weekly paper. It must be posted tonight. Miss Childerstone, abandoning the scarcely touched food, rested her head upon her hands for a few moments.

'I've done something I'm proud of,' she said at length, 'and I may as well have the satisfaction of telling you. My sister has just gone off to Natal, to be married there. I provided her outfit, paid her passage, and gave her fifty pounds. All off my own bat, old boy! Not bad, is it?'

'Your sister? Why, you never told me she was going to be married.'

'No. It wasn't quite certain—all along. Two years ago she engaged herself to a man who was going out yonder—a man of no means, and not quite up to her mark, I thought. (I must eat something; I'll try the potatoes.) A very decent sort of fellow—handsome, honest. Well, she's been in doubt, off and on. (Are these potatoes bad? Or is it my taste that's out of order?) She stuck to her teaching, poor girl, and had a pretty dull time of it. In the end, I made up my mind that she'd better go and get married. There couldn't be any doubt about the man's making her a good husband; I read his letters, and liked them. Good, plodding, soft-hearted sort of creature; not at all a bad husband for Cissy. Better than the beastly teaching, anyway. So she's gone.'

'That's a disappointment to me,' said Langley. 'I hoped to meet her some day. And you promised I should.'

'Yes—but I altered my mind.'

'What do you mean? You didn't wish me to meet her?'

'The probability was you'd have unsettled her. She never knew a man of your sort. She might have fallen in love with you.'

Miss Childerstone spoke in a matter-of-fact voice; her smile could not have been less ambiguous. Langley, gazing at her with surprise, exclaimed at length:

'Well? And why not?

'Why not? Oh, my dear boy, I would do a good deal for you, but I couldn't indulge your vanity in that direction. I'm fond of my little sister.'

'Of course you are. And why shouldn't I have been? Describe her to me.'

'Fair—pretty—five-and-twenty. An old-fashioned girl, with all sorts of beliefs that would exasperate you. The gentlest creature! Vastly too patient, too good. Will make an ideal housewife and mother.'

Langley smote the table with his fist.

'But you're describing the very girl I want to find, and can't! How absurdly you have behaved! And she's gone to the end of the earth to marry a man she doesn't care about—this is too ridiculous! Why, I want to marry, and the difficulty is to find such a girl as this. I shall never forgive you.'

His companion looked searchingly at him, with mocking lips.

'Bosh!' she replied.

'It isn't! I'm desperately serious.'

'In any case, I wouldn't have let her marry you. You've been too frank with me. I know you too well. Of course, I like you, because you're likeable—as a comrade-in-arms. We've fought the battle together, and done each other a good turn now and then. But you're very young, you know. You have money in your pocket for the first time, and—by-the-bye, I heard about that supper at Romano's. How much did it cost you?'

'Oh, ten or fifteen pounds—I've forgotten.'

He said it with a touch of bravado, his smile betraying pleasure that the exploit had become known.

'Precisely. And your Dulcinea of the footlights—Totty, Lotty —what's her name?—was there. My dear boy, you mustn't marry for another ten years. It would spoil you. You're only just beginning to look round the world. Go ahead; enjoy yourself; see things; but don't think of marrying.'

'I think of it perpetually.'

The other moved an impatient hand.

'I can't talk. My head is terrible. I must go home.'

'You've been working yourself to death to provide for your sister. And very likely made her miserable after all.'

'Mind your own business. Where's the waiter? Call him, will you? I'm turning blind and deaf, and I don't know what.'

'I shall take you home,' said Langley, rising.

'You can put me in a cab, if you like.'

She looked very ill, and Langley kept glancing at her with uneasiness as they went together from the restaurant. His resolve to see her safely home was not opposed. In the hansom they exchanged few words, but Langley repeated his promise to do the bit of literary work for her editor. 'Tomorrow morning,' he added, 'I shall come and ask how you are. Send for a doctor if you're no better by night.'

His own rooms were in the same district, that of Regent's Park, and after leaving Miss Childerstone he went off to perform the task he had undertaken—no difficult matter. Though it was holiday time with him just now, he spent the whole evening in solitude, more discontented than usual. The post brought him news that the first edition of his book was sold out. Satisfactory, but it gave him no particular delight. He had grown used to think of himself as one of the young men whom the public run after, and his rooted contempt for the public made him suspicious of his own merits. Was he not becoming vulgarised, even personally? That supper the other night, in honour of the third-rate actress, when everyone got more or less drunk—pah! These dreary lodgings, which no expenditure could make homelike. A home—that was what he wanted. Confound Miss Childerstone! That sister of her, now steaming away to Natal——

At twelve o'clock next day he called on his friend, and was asked to wait in her sitting-room. He had been here only once or twice; today the room seemed more uncomfortable than on former occasions, and Langley wondered how a woman could live amid such surroundings. But was Miss Childerstone to be judged as a woman? For seven or eight years she had battled in the world of journalism, and with a kind of success which seemed to argue manlike qualities. Since he had known her, these last three years, she seemed to have been growing less feminine. At first he had thought of her with the special interest which arises from difference of sex; now he rarely, if ever, did so. He liked her, admired her, and could imagine her, in more natural circumstances, a charming woman. If, as was probable, her sister resembled her in all the good points——

She came in, and her appearance startled him. She wore a dressing-gown; her hair was tossed into some sort of order; illness unmistakable blanched her face. Without offering to shake hands, she tumbled on to the nearest chair.

'Why on earth did you get up?' Langley exclaimed. 'Have you seen a doctor?'

'No; but I think you shall go and fetch someone,' she answered, hoarsely and faintly. 'Did you send the stuff to Tomlinson?'

'Oh yes, and forged your signature. Go back to bed; I'll——'

'Wait a minute. I want to ask you—I haven't any money——'

The change from her wonted vigour of speech and bearing was very painful to the young man. Money. Why, his purse was hers. In his pocket he had only a few sovereigns, but he would go to the bank straightway.

'Three or four pounds will do,' she replied. 'I don't know anyone else I care to ask. Borrowing isn't in my line, you know. I could sell or pawn some things—but I haven't the strength to get about.'

Langley stepped towards her and put coins into her hand.

'What is it?' he asked, gravely. 'A fever of some kind?'

'I'm not feverish—at least I don't think so. Fearful head. Look chalky, don't I?'

'You do. Go back to bed at once, and leave things to me.'

'You're a good fellow, Wilfrid.'

'Pooh!'

'I feel so wretchedly weak—and I *hate* to feel weak—I——'

She suddenly turned her head away; and Langley was horrified to hear her sob. He moved for a moment about the room, as if in search of something; but it only served to hide his embarrassment. Then Miss Childerstone stood up, and went quickly away. In half an hour's time the necessary assistance had been procured. Nervous collapse, said the man of medicine; overwork, and so on. Langley, finding that no one in the house could act as bedside attendant, obtained the services of a nurse. He did not see his friend again, but had a message from her that she was 'all right;' he might call the next day if he liked.

He paid the call as early as ten o'clock, and had a talk with the nurse, who could give but an indifferent report.

'If I write a few lines for her, can she read them?' he asked.

Yes, she could read a letter. So Langley sat down at the table, and tried to find something to say. To his surprise, he wrote with the utmost difficulty; words would not come. 'Dear Miss Childerstone—I feel sure that a little rest and nursing will soon——' Oh, that was insufferably childish. He bit his pen, and stared at the books before him : novels and plays, heaped newspapers, a volume or two of an encyclopædia, annuals, and dictionaries. She had no instinct of order; she lived from day to day, from hand to mouth. Her education must be very defective. On the moral side, no doubt, she was sound enough, but a woman should have domestic virtues.

What was he doing? Abusing his friend just when she lay helpless, and this defeat of her splendid strength the result of toil on a sister's behalf! He tore the sheet of paper and began anew. 'Dear Bertha'—why not? She now and then called him 'Wilfrid'—'don't trouble your head about anything. I have nothing to do, and to look after you will give me pleasure. Is there anyone you would like to communicate with? Consider me absolutely at your service—time, money, anything. I will call morning and evening. Cheer up, dear old chum! You must go away as soon as possible; I'll get lodgings for you.'

And so on, over another page, in the hearty comrade tone which they always used to each other. The nurse, summoned by a light tap, handed this note to her patient, and in a few minutes she brought back a scrap of paper, on which was feebly scrawled in pencil, 'Good old boy. All right.'

It was the last he saw of Bertha Childerstone's handwriting for more than a month. Daily he called twice. What the nurse, doctor, and landlady thought of his relations with the invalid he would not trouble to conjecture. He met all current expenses, which amounted to not very much. And the result of it was that the sick woman became an almost exclusive subject of his thoughts; his longing to speak again with her grew immense.

One day in July, as he stepped as usual into the parlour, thinking to wait there for the nurse, his eye fell upon a figure sitting in the sunlight. A pale, thin face, which he scarcely recognised, greeted him with a smile, and a meagre hand was held out to him.

'Up? Oh, that's brave!'

He hurried forward and clasped her hand tightly. They gazed at each other. Langley felt a thrill in his blood, a dimness about his eyes, and before he knew what he was doing he had given and received a kiss.

'No harm,' said Miss Childerstone, laughing with a look of confusion. '*Honi soit qui mal y pense!*'

But the young man could not recover himself. He was kneeling by the chair in which she reclined, and still kept her hand, whilst he quivered as if with fever.

'I'm so glad—I wanted so to see you—Bertha——'

'Hush! Don't be sentimental, old man. It's all right.'

He pressed her hand to his lips. She abandoned it for a moment, then firmly drew it back.

'Tell me all the news.'

'I know of nothing, except that I——'

He had lost his head. Bertha seemed to him now not only a woman, but beautiful and sweet and an object of passionate desire. He touched her hair, and stammered incoherencies.

'Wilfrid'—she spoke in the old blunt way—'don't make a fool of yourself. Go a yard or two away, there's a good boy. If not, I hobble back into the other room. Remember that I can't stand excitement.'

Eyes averted, he moved away from her.

'I had a letter from Cissy this morning——'

'I don't want to hear of it,' he interrupted pettishly. 'She was the cause of your illness.'

Miss Childerstone pursued in the same tone.

'——Posted at Cape Town. Very cheerful. She was enjoying the voyage, and looking forward to its end in a reasonable and

happy way. We did the right thing. There's a letter, too, from
the expectant lover; a good letter; you may see it if you like.'

Common-sense came at length to Wilfrid's support. He sat
down, crossed his legs, and talked, but without looking at his
companion.

'I owe you a lot of money,' said Bertha.

'Rubbish! When can you go away? And what place would
you prefer?'

'I shall go next week to the seaside. Anywhere near. Some
place where there are lots of people. I was dead, and am alive
again; I want to feel the world buzzing round.'

'Very well. Choose a place, and I'll go after rooms for you.'

'No, no. I can do all that by letter. By-the-bye. I've been hearing from Tomlinson. He's a better sort of fellow than I supposed.
What do you think? He sent me a cheque for five-and-twenty
pounds—on account, he says.'

Langley kept his head down, and muttered something.

'I suppose somebody or other has been pitching him a doleful
story about me. It took a long time before people missed me;
now they're beginning to write and call.'

'Yes—you have a great many friends——'

'Heaps of them! Now, goosey, don't hang your head. The
fact of the matter is, we oughtn't to have met just yet. There's
an artificial atmosphere about an invalid. You're not to come
again till I send for you—you hear that?'

'As you please,' answered Langley, shamefaced, but no longer
petulant. And he stayed only a few minutes after this. At parting, their eyes did not meet.

That night he wrote a letter, the inevitable letter, page upon
page, strictly according to precedent. When two days had
brought no answer, he wrote again, and this time elicited a short
scrawl.

'Goosey, goosey gander! I don't like the style of these composi-
tions; it isn't up to your later mark. Go and see Totty—Lotty—
what's her name? I mean it; you want the tonic of such society.
And pray, what work are you doing? Come tomorrow at three
and tell me.'

He would have liked to refuse the invitation, but had fallen into so limp a state that there was no choice save to go and be tortured. Miss Childerstone looked better.

'I pick up very quickly,' she said. 'In the early days, before I knew you, I had a worse floorer than this, and astonished everyone by the way I came round. Well, what are you doing?'

'Nothing much,' the young man replied carelessly.

She pondered a little, then laughed.

'Now isn't it an odd thing, how far we were from knowing each other? I misunderstood you; I did indeed; as it goes without saying that you quite misunderstood me. I didn't think you could have written those letters.'

'I'm not ashamed of them.'

A certain quiet manliness in the words had its effect upon Miss Childerstone. She smiled, and regarded him kindly.

'Nor need you be, my dear boy. For my part, I'm considerably proud of them; I shall store them up and read them in years to come when they have a value as autographs. But I suppose you had purposely misled me, with your random talk. If I had known —yes, if I had known—I don't think I should have let Cissy go to Natal.'

'Stop that nonsense,' said Langley, 'and answer me a plain question. Is it hopeless?—or can't you make up your mind yet?'

'I *have* made up my mind—since receiving your letters.'

'Before, you were in doubt?'

'Just a wee bit. Partly, I suppose, because of my weakness. I like you so much, and I have such hopes of your future—it was tempting. But—No!'

Langley looked at her with eyes of thwarted passion.

'What do you mean? Just because I have really and honestly fallen in love with you——'

'Just so,' she interrupted, 'and shown yourself as I didn't know you. I like you as much as ever—more, perhaps. I more than half wish I could bring Cissy back again. You would have suited each other very well. And yet, it would have been an unkindness to *you*, however kind to *her*. It meant, for you, a sinking into the comfortable commonplace. You are too young for marriage. I had rather see you in any kind of entanglement. That longing for domesticity gave me a shudder. It's admirable, but it's the part of you that must be outgrown. Oh, you are so much more respectable than I thought.'

She broke off, laughing.

'And you mean to say,' exclaimed Wilfrid, 'that if I could have given proof of blackguardism you might have been inclined to marry me?'

Miss Childerstone laughed uncontrollably.

'Oh, how young you are! No, I shouldn't have married you in any case. I might have promised to think about it. I might have promised to do it; but when the time came—*via!* Dear boy, I don't want to marry. Look at this room, dirty and disorderly. This is all the home I care for. Conceivably, I might marry a man with a big income, just for the sake of a large life. But it's only just conceivable. In poverty—and anything you or I can count upon would be poverty—I prefer the freedom of loneliness.'

'You imagine I should lay any restaint upon you?'

Again she broke into laughter.

'I have a pretty good theoretical knowledge of what marriage means. Unfortunately, one can't experiment.'

Langley turned from her, and stared gloomily.

'Look here,' said his companion. 'In a few days I think I shall be strong enough to go away, and I shall not tell you where I'm going. Let us say good-bye, and see each other again when we're both recovered. In the meantime, live and work. Give fifteen-pound suppers, if you like. Anything to keep your thoughts off domesticity. Cultivate blackguardism'—her voice rang mirthfully. 'Then we shall get back to the old footing.'

'Never!'

'Well, that's as you please. I should like it, though.'

He left her, and determined neither to write nor to call again. In a day or two the former resolve was broken; he wrote at greater length than ever. When the silence that followed became unendurable, he went to the house, but only to learn that Miss Childerstone had left that morning.

For the mere sake of talking about her, he spent the evening with people who had known his friend for a long time. They, it appeared, were ignorant of her movements.

'Gone as war correspondent, I shouldn't wonder,' said a young man; and the laughter of the company appreciated his joke.

'Oh, she really is too mannish,' remarked a young matron. 'I suppose you study her as a curiosity, Mr. Langley?'

'We're great chums,' Wilfrid answered with a laugh.

'Well, at all events we needn't bid *you* beware,' jested the lady.

On reaching home, late, he found in his sitting-room an object which greatly puzzled him; it was a large and handsome travelling-bag, new from some shop. By what mistake had it got here? He examined it, and found a ticket bearing his name and address. Then, turning to the table, he saw a letter, the address in a well-known hand.

'DEAR OLD MAN,— I shall not offer to pay back the money you have spent upon me, but I'm sending a present, one of the useful order.

'Yours in *camaraderie*,

' B. C.'

After a day or two of brooding he saw the use of Bertha's gift, and for a month the travelling-bag did him good service.

He and she had long been back in town, and were again tugging hard at the collar, before they met. It was a miserable day of November, and amid sleet, fog, slush, they came face to face on the pavement of the roaring Strand. Their umbrellas had collided, and as they shook hands the hurrying pedestrians bumped them this way and that.

'All right again?' asked Bertha merrily.

'Quite,' was the stalwart reply. 'Come somewhere and talk.'

'Can't. Appointment in ten minutes.'

'Move on, please!' shouted a policeman. 'Mustn't stop the way.'

'Lunch at the old place tomorrow?' said Wilfrid hurriedly.

'Yes. Two o'clock.'

Each plodded on, and Langley had no cardiac tremor as he thought of Miss Childerstone. For all that—for all that—he could not forget that he had kissed her lips.

Hubert Crackanthorpe

1870-96

HUBERT MONTAGUE CRACKANTHORPE, son of a Queen's Counsel and Doctor of Civil Law, was born on May 12, 1870. Both his parents evinced a high literacy of opinion, his father writing on eugenics and other social problems in the more serious periodicals, while his mother had attracted much attention with an essay entitled *The Revolt of the Daughters* published in the 'eighties.

Crackanthorpe was tutored by George Gissing (fit mentor for the most committed realist writer of the 'nineties). Following a disagreement with the University authorities, Crackanthorpe left Cambridge in his first year and spent some time travelling and studying in France.

In 1893, he married Leila Macdonald, descendant of the famous Flora. For a while they lived in domestic peace in a workman's cottage in Chelsea which Roger Fry had decorated for them. Between 1892 and 1893 Crackanthorpe edited the *Albermarle* magazine with distinction. The seven severe studies in the objective Gallic vein contained in his first volume *Wreckage* (1893) sufficed to bring his name to the fore. As Le Gallienne remarked of them, they were 'one of the sensations of the period.' He contributed to *The Yellow Book*, edited by Henry Harland; and he and his wife and the Harlands made up many parties to attend the music hall. 'He was,' wrote Ella d'Arcy, 'a charming creature. Everyone loved him.'

His wife, however, ceased to do so and left him for another man. Her desertion broke Crackanthorpe's spirit. He threw himself into the Seine; and when his body was recovered, some months later, it was so changed that his brother could identify him only by his cuff-links. It has been said that he died like a character from one of his stories, and one newspaper ever averred that it was 'the judgment of God for adoring French idols.'

Those who knew him well, however, remarked on the distintion between the author and the man. 'The self,' declared Richard Le Gallienne, in his book of reminiscences, *The Romantic 90's* (1926), 'was indeed strangely different from his work, so gentle and chivalric, and romantic.'

Despite the bleak climate of his tales, there is evidence that Crackanthorpe as a personality was largely gay and optimistic. He collaborated with Henry Harland to write *A Farcical Comedy: The Light Sovereign* (edited and published by 'Lady Harland' in 1917, many years after the dramatists' deaths). Nor was he one, like certain 'nineties authors, to bewail the isolation of fine letters in a mercantile society. 'Young men today,' he professed in the second number of *The Yellow Book* (July 1894), 'have enormous chances and we are working under exceedingly favourable conditions. Possibly we stand on the threshhold of a very great period.'

Bernard Muddiman, in his *Men of the 'Nineties* (1920), hailed him as 'the great imaginative prosewriter of the group.' This praise will be confirmed when a much-needed selection of his work, long out of print, appears.

Both during his lifetime and after his death. Crackanthorpe had his discriminating enthusiasts. Henry James noted the 'purple patches of travel' which went to make up his descriptive *Vignettes* (1896). Le Gallienne spoke of 'a scrupulous, almost fanatical "objectivity" [which] was his aim,' while Lionel Johnson, reviewing his posthumous *Last Studies* (1897), remarked of these pages of 'aching poignancy' that 'the telling of the misery becomes a thing of dreadful beauty, and in its intensity goes nearer to the heart of the dark matter than many a moving sermon. The artist's abstemiousness in Mr. Crackanthorpe, the refinement of his reticence, never chilled his reader. 'The pity of it! The pity of it!" *That* was always the unspoken yet audible burden of his art.'

Crackanthorpe was also the author of *Sentimental Studies* and *a Set of Village Tales* (1895). Frank Harris has left an impression

of him in his *Contemporary Portraits: Second Series* (1917), and
he is featured also in V. Starretts' *Buried Caesars* (1923).

EMBERS

The room was small, but the twilight shadows made it appear
larger. An iron bedstead; two tables, one covered with papers,
the other with a white cloth; a chair by the door, and on it a
mud-splashed pair of trousers and a dirty shirt, with a pair of
old slippers, trodden down at the heels, underneath; a black, shiny
armchair, its horsehair stuffing protruding in places; a deal chest
of drawers—this was all the furniture. No kind of ornament,
bare walls, not a spot of colour to relieve the cheerlessness.

Yet presently, as one looked, two or three details betrayed
something of the individuality of the occupant.

The papers on the writing-table were arranged in neat stacks;
the shirt on the chair had been carefully folded; the slippers
lay side by side; but it was the mechanical precision of habit,
and not a love of tidiness; for the room was far from clean, and
looked almost squalid.

But when he came in, he noticed none of these things.

A lean young man, with a hesitating gait and tired stoop;
lank hair streaked with grey; a yellow parchment-like skin that
puckered in wrinkles round the eyes, and gave a shrivelled look
to the whole face; and in the eyes a startling dullness.

He lit the little lamp with the green cardboard shade, hung
up his hat and his overcoat behind the door, took off his boots
and laid them together, just as he had done every evening for the
last five years.

He lifted up the dirty shirt, and, after looking closely at the
cuffs, folded it again, and replaced it on the chair. Then he fetched
a brush from off the chest of drawers, and began carefully to
clean the mud-splashed trousers.

When he had nearly finished, the servant-girl brought in his
dinner.

'Good evening,' he said, without looking up.

'Good evening, Mr. Gorridge,' she answered.

And he began to eat the cold mutton and the boiled potatoes methodically.

As a rule, when his dinner was finished, he seated himself at the writing-table, to copy manuscripts at a half-penny a folio or to address envelopes at fourpence a hundred. It was not so much for the sake of the money, for he had but few wants, and his salary was more than enough to supply them. He had taken to it long ago, when the mechanical work had kept him from brooding over his trouble; and gradually the habit had grown upon him, till it was an inseparable part of his existence. Narrower and narrower had become the groove in which his life ran, and now each day was a counterpart of the preceding one.

But tonight, when the servant-girl had taken away the half-finished leg of mutton, he turned round his chair and stared into the empty grate.

February 18th, said the almanack on the wall opposite. February 18th, the day on which she had gone. With a yearning, dull and immense, like the yearning for home of the solitary traveller, he was thinking of his married life—quite hazily; for five years of unconscious retrospective crystallisation had vaguely beautified them for him.

And then he lived over again the moment when he had come back from the City to find her gone, gone with not a word of explanation.

Most of that night and all the next day he had spent in wild search for her. The next three days he was in bed, unable to get up. On the morning of the fourth day, fearing to lose his place, he had dragged himself down to the City as usual. And afterwards, for weeks, every evening as he mounted the stairs, his heart thumped excitedly with the hope that he would find her back again. But she never came.

He changed his lodgings, for the hundred and one little things that brought her back to him made the rooms unbearable.

Outside, a drizzling rain. The gas lamps shone a dim, filthy yellow, streaking the slimy pavement with their reflections. There

was no sky, only a murky atmosphere overhead. And, save for
a woman creeping along, the street was deserted. Her slatternly
clothes hung loosely about her; her skirt trailed in the mud. She
was quite wet, for she had no umbrella.

Underneath his window she stopped, and for a moment she
stood in the doorway out of the rain.

During that moment, the thoughts of the man in the little
bedroom above, sitting staring into the empty grate, and the
thoughts of the bedraggled figure in the doorway below, went
out towards each other.

She could only think in a foggy sort of way, for she had already
had a drink or two. There were many things which were blurred;
many things about which she was not sure. Her recollection
of their separation was dim; she scarcely understood how it had
come about. She wondered feebly where he was, what he was
doing. Yet her cunning instinct told her he would take her back,
in spite of it all, and that once more she could do with him what
she would. It seemed that they were together. He was so simple,
so confiding, that during the day when he was down at the City,
she did what she liked. She was careful, of course, so that he
never found out anything.

Then she moved out again into the wet, and stumbled along
towards the lights of the public-house at the corner.

It was inevitable that it would come, sooner or later, for she
slept over the public-house at the end of the street, and he passed
it every day on his way to the City. Yet it was several days
before she saw him. When he went by in the morning, she was
seldom out of bed, and when he came back in the evening, she
was generally drunk.

But once she woke early, and looked out through the grimy
window-pane.

There he was! She could see his back, as he hurried down
the street. But there was no mistaking the narrow, sloping
shoulders, the jerky, nervous gait, with the head thrust forward.
She even remembered the black overcoat; he had bought it just
after their marriage. It used to be a shiny one, several sizes too
large for him, and to hang in baggy wrinkles about the armpits.

And she fell to dreaming, recalling vague, half-blurred little incidents.

He was found now. A quarter to nine. He was on his way to the City; well she knew that, when evening came, he would return by the same way. All she had to do was to wait for him, and to keep her head clear. So back she went to her dirty bed and fell into a fitful sleep.

About three o'clock, with a low, sickly feeling, she awoke. But, as she slipped into her tawdry garments, her spirits rose. This was the last day; tomorrow she would be a respectable married woman in comfortable lodgings, with a man to earn money for her. She went down to the bar and ordered a large pewter of beer. She always lunched off a large pewter, never having any appetite till evening.

Presently two women, one of whom she knew, came in. She felt in her pocket. Half a crown. Her last. But what odds? Tomorrow he would give her plenty more. So she recklessly stood drinks to the new-comers.

And thus through the afternoon, and with the idea that she must catch him on his return increasing in force as she grew more and more drunk.

She talked loudly and volubly, explaining to the two others all about him, and dilating on all the things she would do when he had taken her back. They listened stupidly, nodding gravely at intervals.

About six o'clock they found themselves with no more money and with nothing more to drink, so, holding each other by the arm, they sallied forth into the street to wait for him.

He was hastening home, thinking of the bundle of manuscript which bulged his pocket, whether he would be able to copy it all before eleven, the hour when he always went to bed.

Of a sudden something clutching at his arm—a woman!— looking up into his face, with the glare of the gas-lamp lighting up her senseless leer. She did not speak, only leered the more, and hung heavier and heavier on his arm.

He made a half-frightened, half-indignant movement to shake her off. Next he recognised her. She did not know he had done so, for he did not start, nor make any sound. Only first his features, then his whole body stiffened, till he stood as if petrified.

'Don't you know me, Frank?' she stuttered.

There was no reply, and it dawned upon her that he did.

'What are you looking so scared at? One would think you'd never seen me before,' she continued with a sickly smile. 'I'm not as I was, I know that. I've had a hard time of it, a cruel hard time of it,' she whined; 'but I've come back to be your dutiful wife once more,' and she leered the same, senseless leer. 'Where are your digs? Somewhere along this way, eh?' And pulling him by the arm, she dragged him down the street. His feeble resistance only lasted an instant.

When they reached the door, his hand shook so violently that it was nearly a minute before he could fit the key into the keyhole. Automatically he lit the little lamp with the green cardboard shade, hung up his hat and overcoat behind the door, and was about to take off his boots, when his eyes fell on her. With a start he stopped short.

She was lying in an armchair, looking round the room.

'No great shakes, this drawing-room of yours. Just you wait till I've been here a day or two, and see how I'll smarten it up. It's beastly cold and no fire.'

At this moment the servant-girl came in to lay the cloth. On seeing the stranger, she stepped back, looking in astonishment from one to the other.

'Well, stupid, what are you staring at? Look sharp. I'm hungry. Let's see. Soup—soup to begin with. Fish, no, no fish —beastly smelly stuff, I can't stomach it. Tripe and baked potatoes to follow, and here, fetch a bottle of beer, look alive; don't stand there like a blasted lamp-post.'

The servant-girl fled, slamming the door behind her. And the two relapsed into silence, he, standing staring at her, in terror-stricken rigidity.

Exasperated, she turned to him.

'What's the devil's the matter with you? A nice way to receive back your loving wife, after all these years. Good God! man, you look like a blooming mummy!'

The door opened violently. In burst a heavy, stout woman, her face flushed with passion.

'Now, Mr. Gorridge,' she cried. 'What's the meaning of this? I'm not going to stand it, d'ye hear? What are you looking so dazed at? Why, God bless my soul, I believe the man's off his head!' And raising her voice still louder: 'Now then, hussy, clear out quick. What do you take me for, I should like to know? I've always kept a respectable house, and I ain't goin' to begin to have the likes of you about now!'

'Dry up your damned impudence,' stuttered the other, staggering to her feet. 'Why, I'm his lawful wife. We were married in church. I've been away on business, these last three years. And it's a hard time of it that I've had,' and she wound up with a whine.

'Get out, you drunken beast,' shouted the elder woman, 'or if you don't I'll soon make you.'

And, seizing her by the shoulders, she began to push her towards the door. The other kicked and struggled, but it was of no use. There was a scuffle on the staircase, an oath from the drunken woman, a crash as of something falling, and the front door banged.

'If you ever dare to set foot inside my house again,' called the landlady through the door, 'I'll send the police after you.'

And, as she re-entered the room: 'Mr. Gorridge, just you understand that, I'll have none of these goings on in my house. You ought to be ashamed of yourself, at your age.'

But he lay in a heap in the armchair, staring fixedly into the empty grate.

Seeing that he paid no heed, she bounced out of the room with a snort of contempt.

Quite still he lay, his limbs huddled together, while the servant-girl, openly casting indignant glances at him, prepared his dinner.

Half an hour passed. The food was untouched. He had not moved.

'Ain't you going to have no dinner, Mr. Gorridge?' asked the girl, with a touch of compassion in her voice.

He made no sound, so she took away the things.

How long he had been there he did not know. He was cold; the cramped position had stiffened his legs; the lamp had gone out; it was quite dark.

He struck a match, and clumsily lit it again. Then, undressing, crept into bed.

When he awoke his mind was blank. Mechanically he looked at the chair on which his clothes always lay folded. It was empty. In a heap, there they were on the floor.

A quick spasm, contracting his features, and he remembered, and, with a gesture of indescribable weariness, began to dress.

That day he did his work at the office as usual, only he looked more yellow and more wizened than over. But no one noticed it.

In the evening, he no longer hurried along the street towards home, absently with his head thrust forward. Slowly he crept, with cautious, cat-like movements.

From a doorway, out burst a boy with a basket. He started aside like a frightened animal.

It was only when he had passed the spot where she had met him yesterday that he seemed reassured. Quickening his pace, he fell again into his accustomed, jerky gait.

But presently, he caught sight of something coming in the distance. By instinct he knew that it was she. On he hastened, his eyes on the pavement, till they came face to face.

'Frank,' she began in a voice broken by maudlin sobs, 'don't you think that I'm going to bother you any more. I'm a miserable, lost creature. I know I am. I'll never trouble you again, Frank; only give me something to keep body and soul together. I haven't a blessed sixpence,' here she stopped, watching him intently.

He had pulled out his purse, and was emptying its contents into his hand. Three half-crowns, a shilling and four coppers— he handed them all to her, and, without a word, turned to go in.

'Good-night, Frank, my darling,' she called after him. 'You're a trump, you are.'

The next three days passed, and she never appeared.

Back his life dropped into the old groove, till it all seemed like a bad dream, and sometimes he wondered whether it had really happened.

Then she met him again, with the same maudlin tears. He gave her a sovereign, for that morning he had received his salary.

After this she took to waylaying him almost every evening. Sometimes, he could only give her a copper or two, sometimes half a crown, sometimes—on Saturdays—gold. He scarcely ever spoke to her, and seemed relieved when she left him on the door-step. Once she spoke of coming up.

'Tomorrow is Saturday,' he said in a hurried voice. She understood, and went away.

At the end of a fortnight, he was unable to pay his weekly bill. This was the first time since he had lodged there, and the thought gnawed him night and day.

His landlady said nothing but, when at the end of the second week no money was forthcoming, she grumbled sullenly.

And he began to age strangely, thinner and thinner his hair became, till he was almost quite bald.

. . . About three weeks later—night-time—the little street was black and still—on the doorstep, two figures.

'I am going on Saturday,' said he.

'Going? Why? Where?' she answered.

'I can't pay the rent,' he said simply.

Face to face they stood. In his eyes the vacant stare of complete weariness; in hers a look of silent suffering. Quicker and quicker her face quivered. Big tears rolled down her cheeks.

And as he watched her, his vacant stare passed away; in its place came the soft light of compassion.

'Don't cry, Mag,' he said gently.

At the sound of this little pet name, coming again for the first time at the end of all these years, she broke down.

It was the hysterical sobbing of a ruined nervous system; it was very painful to hear.

'Don't cry, Mag,' he repeated.

But she sobbed on, her frame rocking with convulsive throbs.

Bewildered he looked about him. Then timidly, he put his arm round her, saying once more:

'Don't cry, little Mag.'

By degrees the fit spent itself. She stood quite still at last, her head resting on his shoulder. After a moment, she stepped back and looked again into his eyes.

The features were quite composed, but the lips were bloodless.

'Frank,' she said with an intenseness that revealed the tumult within. 'Frank, will you forgive me?'

The old spasm of pain, contracting the features, came back. She saw it.

'I don't mean that,' she said hurriedly, 'I'm too bad for that. Only say that you forgive me.'

He pondered a moment perplexed, his eyes blinking rapidly.

Then, looking at her, and seeing that she was waiting for his answer:

'I forgive you,' he murmured.

Holding out her hand—'good-bye,' she said.

'Good-bye,' he answered mechanically.

And she stepped on to the pavement, and moved slowly away down the street.